PAYBACK IN THE KEYS
A LOGAN DODGE ADVENTURE

FLORIDA KEYS ADVENTURE SERIES
VOLUME 13

Exotic Latitudes
Press

LOGAN DODGE ADVENTURES

Gold in the Keys
Hunted in the Keys
Revenge in the Keys
Betrayed in the Keys
Redemption in the Keys
Corruption in the Keys
Predator in the Keys
Legend in the Keys
Abducted in the Keys
Showdown in the Keys
Avenged in the Keys
Broken in the Keys
Payback in the Keys

JASON WAKE NOVELS

Caribbean Wake
Surging Wake
Relentless Wake

Join the Adventure!
Sign up for my newsletter to receive updates on
upcoming books on my website:

matthewrief.com

Acknowledgements:

I would like to thank my exceptional editor, Eliza Dee (clioediting.com), for always going above and beyond to not only correct my mistakes, but also educate me in the process. Much of the success of this series can be attributed to her, and I can't thank her enough.

I'd also like to thank my invaluable, sharp-eyed proofreaders:
Nancy Brown (redlineproofreading.com), and Donna Rich (donnarich@icould.com).

A special thanks as well to Richard Irwin for always being willing to educate me on the art of everything aviation. Lastly I'd like to express my gratitude to a favorite musician of mine (whose name you'll find later on) who's generously agreed to make an appearance in this book.

ONE

Naval Station Norfolk
2000

When my name was called, two armed guards opened the double doors and I marched into the courtroom. I was greeted by the smell of freshly waxed hardwoods mixed with residual aftershave from my rushed shower and change following an early-morning exercise. Breaking a sweat was usually effective at putting my mind at ease, but it hadn't worked today.

Nothing will work today, I told myself, already feeling my pulse begin to quicken.

Every pair of eyes locked onto me as I pressed down the aisle, feeling the severity of the storm I was about to conjure. Most of the four rows of seats were occupied, the high-profile case having garnered the attention of much of the country. The scene was silent aside from my shined black shoes clapping against the floor and the hushed chatter and shuffling of papers at the prosecutor's desk.

I focused on the judge's bench, where a captain sat on a tall polished-oak number with flanking Navy and American flags and a wooden decoration ornamented with a bald eagle carving at his back. A panel of officers sat in the jury box at the back left corner of the room, and on the right sat the court clerk.

I pushed through the low swinging doors, and just as I passed the defense and prosecutors, I shot a quick glance over my left shoulder. Nathan Brier sat between the defense station and the jury. Like me, he was decked out in his clean and pressed dress white uniform. My brother in arms shot me a severe look that reminded me of the heated private conversation we'd had in his cell the previous day.

I turned around once in front of the witness stand.

"Please state your name, rank, and current billet for the record," the court clerk said.

"Chief Petty Officer Logan Dodge," I said. "Operations leading chief petty officer for Task Unit Charlie, SEAL Team Four."

Then I gave an oath to tell the whole truth and nothing but the truth, and sat.

A lieutenant commander JAG officer stood from the prosecutor's table and ambled toward me. He looked my way confidently. His rank indicated that he was clearly experienced in a military courtroom and, judging by his demeanor, was anything but overwhelmed by the momentous case.

"Chief Dodge," he started, his voice articulate and powerful, "on the evening of June third of this year, you met with Lieutenant Brier alone, correct?"

"Yes. He and I spoke in his quarters following a

brief."

"What did you discuss?"

"At first, normal operational specifics. Finer details for the upcoming mission. Then... he asked what I planned to do after I got out of the Navy."

The prosecutor placed a finger to his lips. "Interesting. And how did you respond?"

"That I'm third-generation Navy and the son of a man who served thirty years. I wasn't planning on getting out anytime soon."

The JAG cleared his throat. "And are you aware, Chief Dodge, that at the time of your conversation with Nathan Brier, the lieutenant was up for disciplinary review?"

"No. I wasn't aware."

"Were you also unaware that multiple superiors were deeming him"—the lawyer stomped over to his desk, snatched a transcript, and began to read—"'unfit to command a platoon'?"

"No. I wasn't aware."

He set the papers aside, folded his arms, and paced before me. "Where did the conversation go next?"

I cleared my throat. "He started talking about what he was going to do when he got out. How he was going to find a beach somewhere and never leave it."

The man smiled. "Sounds nice. Hard to pay for a beach life without an income. He say how he was going to finance this lifestyle?"

"I asked if he was planning to do twenty for the retirement."

"And?"

"He just looked down at the floor. Fell silent for a bit. Then he said that men of our skills, intelligence, and sacrifice shouldn't need to, and that he'd found a way to pay for it."

"Interesting." The JAG scanned the courtroom confidently, then turned back to me. "Did you press him on this?"

"No. There are lucrative opportunities in the civilian world for people who can do what we can."

"Are you referring to legal opportunities?"

"Yes. I assumed he was alluding to those. Then…" I shot a quick glance at Brier, seeing the intensity in his eyes. "Then he told me again that he'd found a way. That money wasn't going to be an issue. And that I could get in on it." I swallowed and sat taller. "But he said it would require absolute secrecy. And that most of our men should get out unscathed if we played our cards right."

All the anger and confusion I'd felt when Brier had said those words came back and flooded over me in an instant.

The prosecutor narrowed his gaze at me. "And what was your reply?"

"I didn't have time to reply," I said. "I just scrutinized him, then the door opened at my back."

"Who was it?"

I sighed. "Captain Holt."

A hush fell over the courtroom. You could feel the intensity burning across the space, sparked by my words.

Wyatt Holt, the former task force commander who'd served as an officer for twenty-two years, had been charged posthumously with conspiring to start a civil war in order to make a big payday by working with illegal arms dealers. When the accusations had reached him, followed by a team of military police to put him behind bars, rather than face disgrace, Holt had shot himself in the head.

"And what did Captain Holt say when he walked into Brier's quarters?"

"He asked if everything was all right."

"How did he look?"

"The captain's expression was fixed as stone, as usual. He stood in silence, observing both of us for a moment, then asked me to leave. So, I left. But then I remembered about paperwork I had for the captain. It was regarding information of a confidential nature, and it would have been quicker to have him sign it then rather than meeting him later on."

"What happened when you went back to Brier's quarters?"

I paused, gathering my thoughts. "I was just about to grab the knob when I heard my name and froze."

"They were talking about you." Before I could answer in the affirmative, he added, "And you spied on them?"

"My gut told me to, and it's saved my life handfuls of times, so I've learned to trust it."

"What did you hear?"

"Lieutenant Brier said something about my not being on board, and the captain said that they didn't need me. Brier then said that he'd received confirmation from both the rebels... and Muerto."

The prosecutor's eyes lit up. "El Muerto? As in the notorious Bolivian illegal arms dealer?" Before I could answer, he added, "What did they do then?"

"They mentioned that they had to move quickly and marched for the door. Before I could move away, they exited right in front of me."

"What happened next?"

"They both stared and studied me for what felt like a minute. Probably five seconds, though. Holt seemed to know that I'd heard them. He read my eyes and posture as I handed him the paperwork. I was about to take my leave when he grabbed me by the arm. He told me that if I said anything, they'd kill me."

"And during this threat, the lieutenant didn't jump in to defend you?"

"No. He didn't. The captain just looked me deep in the eyes, then let go and they both stormed off."

The prosecutor fell silent for a moment, letting the revelation settle with the jury, then said, "Did you tell anyone about the encounter?"

I paused again. Up until that point, the tip had been anonymous. Even Brier didn't know the truth.

"Yes," I said, nearly causing enough murmurs for the judge to strike his gavel. "I called Rear Admiral Lewis, having no choice but to jump my chain of command. He ordered an immediate investigation, and less than half an hour after our conversation, a communication between Holt and El Muerto was discovered. Then charges were filed against him and—"

"The captain ended his own life."

"Yes."

The officer stepped toward the jury and held out his hands. "The evidence, combined with this interaction, clearly paints Lieutenant Brier as a coconspirator." He turned back to face me. "Would you agree with this conclusion? That Nathan Brier conspired to threaten American lives, not to mention

10

countless Colombians and Venezuelans, all for personal financial gain?"

Occasionally, a decision comes along that you know will change everything. It's in these moments that you're forced to decide—at the foundation, the core of your being, who are you and what do you stand for? What do you believe in? Because for the rest of my life, I'd have to live with whatever decision I made. Not just the external consequences, but the internal ones. The ones of the mind and heart. The ones that overpower everything else.

"Chief Dodge?" the prosecutor said, raising his eyebrows.

I leaned closer to the microphone. "Yes."

Hushed voices filled the courtroom.

"You believe that Nathan Brier was working alongside Captain Holt in this endeavor?"

"Yes, I do."

I shot a quick look at Brier. His face had turned deep red, and his eyes narrowed at me. I could feel the all-consuming hatred oozing off him. I knew what I'd done; everyone there knew the significance of my testimony. Nathan Brier was guilty, and soon the charges would be given, and he'd be disgraced and slapped with a hefty sentence.

The prosecutor eyed the jury again, then turned to the judge and stepped backward. "No further questions."

"The witness is dismissed," the clerk said after a nod from the judge.

The defense had turned down the chance to cross-examine me, knowing that the damage was already done and that they couldn't fix it.

I rose from the stand and tucked my cover into the crook of my right elbow. Standing tall, I flattened my uniform. I felt good knowing that I'd spoken the truth, that I'd held on to my convictions despite wanting to help a man I'd once called brother. Deep down, I knew that I'd done what was right. That I'd honored my commitment and my oath.

I strode confidently back toward the aisle, ready to put the incident behind me and move on with my unit as best I could. Just before I cut between the attorneys' desks, Brier pushed back his chair.

"You son of a bitch!" he shouted, springing toward me like a provoked cobra.

He was so fast that by the time I turned to ward off the engagement, his charging frame pummeled into me. The furious man knocked me off my feet and we crashed into the side of the prosecutor's desk. He managed to slug me across the face before I struck back, shoving him away. A horde of special warfare personnel closed in, pulling Brier off me as armed guards flooded in to secure him.

"You betrayed me!" Brier shouted, struggling as four men held him back.

I wiped my jaw and staggered to my feet. Blood dripped down my face, staining the flap of my bleached uniform.

As Brier was forced out of the courtroom, I made eye contact with him one final time, then he belted out, "I'll get you for this, Dodger! I'll find you and make you pay. As God is my—"

His words were cut off as he was forced out through a side door, the thick maple slamming shut and silencing his vow.

TWO

Key West
11 Years Later

I stared out over the brightly lit football field just as the fourth quarter was about to commence. My heart rate spiked, and adrenaline flooded my veins as I processed the words I'd just heard.

With my phone still glued to my ear, I blinked and snapped my head sideways as my daughter grabbed me by the hand.

"Dad, is everything all right?" Scarlett said, reflecting my shocked expression back at me.

I was just about to reply with my best attempt at a reassuring statement when the familiar voice came over the small speaker once again.

"You'd better not make me repeat myself, Dodge," Nathan Brier said across the line. "Are you reading me?"

The man's words continued to sprint circles in my

mind. My former comrade had just told me that if I didn't follow his instructions, he'd kill everyone in the stadium.

I swallowed hard. "Loud and clear."

"Good," he said with a curt laugh. "Now tell your daughter that everything's fine."

I glanced back at my sixteen-year-old. She was decked out in the hometown school colors of crimson and white. She brushed aside a strand of brunette hair and stared at me with her hazel eyes.

"Everything's fine, Scar," I said, placing a reassuring hand on her shoulder.

I tried my best to clear out of the chaos, to quell the tempest raging in my mind and keep my composure.

The fourth quarter began with a kickoff to the opposing team from Marathon, and the thousands of gathered spectators let out booming cheers as the kick was hauled in and its carrier sprinted into battle.

"Go back to your friends," I said, motioning to the cluster of teenaged girls leaning against the fence, their attentions fixed on the game. "I'll send you the picture," I added, referring to the one I'd just taken of her and her friends.

I gave her another pat on the shoulder and a smile, then turned away. Her body language made it clear that my words hadn't convinced her. Not even close.

I could feel her inquisitive eyes boring into my back as I turned and focused my attention back on the phone call.

"That was pathetic acting," Brier said. "Not that it matters. Head straight on your current line. Thirty paces."

With the crowd excited and cheering like mad, and with the Friday night lights blazing into my side, I did as Brier said, striding forward and weaving through the thick mass of islanders.

After taking two steps, I peeked over my left shoulder and found Angelina sitting in the bleachers in the second row down from the top. We locked eyes for half a second. I'd known my wife for seven years, and we'd been married for two. The former mercenary knew all of my expressions and could read my mind better than anyone alive.

Even from thirty yards off, and even surrounded by the chaos of a nail-biter football game between rivals, she knew that something was happening.

That something was very wrong.

I scanned over the crowd, steering my gaze forward as I continued along the track. Pacing parallel to the field, I headed toward the entrance into the sporting event.

As the shock of the initial revelation settled, my mind went to work. Having served eight years in Naval Special Forces, and another six as a gun for hire, I was no stranger to high-risk, dangerous situations. As casually as I could, I homed in on the corners of the field. The nearby structures. The high places. Attempting to pin down where Brier was watching me from.

When I reached twenty-five paces, I spotted a familiar face up ahead. Jack Rubio, one of my closest friends, stood in line at the concessions stand. The tanned, curly-blond-haired beach bum turned on his flip-flops when he noticed me and threw a wave.

"Just wrapped up a *late* charter, bro," he said, his

voice raised to travel over the sounds of the people. "Looks like I arrived just in time. You want anything?"

I continued on my trajectory, focusing on Jack but not replying.

"Watching you like a hawk, Dodge," Brier snarled. "You mention me and you're all dead."

His words were like a sharp blade digging deeper into my gut, but I remained calm as best I could.

"No, thanks, Jack," I said, waving him off. "I've had more than my fill of junk food today already."

I hit thirty paces just a few strides from Jack, and when a group of rowdy high schoolers cut between us, Brier's voice returned.

"Veer left. The side path to—"

"You forgetting my popcorn refill?" Angelina said from behind me, cutting off Brier in her faint Swedish accent.

She wrapped her arms around me and kissed me playfully on the cheek. It was far from a fun, innocent gesture. She was checking my pulse. She was in tactical mode—choosing her actions carefully and calculating the issue at hand.

I guessed that I was running close to a hundred beats per minute, far higher than my usual resting.

"One large popcorn it is," Jack said. He was next up in line and eager to get his snacks and watch the end of the game. "I've never seen this place so packed," he added, gazing at the crowd. "I had to park two blocks down Third."

I paused a moment as an idea slid into my mind. "Reminds me of that stadium in Trinidad," I said, shooting my wife a look.

Sharper than my dive knife, Ange hopped onto my train of thought in a fraction of a second. She chuckled and replied, "At least these bleachers have slightly higher safety standards."

Jack stepped up to the counter and placed his order. I shot another glance at Ange, then held up my phone and said, "I've gotta take this."

She nodded playfully. "Just don't be too long. Looks like the Conchs are about to force a fourth down and get the ball."

"You're catching on quick," I said, kissing her on the cheek before turning away.

It was her first time watching an American football game. It was supposed to be a fun, entertaining night out until—

"Slip out through the entrance," Brier said.

A girl stamped the top of my right hand so I wouldn't have to pay to get back in, then told me that I'd better make it quick.

"Most exciting game of the year," she beamed. "And really gonna start heating up soon."

You have no idea, I thought, hoping that her prediction only applied to the game.

Exiting the sporting grounds, I strode onto the main path that snaked through the heart of the campus. It was much quieter there. Just me and two or three stragglers hustling by to catch the final minutes of the bout.

"Cut right," Brier said when I reached an intersecting path.

I turned on my heel, trekking toward the school's gymnasium. Along the right side of the structure was a utility shed, a patch of grass, and a row of tennis

17

courts beyond. To the left was a wide walkway leading to a side road.

With every step, I ran through scenarios. I couldn't help it. It was a facet of my character that'd been developed over years of deadly encounters.

I couldn't trust Brier. That much was certain. I'd dealt with the man enough to know that he'd go against his word at the drop of a hat, that even if I did everything he asked—even if I lay dead in a pool of blood at his feet—he'd still blow up the stadium out of spite. Every move I made, every order of his that I followed, was nothing more than a stall. Time for me to work out a strategy, and time for Ange to catch on to the hints I'd dropped and try and locate whatever it was Brier was threatening to use to blow the stadium sky-high.

"Around the back," Brier said. "Left side."

I skirted around the outside of the gym, keeping to the shadows as I headed toward the rear. There was nobody around, and no sounds but the distant chorus of cheers, claps, and the occasional referee's whistles. Though it was past nine o'clock, the Conch Republic was in the lower seventies, with barely a whisper of wind. I felt my forehead dampen and wiped the residue as I crept around the corner to the back of the gym.

I faced a spread of dark tennis courts, an auxiliary parking lot with every space occupied, and a back entrance into the structure.

"Head to that row of dumpsters," Brier said. "Sig in the green. Knife in the black."

I swallowed hard. Brier knew me well and knew that I'd be packing my two favorite weapons. My trusty Sig Sauer P226 9mm, and my titanium dive knife. I rarely went anywhere without the two items that had saved my life so many times I'd lost count.

I approached the two dumpsters, then paused.

"Today, Dodge," Brier said.

I clenched my jaw. He was still watching me. A quick focus on my peripherals and I decided that he had to be posted either on the rooftop of a house across the street or up on top of the gymnasium.

Reaching to the back of my waistband, I withdrew my Sig, then pried open the lid of the green dumpster and tossed it in. I kept my knife in a sheath that runs parallel along the back of my belt. A quick slide and a fling into the other dumpster, and I found myself unarmed.

"Ladder at your three o'clock," Brier said as my blade rattled against the bottom of the empty receptacle. I turned and saw a ladder bolted to the side of the building, its bottom rungs covered by an eight-foot-long steel guard. "Don't tell me the islands have made you too soft to scale that."

I cut the distance to the base of the gym and looked up. The metal plate was raised off the ground, leaving me with over ten feet to conquer. Hesitating only to buy Ange more time, I took a breath, twisted my right foot into the pavement, then bent down and pushed off. I launched myself up and my fingers gripped the top of the guard. Reaching overhead, I snagged the nearest rung, then hoisted myself up until I could push with my feet.

Brier's "soft" jab died off in the breeze, and I relished my enemy's silence as I scaled the rest of the ladder.

The roof was still and dark. Patches of clouds blotted out the moonlight, shrouding the scene in blackness. I could see the field in the distance, the scene melding into a chaotic blur of activity from that far off.

I scanned over the massive rooftop while striding forward. I expected Brier to chime back in and give me further instructions, but I heard only silence apart from the far-off sounds of the game.

As I approached the opposite corner of the roof, I spotted a figure crouched down near the edge. I advanced carefully, not wanting to slip on the smooth metal and tumble to the ground forty feet down. When I moved closer, I realized that it was Brier.

A whistle blared out and the crowd roared, but I kept my eyes fixed on Brier.

"Quite the show," he said once we were within ten feet of each other. "It's a shame that…" He tilted his head and stared daggers at me.

"This is between you and me," I snapped. "There's no reason to bring all of these people into this. You and me, Brier. Tonight. Let's finish this."

Brier chuckled, then rose to his feet, the metal roof warping under the soles of his tactical boots as he paced toward me. He turned back to gaze at the field. Raising a monocular, he did a quick scan, then lowered it to his side.

"Funny how your wife disappeared right after you spoke with her," he said, then snickered. "Not that it matters. If she's looking for the explosives we've planted, I can assure you she's wasting her time."

I shook my head. "What do you want, Brier?"

I heard the shuffling of feet at my back and

whirled around. Two men climbed up through a small hatch and stomped toward me, both carrying submachine guns. They raised their weapons at me in unison, and I held up my hands.

When I turned back to Brier, he lunged and slugged me with a strong fist to the gut. I lurched forward, the blow knocking the air from my lungs and the sting of pain rushing through my body. I wanted to retaliate—to pin the man to the roof and strangle the life out of him. But the barrels of two firearms held me back.

"What do I want?" Brier snarled, gripping me by the back of the neck. "I want you to feel as I felt. I want to watch as your life is ripped apart. As everything you hold dear crumbles before your eyes." He let go, took a step back, and gestured toward the stadium. "This show is just getting started, Dodge."

THREE

Angelina watched Logan carefully as he meshed through the people, making a beeline for the exit with his phone pressed to his ear. Jack wrapped up at the concessions stand, gripping two hot dogs in one hand, balancing a tray of nachos in the other, and tucking a soda under his elbow.

"Popcorn's on the counter, Ange," Jack said.

She didn't hear him. With her gaze fixed on her husband, she ran through the words that he'd said just before excusing himself. She and Logan had been in Trinidad the previous year, helping to prevent a terrorist attack on the Caribbean island. The intended targets had been a moored cruise ship as well as a stadium filled with people. The cryptic message Logan had sent her was clear as day. Somebody was trying to blow up the stadium. And whoever Logan was on the phone with, they sure as hell weren't friendly.

"Hey," Jack said, nudging her shoulder. "Earth to

Ange? Your popcorn's—"

Ange blinked and turned her focus on Jack. The laid-back islander stared at her quizzically when he saw her serious expression. Before Jack could say another word, Ange slid a hand under his arm and ushered him around the back of the concessions hut.

"Hey, what the hell's going on?" Jack said, trying his best to keep the food from falling.

Ange turned and peeked over the top of the kiosk, eyeing the rooftops of the distant school buildings for a moment before striding back under the eave.

She snatched the food and drink from Jack's hands and set them down. "We're in big trouble." She bit her lip, running thoughts around in her mind, then added, "I'm sure they're watching me."

"Who?" Jack said, his eyes bulging.

"I don't know. But whoever they are, I think they've planted a bomb in this stadium."

Jack's jaw hit the ground. "What? Why would anyone want to set off a bomb here?"

Seeing that a few nearby kids had heard Jack's words and stared at them curiously, Ange shushed her friend and pulled him out of earshot of passersby.

"We need to keep this between us," Ange said. "If people start panicking, whoever's holding the trigger will get jumpy. And bad things happen when killers get jumpy."

The islander thought for a moment. "So, we need to find this thing."

"And disable it. Yes." Ange glanced around the corner, catching a final glimpse of her husband as he strode beyond the entrance, vanishing around the corner as he reached the main part of the school.

23

"Logan must be trying to buy us time. That's why he's listening to whoever called him."

Jack nodded, thinking over her words. He gazed beyond her, toward the ongoing game and the thick clusters of people along the side. "If I were a mad serial killer, where would I place a bomb?" he whispered, more to himself than Ange. "The bleachers?"

"Strike at the thickest concentration of bodies," Ange said. "Amassing as many casualties as possible. That's where I'd look first."

"Start on opposite ends and work our way to the middle?"

Ange shook her head. "Whoever's watching Logan's most likely keeping tabs on me as well. We can't risk it. But I'll do what I can after I find Scarlett."

"You and Logan are the professionals. I'm just a guy who likes to fish and dive. What would I even be looking for?"

"You've held your own on many of our escapades over the years." She paused as the crowd erupted in a powerful roar. "It has to be you, Jack. You can do this."

Jack swallowed hard and narrowed his gaze. After agreeing, Ange gave him a ten-second rundown on identifying improvised explosives.

"Call me right away when you find it," Ange said, then Jack turned and blended into the crowd, heading for the back of the bleachers.

As Ange backtracked to where she'd last seen Scarlett, she made a pit stop at the school merchandise stand. She bought a long-sleeved Key

West Conchs shirt and hat. Throwing the red shirt over her tank top, she tied her hair back into a ponytail and tightened the ball cap.

Her walk back toward the front of the bleachers was calm and calculated. Her mind went to work, surveying every inch of the scene as she blended through the people, keeping her head down.

She found Scarlett up against the fence, still watching the game with her friends. The insightful teenager noticed Ange approach and turned toward her mother.

"Mom, what's wrong with Dad?" she said, keeping her voice low so that her friends wouldn't hear.

One of them, a short girl who was waving a strand of ribbons, turned and beamed at Ange. "Love the school spirit, Mrs. Dodge."

Angelina smiled back, then ushered Scarlett away from the group.

"Okay, now what's wrong with you?" she said.

Once they were out of earshot of Scarlett's friends, Ange stared deep into her daughter's eyes. "I need you to listen to me carefully." Her voice was stern and resolute. It caused Scarlett to turn rigid as stone in a blink. "I need you to tell your friends that you're going to the bathroom, then walk casually out the entrance, to the parking lot, and get in your car." Ange peeked at her watch. "If you don't hear from me by nine thirty, drive to Jack's house and stay there."

Scarlett's intrigue drifted to the fringes of fear. "Mom, what's going on?" She scanned around the game, then leaned in even closer to Ange. "Are these people in danger?"

"Scar," Ange said, grabbing her by the shoulder. "Do what I say. There's no time to explain, and if we cause a panic, it'll likely only make things worse."

Scarlett nodded, feeling the severity of the situation oozing off her mother. She swallowed hard, then stood tall.

Ange watched as she marched back to her group, noticing the gravity of their conversation weighing on her. When Scarlett broke away, the short girl with the ribbons followed her and they both strode toward the exit.

No harm, Ange thought. *Two girls sauntering out of the stadium won't make a scene.*

Scarlett's words resonated in her mind as she went back into tactical mode, scanning the scene for anything out of place.

Yes. All of these people are in danger.

She wanted to warn everyone there. Many of them were familiar faces. Friends, teachers, local store owners, friendly faces around town. Over two thousand people had turned out to enjoy the bout between the island rivals. Then there were the players, coaches, cheerleaders, and band members.

But she couldn't warn them. The best way to ensure their safety was to keep them in the dark and to locate the bomb. Just as Ange turned to inspect the side of the bleachers, she froze as she locked eyes on Jack, who was climbing over the chain-link fence and hustling onto the football field. Ahead of their local friend, she saw a large black case resting on the grass at the corner of the home team's bench.

FOUR

Sticking to the shadows, Jack crept along the outer fence, then made sure that nobody was watching him before ducking under the bleachers. The scene was dark and gloomy outside the reaches of the beaming stadium lights. The rumble of the excitement overhead made the metal frame tremble and creak.

Jack pulled himself together and searched every inch of the structure. He knew Logan and Angelina well enough to understand that if they believed that the place could be rigged with explosives, there was a good chance that it was. Though Jack's expertise lay in the art of showing tourists around his island paradise, he'd accompanied the two on his fair share of wild and dangerous adventures.

He moved carefully, climbing under horizontal metal beams and traversing through the sea of soda cans, popcorn, and various other trash that had fallen through the cracks overhead. The frame was narrow and mostly bare. If something were attached to it, even small, bang-for-your-buck plastic explosives, he was confident he'd spot it in the first sweep.

While nearing the middle, he heard soft chuckling, then spotted dark movements up ahead along one of the big vertical support bars. It was two teenagers making out. The couple pushed off each other, startled by Jack's sudden appearance.

"You two see anyone else back here?" Jack said.

The girl shook her head.

"How about any items that aren't usually here? Anything strange?"

Again she shook her head.

"Please don't tell on us, man," the kid said, referring to the half-empty bottle of Red Stripe on the ground beside him. "The superintendent's here and—"

Jack waved him off, focusing all his attention back on his crucial search.

Ranging back and forth between the low-lying front regions and the back that opened up to a tall chain-link fence, he left no nook or cranny unchecked. But by the time he reached the other side of the bleachers, he hadn't seen anything unusual.

He shifted his position, trying to look casual as he scanned over the field, looking for plan B. A glance at his phone told him that it'd been three minutes since he'd left Ange. He didn't know the extent of what was going on, but he was certain that every second counted. Every moment that slipped away brought them and everyone in that stadium closer to a potential catastrophic doom.

As he peered over the scene, doing a full three-sixty, he focused on the fence bordering the stadium

28

behind the bleachers. Beyond it was a soccer field, a baseball field, and three smaller school buildings far off in the distance. There were no roads within a hundred yards of the bleachers.

How in the hell could someone plant a large haul of explosives without attracting attention? he thought.

He ran through scenarios, trying to think of the kinds of people who wouldn't draw suspicion loading bags or boxes into the stadium.

Maybe they were dressed as janitors? Or maintenance workers?

He performed a second, more frantic and thorough search of the bleachers. After coming up empty a second time, and with the clock ticking down, he strode in front of the stands and eyed every row, searching for anything that could house a bomb. When he peered toward the football field itself, he spotted an unattended long black case lodged under the home team's bench, beneath helmets and a Gatorade cooler. As he gravitated closer and focused harder, he thought that it looked out of place. Different from the equipment bags nearby.

With no other options jumping out at him and with the lives of everyone there at stake, he pushed up against the fence, then pressed his hands against the top and flung his body over. Few people noticed and no one said anything as he landed on the grass and closed in on the bench. Kneeling, he gripped the hardcase, his heart pounding as he slid it out. It was big, roughly four feet long and two feet wide. Spinning it around, he reached for the latch that was secured by a combination lock.

"Hey, what are you doing?" a low voice grumbled.

Jack kept his attention focused on the case as an assistant coach stomped toward him, lowered a clipboard, and reached for Jack.

Ignoring the coach, Jack whirled around, searching for anything he could use to break the lock.

"Hey, get off the field!" the coach demanded.

"What's in this case?" Jack said, ignoring the man's order. "Do you recognize it?"

The guy's face scrunched up and he shook his head. "We've got a lot of gear."

"Do you recognize it?" Jack said again.

A few players and another coach moved in as the team huddled for a timeout. With no time to argue with the guy, Jack resumed his search.

"Jack?" a young male voice said. Cameron Tyson, the hometown quarterback and Scarlett's boyfriend, eyed Jack skeptically. His uniform was covered in grass stains, his dirty blond hair drenched in sweat.

"Looking for this," Ange said, dropping down behind Jack with a pair of bolt cutters in her hands.

Jack gave a relieved sigh, then grabbed hold of the tool.

"Hey, what did I tell you?" the assistant coach said, reaching for Jack again.

Cameron cut in front of the man. "This is Jack Rubio. He's a friend."

"I don't care who he is, he's not allowed on this field during a game."

Jack ignored the conversation. He and Ange had far more important things to attend to. Gripping the bolt cutters, he positioned the two short blades around the brass lock, then pressed the grips together. The shears drove into each other, and the lock tumbled to the grass. Dropping the cutters, Jack unlatched the case, then pried open the lid. Lights illuminated a large hollowed-out space lined with felt. It was empty.

Just as the realization took form, a series of mechanical clicks filled the air. The overhead lights switched off, and the whole stadium went dark.

FIVE

I fought to catch my breath and ignore the pain radiating from my midsection. Brier's punch had been solid and had caught me off guard. Nearly identical to my six foot two and a hundred and ninety pounds, Brier was solid muscle and knew how to throw a punch.

My adversary gazed out over the football game, then planted his hands on his hips and turned back to me. "Given our history, you must've known that I'd return one day."

I forced myself to a knee, then stood. "I was wrong to suspect that if you did, you'd face me like a man. That you'd challenge me to a standoff and leave innocent people out of it."

Brier paused. "Well, you were wrong about many things."

"Then the man I knew is gone completely. There's no trace of the honorable Nathan Brier I once called brother."

"Honor?" Brier spat, stomping toward me and shoving a finger in my face. "Don't you fucking speak of honor. There's no honor in hanging your *brother* out to dry. In kicking him to the wolves just to save yourself."

I threw my shoulders back, letting him know he could do a lot of things, but intimidating me wasn't one of them. "We were both bound by the same oath, the same code of conduct. And you chose to break it."

"You still don't get it, do you?" Brier said with a coarse laugh. "As I told you back on the sixtieth floor of the Wake Tower in Miami—we were never anything more than pawns. Cogs in a system that never cared about us. A system that turned its back on me. No, I've seen behind the curtain, Dodge. And tonight, I'm going to show you the price that comes from stabbing me in the back."

"By targeting civilians? How do you justify mass murder, Brier?"

The man rubbed his chin, then sneered. "Sometimes sacrifices must be made for the greater good. A message must be sent."

"What message?" I said, certain that I was dealing with a bona fide psychopath. "And who are you sending it to?"

"First you, Dodge. And then the rest of the people holding the reins of this country."

There was no reasoning with him—no sense in trying to shift his thoughts. They were too powerful, and far too burrowed into the depths of his psyche. Brier had betrayed us, not the other way around. He and Captain Holt had planned to lead our platoon into certain death that humid evening in the jungles of

33

South America. And if I hadn't overheard their conversation and notified our chain of command, many American soldiers would've died that night. And Brier would've reaped the financial rewards of working with illegal arms dealers and starting a war.

"How cute," Brier said, turning and focusing through his monocular. "Looks like your beach bum friend is trying to find our explosives." He chuckled and added, "He'll never find them." When he looked over at me, he saw the stunned expression on my face. "That's right. I know all of your little island friends. You see, I've been lurking in the dark for a while now. You struck a hard blow in Miami—nearly killed me. But you failed to finish the job and I've been lying quietly, like an alligator patiently waiting for an opportunity to pounce. And... just a few months ago, you handed me an opportunity that was far too appetizing to pass up. You handed me a partner who hates you almost as much as I do to help finance and orchestrate this whole endeavor."

I shook my head, not knowing where he was going or what he was referring to. Then Brier raised his radio and said, "Come on up."

The same hatch where the two men with submachine guns had appeared from minutes earlier hinged open again. This time, a man stepped out who I recognized instantly. His dark blue suit, his red tie, and his weathered face and slicked-back gray hair were unmistakable.

"Hello, Logan Dodge," Vito Bonetti said.

The last time I'd seen the Italian crime boss was ten days earlier in his restaurant in Coral Gables. After I'd stabbed a knife through his hand and knocked him out, he'd managed to slip away from the scene and escape a swarm of searching police officers.

Of course. It all made sense the moment I laid eyes on the man. Brier had been there that rainy night. He'd seized a moment of opportunity and saved the rich, powerful Italian in exchange for my downfall.

Vito held a silver-plated Colt 9mm in his right hand. Before I could say a word, the Italian continued, "Your reaction is priceless and well worth all of these theatrics. Usually, I'd simply track you down and put a bullet in your head when you least expected it, but this... this was quite the idea."

Brier glanced at his watch. "It's almost time." He smiled and motioned for the armed men to prod me toward the edge for a better view.

Once near the corner, Brier pointed at the stadium, then turned to look back at me.

"You don't have to do this, Nate," I said, planning out the best time and way to strike. "You're a better man than this. Deep down. This isn't you."

Brier held up the radio. "Yes, it is, old friend. This is the result of your actions." He held the talk button and spoke into the radio. "Do it."

I chastised myself for not acting sooner, wondering if it was too late and hoping that I'd given Ange enough time. Seconds after the words left his lips, the stadium lights shut off at once, drowning the scene in darkness. Referees blew their whistles. The crowd let out a chorus of murmurs. And Brier stuck his hands on his hips. But no bombs went off—no explosions filled the air and consumed the spectators.

For a moment, I thought we'd succeeded. That

Ange had discovered and disabled whatever explosives Brier and his newly formed team had planted.

Then, my old comrade tilted his head toward me and smiled. "Now, time for the real fun to begin."

A loud, piercing siren filled the air, echoing across the island in such a high pitch that it made my ears ring. It sounded three times, then an altered low voice boomed, "Evacuate the area in an orderly fashion. I repeat, evacuate the area in an orderly fashion." The siren blared once more, and the cycle repeated itself.

Confusion filled the dark scene. On the field, the referees again blew their whistles and directed the players to the sidelines, where the coaches took over. Teachers came forward, taking the lead and directing people along the walkways. The bulk of the crowd drained from the bleachers and the thick cluster of people funneled at the exit, marching through the center of the high school.

I shifted my attention from the scene below to my old friend's face. He wore a satisfied expression. "Like sheep to the slaughter," he said. Brier turned to look at me. "I'm sure you're familiar with the battle of Teutoburg Forest?" I was, but he didn't wait for a response. He wanted to paint the picture clearly for maximum effect. "I've always been fascinated by it. Arminius, a Germanic-born Roman military commander, convinced the generals to lead an army of three legions into the mountains. Once there, the spread-thin Roman soldiers were ambushed by hordes of rebel tribes united and led by none other than Arminius himself." Brier sneered. "Imagine that. Betrayed by one of their own. The mass of men led away, then unable to stop their thousands being decimated before their eyes."

As Brier's face had given away, the lights going out and the alarm were all part of his plan.

We watched, intense anger knotting up in the pit of my stomach as the crowd continued to move between the school buildings. A carefully placed strand of yellow tape forced the group to stick to the main walkway to the parking lot.

"Here," Brier said, shoving the monocular into my chest. As I clasped the instrument, he pointed toward the parking lot. "Zoom in near the drop-off area."

I did as he said, raising the monocular and bringing the magnified image into focus. My mouth fell open as I realized that there was a tall fence in place between two buildings, blocking the way to the parking lot.

"Now follow the path back thirty yards," Brier added.

Slowly, I panned sideways, scanning over the first people to arrive at the fence and realize that they'd reached a dead end. Roughly thirty yards from the fence, I spotted a maintenance van parked in the center of the path.

"You see, Dodge?" Brier said. "I told you your wife's pathetic attempt was futile. At first, I didn't think I had enough C-4 to take down this large of a crowd. But all squished together like a can of sardines, I think I'll have a chance."

As the mass of attendees congregated at the fence, the people at the front trying to push it aside or find a way through, Brier reached into his pocket and pulled out a switch with a plastic cover. A few people down below started yelling for the crowd to push back and use an alternate exit. We were nearing the moment of maximum damage, when nearly the entire crowd pushed into each other around the van.

This was it. I'd stalled long enough—come hell or high water, it was time for me to make a move.

I noted each of my four assailants' positions carefully, using my peripherals to see where each of them stood along the slopes of the sleek metal roof. Brier was two strides away, his back facing me and his eyes gazing over the scene below. Vito was to my right, watching the spectacle but keeping his weapon locked onto me. The two others were still at my back, just half a stride away, their submachine guns at the ready.

"Now, it's time for you to watch," Brier said. He held up the detonator, took one more satisfied look at me over his shoulder, then turned to face the crowd.

Just as he was about to flip open the cover and reveal the switch, a loud commotion coming from below caught all of our attention. A gunshot went off, then another.

This was my chance. My only window of opportunity.

The guy to my left stepped forward instinctively and adjusted his aim just enough for the barrel of his weapon to be within arm's length. As fast as I could, I twisted, snatched the barrel, and lunged behind the guy. As I'd hoped, the trigger-happy Vito opened fire, sending a round screaming into his own man's chest.

The guy shook and groaned on impact, his body protecting mine. Still gripping tight to his weapon, I completed my spin with a roundhouse kick to my second opponent, bashing my foot across his face and knocking him out.

Just as Vito was about to have a clear shot at me, I ripped the SMG from my gunned-down adversary and hurled it as hard as I could. The seven-pound steel-and-polymer firearm smacked into Vito, causing the crime boss to fall out of sight and his pistol to tumble and slide down the roof.

By the time I turned back to focus on Brier, my old brother in arms had turned, released his monocular and withdrawn his sidearm. As I sprang toward him with reckless abandon, the man took a fatal step backward, his sole striking the opposite side of the angled roof. It threw him off-balance, and he slipped, pulling the trigger and firing a bullet skyward just before I reached him. I leapt and drove my right shoulder into his chest. He lurched backward and heaved from the blow, relinquishing control of his weapon as we both pounded into the roof.

We rolled twice, exchanging quick blows and fighting for position as we slid to a stop right beside the edge. I grabbed Brier by the wrist, squeezing with all my strength to try and free the detonator from his grasp.

He growled back, baring his teeth as he used his free hand to grab a blade from his hip. The twelve-inch steel flew toward me, and I just managed to let go of his other wrist and stop it before the tip punctured my throat.

"It's useless to resist, Dodge," he snarled, pressing the knife down harder until it was just inches above my flesh.

In a blink, I jerked my upper body to the side and

relaxed my arms. Still putting all of his weight into the knife, the steel screeched into the roof beside my right ear. As he jolted forward, I pounded my forehead into his face. He wailed and released control of his knife. Kicking him off me, I slugged him in the breadbasket and tackled him to the ground, struggling with everything I had to pry the detonator from his hand.

Grabbing his wrist with both hands, I pounded his fingers into the roof and the little device bounced free, sliding down the smooth surface.

"Never turn your back," Brier growled, punching me in the side of the face, then kicking me in the chest. I flew backward, rolling to a stop and struggling to a knee, pain coursing through my body. "On a raging beast," Brier added.

With the detonator resting on the roof between us, we both made a mad dash. I took two steps before diving and reaching as far out as I could. But Brier had been closer, and by the time I landed, he'd already swiped the device and held it up.

"Game over, Dodge," he said as he swiftly flicked the cover and pressed the switch.

SIX

Ange stared into the large hardcase, realizing that it was empty just before the stadium lights shut off. As the world turned dark, she whirled around and scanned over the sea of confusion. Players ran off the field and huddled with their coaches to the sound of whistles. The crowd shuffled and murmured in confusion. Then a blaring alarm sounded, followed by the instructions for everyone to evacuate the stadium.

As the players and coaches made a beeline for the home team side of the field and the audience shuffled for the exit, Ange remained frozen, wondering what was happening.

Maybe Logan did it, she thought. *Maybe he took down whoever was threatening the stadium and is now clearing everybody out just in case.*

"Hey," Jack said, nudging Ange. "I'm all out of guesses," he added, gesturing toward the empty case. "What's the plan now?"

Ange didn't know how to answer that. She

wondered whether they should continue looking for an explosive device or if they should clear out with the others and let a bomb squad handle it later on.

"Come on," she decided, beckoning Jack to join her as she cut back toward the side of the field, then moved parallel with the fence, heading for the exit.

As they reached the corner and were about to exit the field through a gate onto the track, Ange spotted a man in a suit that she recognized as the superintendent of the school district. He was talking animatedly to a woman who she realized was the assistant principal of the high school.

"Any clue what's going on here?" the superintendent asked, apparently reasoning they were far enough from the crowd that no one would hear them.

"No idea," the woman replied.

"And when did the school get a new alarm system? I've never heard that message before."

"I didn't know we had."

The words struck a chord in Ange's psyche. Neither of the school administrators had heard the alarm before… because it was new. It wasn't theirs at all. Whoever was threatening to blow the place had killed the lights and set off the alarm. Ange was far from certain that she'd reached a viable conclusion, but if there was even the slightest chance that she was right, she needed to move.

"Come on," Ange said, shooting Jack a stern gaze.

She didn't bother waiting for a reply. There wasn't time for that. Taking off into a sprint, she quickly reached the edge of the grass, dashed through the opening, and weaved through the exiting mass of

42

people.

"Everybody just stay calm!" one of the teachers shouted. "There's no need to rush. We'll all get out of here."

Ange had a need to rush—deep in her gut, she knew that every second could be vital. She cut through the group, hustling around the outskirts, scaling the side fence and racing along a narrow walkway into the center of the school. In the quad, she reached the front of the advancing crowd and spotted a strand of yellow tape strung across the alternate route to the parking lot—a strand that hadn't been there when she and Logan had arrived for the game two hours earlier. The tape further solidified her conclusion, and she ran over and quicky removed the strand before cutting back and continuing down the main path.

Heading for the lot, she flew by a giant statue of a conch shell and a parked maintenance van, then staggered to a stop as she saw that the exit was blocked off by a newly placed chain-link fence.

"Holy crap," she whispered, the scheme becoming clear in her mind.

When she turned back to face the direction she'd come, she saw the throng of people heading straight toward her. For a moment, she thought that the best move would be to somehow batter down the fence. As she searched for possible methods, she homed in on the maintenance van parked beside the statue.

That wasn't there before either, she thought, scrutinizing the vehicle. *And how did it get here with the fence in place? Unless...*

After cutting the distance, she tried the back door

of the van, but it was locked. Prying loose one of the bricks lining the walkway, she fired the heavy object into the window, shattering the glass. Reaching a hand inside, she gripped the handle and opened the door. There, resting in the back of the van, were eight M112 demolition blocks of C-4 plastic explosives, wired for synchronous detonation.

Ange gasped, her jaw hitting the floor as the objects came into focus. With no timer ticking down to initiate the blasting cap, the explosives could be detonated at any second.

"Ange!" Jack shouted.

The islander had kicked off his flip-flops and finally caught up with Ange after her impressive dash across the campus.

As the name left his lips, gunfire erupted. Bullets pelted the side of the van, let loose by two men rushing toward the vehicle from a side path. Jack dove, then took cover behind the van as the bullets continued to whiz by and spark against the frame.

Nearby, people let out cries of terror as they scrambled away from the scene. Some who'd already reached the fence scaled the chain link and tried to batter it down to escape to the nearby parking lot.

Ange dropped down into the van, lying flat to minimize her target size as she withdrew her Glock 26. She readjusted her position, then peeked around the corner and took aim toward the shadows, firing two rounds at the shadowy figures closing in with their weapons raised. The two men took cover, and Jack crawled around and rushed into the back of the van during a brief break in the assault. As he landed, he looked up and then froze, his eyes massive as he gazed upon the bombs.

"So glad I took cover in here," he gasped. "Please tell me you can disarm this thing?"

Ange fired another round, then turned back and handed the pistol to Jack. "Keep me covered."

With laser focus, she and Jack switched positions and she crawled carefully over to the detonation mechanism. Her husband was the real expert when it came to explosive disposal, but she was far from inexperienced. Knowing that the most important thing with C-4 is the removal of the blasting cap, she knelt down and reached for the plastic housing covering the detonation circuitry. With no proper tools, she removed her knife and used the tip to pry open the shell. Once inside, she expected to give the wires a quick snip, rendering the explosives useless, but all the components were wrapped in layers of duct tape.

Of course, she thought, going to work to tear and cut away the strong adhesive.

Jack fired two more rounds at their attackers, then dropped back as they both let loose, peppering holes through the side of the van.

"Can't hold them off much longer, Ange!" he shouted. "They're breaking apart to come at us from both sides."

He peeked around the door, contorting his body just enough to get a view, and fired another round. This one struck home, blasting into one of their attackers' shoulders and causing him to tumble forward.

Keeping her focus fully engaged on the task at hand, Ange finally forced her way into the wires. Her heart pounding like a jackhammer, she placed the cutting edge of her knife to the rubber coating and held her breath. A quick slice and the wire was severed. She gasped, then inspected the device, relieved to find that the illuminated LED on the housing had gone dark.

As she turned back toward Jack, the man he'd shot staggered into view. Before Jack could fire at the guy again, the bloodied man aimed his weapon around the corner. Ange didn't hesitate. She spun rapidly and hurled her knife toward their assailant. The blade flew across the back of the van, right past Jack, then burrowed into the guy's abdomen. He fired a bullet into the roof of the van as he fell back and collapsed on the pavement.

Again gunshots erupted, but this time, they came from the direction of the retreating crowd. The second attacker fell to the ground, sprawling out beside his buddy. Jane Verona, the chief of the Key West Police Department, rushed into view. Off-duty, the Latina wore jeans and a black tank top. She held her government-issued Walther handgun out in front of her as she closed in on the van.

"What the hell's going on?" she demanded. Then her eyes rested on the explosives. "Is that what I think it is?"

"Exactly what you think, Jane," Ange said, retrieving her weapon from Jack and climbing out of the van.

"Please tell me it's disarmed," she added.

"It is," Ange said, looking around the scene with her Glock at the ready. "But it could be rearmed. It needs to be watched until a bomb squad arrives."

Seeing Ange peer toward the parking lot and focus

her gaze, Jane said, "Backup's on the way. What do you see?"

Ange zeroed in on a third gunman racing toward the parking lot. Hoping that the fleeing terrorist could lead her to her husband, she took off.

"A straggler," she said. "Keep an eye on that bomb," she added over her shoulder.

Sliding her Glock into the back of her waistband, she jumped onto the fence and launched herself over the top. As her feet hit the blacktop, she sprang toward the lot, following the line of the man who'd vanished behind the cars seconds earlier. Keeping her eyes peeled, she moved between the vehicles, trying to catch a glimpse of him, but it wasn't easy with all the people who'd managed to reach the lot running for their cars, motivated by the sound of gunfire booming across the campus.

Catching sight of the guy just before he crept behind a parked Marathon High School bus, she cut left and picked up her pace. Sweat coated her body from the exertion and humidity. Her heart continued to race, but she kept her breathing under control as she reached the bus. Snatching and raising her Glock, she sprang around the opposite side and prepared to open fire. But the attacker was gone. Creeping forward, she kept the sights leveled, expecting to have to shift her aim and pull the trigger at any second. She popped out at the back of the bus, still not seeing any sign of the guy.

As she strode back toward the other side, seeing and hearing nothing, the sound of a grumbling engine filled the air. There a powerful rumble and a screech of tires against the pavement. Ange popped back around just as a blue Ford Bronco rocketed toward the yellow bus and the third attacker as he hid around the corner, waiting to pounce on her. The man redirected his aim and pulled the trigger, sending a bullet into the raging SUV just before the vehicle smashed into his body, shattering bones as he was pummeled against the side of the bus.

SEVEN

I watched from just a few feet away as Brier stabbed the detonator switch with his thumb. My heart sank as the mechanism clicked, and my mouth dropped open as I anticipated the sound of an explosion roaring across the evening air.

But the sound didn't come.

Only the noises of fleeing people and shouts of panic could be heard from below, punctuated by the occasional gunshot. Brier lowered the detonator, his face burning with anger as he pounded it against his thigh, then thumbed the switch back for another go.

I pounced on my old friend, spinning and battering my leg into the back of his knees. He buckled and hit the roof hard. I shifted around and ripped the knife from his hands. As he struggled to retaliate, landing a quick jab to my side, I forced him around and jammed the blade toward his neck. He managed to keep the knife away and elbowed me in the forehead.

We rolled again, fighting for the upper hand until

we reached the edge of the roof. I slashed a gash across his shoulder, and he twisted and winced in pain before striking back. Using his anger against him, I went with his momentum, forced him onto his back, and shoved a knee into his chest. As I put all my weight into the knife, wanting to put an end to Brier for good, he glanced toward the apex of the roof.

A sinister smile formed on his face.

"Like I said. Game over, Dodge," he hissed, baring his teeth at me.

I glanced up just as Vito took post at the crest of the roof, his Colt clutched in his right hand. The crime boss wiped the blood from his chin from the blow I'd dealt him moments earlier, then sneered at me as he arched the barrel of the pistol my way. With Brier holding me back, I couldn't finish him off before Vito pulled the trigger. Brier had a knife inches from his body, but it was I who faced imminent death.

With no other way out, I forced myself away from Brier, yanking my body backward. He held on to me as I jerked over the corner of the roof, but let go as I rounded the edge. Vito pulled the trigger, sending a round into the metal right beside us as I tumbled over nothing but open air. Remembering the location of the utility shed, I spun wildly, picking up speed before bashing into the roof of the outbuilding. I struck hard and rolled along the angled slope before falling again. I did my best to roll with the landing as I slammed against the grass, grunting from the hefty blow as I twisted, pain resonating from all corners of my body.

The second my body came to a stop, I locked eyes

on the shadowy figure of Brier up on the roof. He pointed at me and yelled. I rolled back in the direction I'd come and managed to reach the cover of the shed just as Vito arrived with his weapon raised. Still clutching Brier's tactical knife, I rose up onto a knee and prepared for round two. I was battered and delirious from the fight and fall, but ready to finish the criminals off for good. The whine of police sirens filled the air as I waited in the shadows.

After taking a second to catch my breath, I peeked around the shed and focused on the top of the gym. Brier and Vito were gone. I came to my feet and staggered along the side of the building, heading toward the back and the ladder I'd used to make my ascent. When I popped out, knife at the ready, I saw that the two men had already reached the bottom, having used a set of ropes dangling down the building to rappel down. I spotted their two shadowy figures as they raced around the tennis courts, heading across a small lot toward a side road.

I took off as fast as I could, willing my body to ignore the discomfort. I took a narrow path through the courts, cutting the distance between us as I reached the other side and watched them hightail it across the road. When I reached the sidewalk, I stood behind a hedge as they climbed into a parked Porsche SUV. Too far off to make a move, I focused on the license plate and managed to catch the number under the glow of a streetlight just before they took off.

Brier floored it, burning rubber and accelerating away from me. The vehicle rounded a corner, disappearing from view. I sighed in anger as I planted my hands on my knees and slowed my breathing.

Just as I thought the ordeal was over, a gunshot echoed from the main parking lot, followed by a loud crash.

EIGHT

Drawn by the sudden commotion, I turned and bounded toward the main parking lot. I followed the side road until I reached one of the school's main buildings, then cut and raced toward the opposite side of the lot. The place was a madhouse. People running frantically for their vehicles. Cars peeling out and thundering toward the exit. Police interceptors flying into view, avoiding the chaotic traffic and cruising toward the main walkway.

I wanted to search across the lot for the source of the gunfire, but I had to keep all my senses focused on my surroundings to avoid being hit by a renegade vehicle. Weaving in and out of the bustling traffic, I reached the opposite side of the lot and gazed upon the place where the sound had come. I instantly laid eyes on my daughter's blue Bronco, its grille and hood smashed in against the side of a yellow school bus.

Scarlett, I thought, gasping as I eyed the wrecked

SUV.

With newfound vigor, I darted across the remaining pavement, preparing for the worse and still gripping Brier's knife in my right hand. As I rounded the Bronco, I saw a man sandwiched between the frame and the bus, his motionless, bloodied body draped over the scrunched hood. My heart sank as I saw a bullet hole in the windshield, and I stepped toward the passenger door.

"Logan!" Ange exclaimed.

I turned and saw my wife striding around from the other side of the Bronco, her arms draped over Scarlett. Unable to control myself, I lunged and wrapped my arms around them.

"Are either of you hurt?" I said, relaxing my grip just enough to inspect them.

I noticed a cut to my daughter's forehead.

"We're fine," Ange said.

"But Kate's banged up," Scarlett added. She ushered me over to her friend, who sat in a patch of grass, hunched forward with a hand placed to her forehead.

I knelt down beside the girl. "Are you all right?" I said softly.

She winced and rubbed her brow. "My head hurts."

"She hit the dash when I plowed into the guy," Scarlett said. "We were waiting in the car, just as Mom said, when we saw him holding a gun and waiting to attack Mom when she rounded the bus. I had to do something." She placed a hand on the injured girl. "I'm sorry. I'm so sorry, Kate."

Seeing an ambulance pull down our row, I cut out

into the middle and flagged down the driver. When he pulled beside me, I pointed toward Kate.

"She's hurt," I told the EMT, who parked beside the Bronco.

The team went to work. As they helped Scarlett's friend, Ange brought me aside.

"What the hell happened to you?" she said, looking my battered body up and down. "Who did this?"

I answered her questions with one word. "Brier."

Ange's eyes bulged. "What? How in the… is he dead?"

I swallowed hard. "He and Vito got away."

"Brier and Bonetti are—"

"Yes."

I blinked and looked up as people continued to rush to their cars. Over by the fence that Brier's men had installed, I caught sight of Jane Verona directing the fleeing crowd.

"Stay here," I said, jogging toward the chief of police.

I headed along the side of the lot. Jane took charge, being the well-known and effective leader that she was. She ordered two officers to set up a perimeter surrounding the parked maintenance van, then whirled around upon my approach.

"Logan," she said, eyeing me up and down. "Please tell me you know who left this stack of explosives."

"Nathan Brier," I said flatly.

She took a step back. She'd heard of the man as well. Six months earlier, while trying to lure me out of the islands for his ultra-rich, corrupt employer,

Brier had murdered the mayor of Key West in a gruesome act that had taken place downtown right after he'd given a speech.

"And he's getting away," I said. "There's still time for your men to catch him. I got the plates of their getaway vehicle. It's a black Porsche Cayenne."

I gave her the number, and she snatched her radio and called it in. In addition to putting every officer, off duty or not, who wasn't already at the school on the lookout, she ordered a roadblock to be set up just east of Cudjoe Key on US-1.

"We'll get him," I assured her. "He may have gotten away, but his plan failed. His bombs didn't go off and I'm still breathing."

With Jane bringing order to the scene as well as anyone could, I made my way back to Ange and Scarlett.

"Well done with the bomb," I said, wrapping my arms around Ange again. "And for getting my message."

Scarlett's shoulder slumped and she teared up as the ambulance drove off with her friend.

"You did a brave thing, Scar," I said, consoling her.

"And you might very well have saved my life," Ange added.

"I just hope she's okay."

Jack approached. After telling me his side of the story, I thanked him for having my wife's back. The next hour and a half was spent helping Jane control the scene and clear everybody off the campus and telling local detectives what had happened. Fortunately, we managed to get out of there before reporters from major networks showed up. A bomb scare at a high school would make national news, and the last thing either Ange or I wanted was our names plastered all over the web.

The scene was gloom as we prepared to head home. The spectators had managed to come out mostly unscathed, but the threat and the potential for a catastrophe were felt by every member of law enforcement. Jane seemed especially hard hit and began to show it only when most all of the civilians had cleared out.

"In my fourteen years serving the people of Key West," Jane said, "I've never seen anything like this." She paused, fighting to keep it together. "I've got voicemails from the FBI, Homeland Security, and Fox News and CNN. I've got worried people calling the operator at the station from around the country, making sure that their family members are all right." She straightened her shirt and stood taller. "This isn't a battlefield, Logan. This is my town. These are my people. I'm gonna find this bastard and bring him down."

"I'm with you, Jane. The last thing I want is to put the people here in danger. We'll find him."

NINE

Nathan Brier focused forward, his eyes intense as he mashed the gas pedal, zooming from one island to the next. He took intermittent glances at the police scanner attached to the dash and listened carefully as local law enforcement scrambled to take them down.

"You hear that?" Vito said, following an officer's report. "They're setting up a roadblock on the Kemp Channel Bridge." The Italian crime boss slipped out his phone and checked Google Maps. "That's right after Cudjoe. Just two more miles from he—"

"I know where it is," Brier snapped, keeping his gaze forward and his hands gripping the wheel tight.

Vito shook his head. "Call in your flyboy. Get us the hell out of here."

"Pipe down, old man. I've always got a plan B. And I'm not calling in air support until we accomplish our mission. He'll stay on standby for now."

During a long straightaway, Brier pulled out his

phone and shot off a text to a number he'd called five minutes earlier. Halfway across Cudjoe, and just two miles from the roadblock, a still infuriated Brier got an idea and turned into a gas station.

"What the hell is wrong with you?" Vito said, looking around frantically. As Brier braked to a stop beside a pump, he added, "You're getting gas? Are you crazy? You're going to get us killed. There's a camera right there!" He pointed at a security camera built into the roof that was trained straight at them.

Brier leaned forward, examining the camera's angle carefully before looking back at the road.

"It's stationary," he whispered to himself. "And only catches half the Overseas Highway at best." He nodded. "This will work nicely."

Years of government and private military training and experience, and hundreds of operations in locales ranging from urban environments to jungles, had attuned Brier's senses and instincts beyond those of a normal person. He saw the world, angles, people, and structures differently than others. He saw them like a professional killer.

Brier took one more look around, making sure that there were no cop cars nearby. Before Vito could protest again, he pushed open the door and strode into the station.

He purchased a bag of items with cash, then pushed back out into the humid air. Opening the driver's side door, he leaned inside and pulled a notebook and sharpie from the plastic bag.

"What the hell are you doing now?" Vito said, shifting in his seat.

Brier continued to ignore the man as he wrote a

message on a sheet of notebook paper. Sauntering to the front of the Porsche, Brier held up the paper to the camera and shot a cocky smile. Then, he plopped back into the driver's seat and hit the gas. Only instead of continuing east, he turned right, accelerating back toward Key West.

As Vito opened his mouth in utter confusion, Brier held up a finger. "You have your areas of expertise... and I have mine."

If there was one thing Brier valued when it came to slipping through the cracks of the law, it was unpredictability.

Going against the norm and instilling confusion are the key.

As a line of semi-trucks closed in from behind them, Brier pulled off the gas, hit the brakes, and did a quick U-turn. Driving east, he turned left just after the gas station and floored it north up the island.

Vito looked forward at the dark, sparsely populated land surrounding them. "This wasn't the plan, Brier," he spat. "You promised me that Dodge would be dead. And that I'd be the one who got to pull the trigger."

"You did. It's not my fault your shoddy aim took down one of your own instead."

"This wasn't how it was supposed to go down. You promised me. That's the only reason I agreed to help you."

"Yes, and you promised me that your men would come through with the bomb. So, I guess you failed as well."

"The bomb was placed. It was constructed correctly. The only way for it not to detonate is if it were tampered with, which isn't my fault. That's yours for waiting too long to flick the damn switch."

Brier cocked his head and stared at the crime boss. The speedometer indicated that they were cruising down the empty side road at over ninety miles per hour, but Brier didn't care. "I think you're forgetting, Vito, that I saved your life. That I found you crawling in a ditch on the side of the road, bleeding to death. That you'd be dead at worst and serving a life sentence at best right now were it not for me."

"Would you keep your eyes on the damn road?!" Vito spat.

Brier kept his eyes locked on Vito, then sneered before turning back forward. "You scared?"

"I'm not suicidal."

Brier chuckled.

As they neared the end of the road, Vito said, "How exactly are you planning on getting rid of this car anyway?"

Brier let his foot slip off the gas and onto the brake.

"What's going on?" Vito snapped, looking around again as Brier brought the Porsche to a stop just before a fork in the road.

Without a word, Brier snatched a pistol from the center console and shoved it into the crime boss's gut. "I'm in charge, Vito, understand?" Brier gritted his teeth and shoved the barrel harder. Vito didn't wince, but he tensed up. "If you don't like it, you can get the hell out of the car." He flexed his trigger finger slightly. "Say it. Say I'm in charge!"

Vito's face scrunched up, but he relented. "You're in charge."

Brier smiled, kept the pistol in place a moment longer, then brought it away. Wanting to terrify the old man even more, Brier revved the engine and stared forward. "To answer your question, I'm gonna get rid of the car by sending it into to the drink." He gazed through the windshield down the right side of the fork toward a distant boat ramp. "But to do that, we're gonna need a lot of speed."

The moment the last word left his lips, Brier stomped the gas, sending them hard against their seat backs as the tires spun up smoke and the smell of burnt rubber. They launched forward, the tachometer pegged as the growling engine worked in overdrive, and flew down the end of the road, the waters of Kemp Channel looming dangerously close.

Brier laughed as Vito held on, sheer terror overtaking the hardened man's face. At the last moment, Brier eased off the gas and hit the brakes, stopping them less than a foot from the water's edge at the base of the ramp.

"You're a madman!" Vito said, catching his breath.

Before the Italian could say any more, Brier shut off the engine and shoved open his door, the sounds of an approaching vessel filling the air.

"Time to go," Brier said, smacking the top of the vehicle.

Vito sighed, then climbed out, his face contorted with anger from the incident. They stood along the shore as a boat pulled up, Brier throwing a wave to one of Vito's men standing on the bow. The guy swung a coil of chain, then tossed it when the craft was within twenty feet of the bank. Brier snatched up the links, attached it to the Porsche's front axle, then put the vehicle in neutral.

"You need to learn to trust me," Brier said as they waded into the knee-deep water and climbed up onto the boat. "Your men do."

Once aboard, Brier gave the order and the pilot pushed the throttle forward, accelerating them slowly out into the channel. When the chain went taut, he shoved farther, splashing the SUV into the water and pulling it along the shore into a deep pool that was partly covered by encroaching mangroves.

"We've got a Coast Guard patrol passing by," the pilot said, eyeing a radar screen in the cockpit.

Brier lunged toward the monitor. "How far?"

"Five miles due northeast. Skirting along the islands." He paused, then added, "They're trying to hail me."

The sound of a Coast Guard officer's voice blared through the radio, but Brier pounced over and switched it off. "Don't answer them." Scanning along the taut chain and toward the submerged vehicle, he added, "This is good enough. Reverse."

The pilot did as instructed, giving Brier enough slack to remove the chain and toss it into the water. Once the SUV was released, Brier shot him a thumbs-up. "Get us the hell out of here. Back to the safe house."

Brier held on as the boat quickly picked up speed, keeping his gaze to the north and making sure that their getaway wasn't interrupted by the patrol boat. His backup plan of driving out of the islands until they hit a roadblock, then meeting the boat at the nearest ramp, was working well, but they weren't out of the woods yet. They weaved between islands, and it wasn't until the dock of their hideout came into view that Brier finally took a breath and fully pondered the evening's events.

The pilot idled them up to the covered dock and they tied off.

"What are we going to do now, Brier? Huh?" Vito said. "This all part of your plan?"

Brier thought a moment. "We lie and wait. And... when Dodge least expects it, we'll strike and take him down. It will take the feds a while to find that sunken car. We have time to orchestrate another plan." When Vito didn't reply, Brier added, "If you don't like it, Bonetti, I'd be happy to handle our disagreement right now."

The two men stared at each other for a moment, then Vito said, "All right. We will wait and strike a second time." He strode toward Brier and added, "But if you fail again, you're on your own. Understand?"

Brier chuckled, then nodded. "Whatever you say, old man."

Brier strode arrogantly down the planks, heading toward a house that was mostly hidden by clusters of trees.

When Brier was out of earshot, Vito turned to his men. "To hell with this punk. We don't need him to take Dodge down." He looked at each of his men in turn. "We'll track his movements, figure out his usual hangouts, and finish him ourselves."

TEN

It was just after midnight by the time we pulled into our driveway on Palmetto Street on the New Town side of the island. Jane had ordered two of her officers to sit tight in their police cruiser near our mailbox just in case Brier decided to pay us a visit. She knew we could take care of ourselves, but figured a little backup couldn't hurt.

I threw a wave to the officers, and as the tires of my Tacoma 4x4 crunched the seashells, I spotted a familiar old Chevy pickup parked along the left side of the drive. Cameron Tyson, a senior at Key West High and the quarterback of its football team, sat on the front porch steps. He came to his feet as we pulled in.

"They had the players leave right away and I didn't get a chance to see you," he told Scarlett as we hopped out and approached him. "I wanted to make sure you were all right."

He wrapped his arms around Scarlett as Atticus,

our yellow Lab, bolted from the deck and jumped into us, slathering Ange and me with licks and wagging his tail like crazy.

"Good to see you too, boy," I said, scratching behind his ears. "Glad you made it out fine," I added to Cameron. "Keep it under five minutes, all right, Scar? It's late."

"You too, Mr. Dodge," Cameron said. Like about a hundred other people had in the past hour, he looked over my tattered clothes and bruised body. "What happened, anyway? I heard the gunshots and—"

"I'll tell you some other time," I said, tired of relaying the incident. I eyed my daughter and added, "Scar?"

She nodded. "Five minutes."

Before heading inside, I looked around the property and asked Cameron how long he'd been there.

"An hour maybe," he said.

"You see anyone?"

"Other than the cops and your neighbors rolling out their trash can? No."

Ange and I did a quick sweep of the grounds, making sure that nothing had been tampered with. If Brier had been able to figure out where I'd been that night, he'd have no trouble discovering our address.

Once done with our sweep, I checked the advanced and elaborate security system I'd installed myself after buying the place. None of the cameras or sensors indicated that we'd had a visitor other than Cameron.

Confident that neither Brier, Vito, or any of their men had paid us a visit, Ange and I headed inside.

After downing three glasses of water, I migrated to the master bathroom and ran the shower.

"You look pretty good considering," Ange said, examining me as I peeled off my clothes.

The paramedics had cleaned the cuts. Fortunately, none of them were bad enough to require stitches. The worst blows I'd suffered had come from gravity, purple bruises having blossomed on my left shoulder and hip.

When I didn't reply, Ange added, "You hungry? We've got leftover grilled mahi and vegetables in the fridge."

Jack and I had hit it big our last time out fishing and had hauled in three of the vibrant ray-finned fish, each of them far too large to toss back.

"That would be great, Ange," I said, kissing her on the forehead.

I was still in a haze, and my wife could see that. It wasn't just about the ordeal we'd just been through, and it wasn't the scrapes. I'd been beaten to hell and shot at dozens of times over the course of my life. My body can take a pounding, and with time and rest can rebound. This was another level. This was Nathan Brier hunting me down.

I stepped under the hot waterfall, leaning against the tile as it cascaded over my body. Drops of blood and dirt washed away, gurgling down the drain at my feet. I couldn't get the man out of my head as I washed up, rinsed off, then turned the knob and toweled off. I'd been thinking about what to do next ever since the SUV had peeled out and disappeared from sight. One thing I knew for certain: Brier would be back. Until I finished him off for good, he'd continue to come after me with everything he had.

I threw on a pair of cargo shorts and a T-shirt, then strolled barefoot to the living room. The smell of grilled fish and lemon welcomed me, and I sat down beside Ange. Cameron's truck pulled out of the driveway and Scarlett entered, having spent far more than five minutes talking to her boyfriend. But I didn't say anything about it. It had been a difficult night, and I was glad she had someone her age she could talk it over with.

Without a word, she sat down beside me, clearly still shell-shocked from the ordeal, and barely pecked at her food.

"Kate's gonna be fine, kiddo," I said. "You did the right thing."

She nodded, then excused herself to her bedroom after managing only half her plate. When I pushed my chair back to follow her, Ange placed a hand on me. "She'll be fine," she said softly. "Just give her some time to herself to process what happened."

"I think it's going to take all of us some time."

We both ate in silence for a moment as I finished up. When I started clearing the table, Ange rose and wrapped an arm around me.

"Hey, you did good too," she said, squeezing me tight. "Seems like you said that to everyone tonight, but no one said it to you. If it weren't for you, there'd be a much different story in the news. You saved hundreds of lives tonight, Logan."

My mind didn't stray from Brier and all that the man had said to me on top of the gym. "They wouldn't have been in danger in the first place were it not for me. I was the only reason that Brier was there."

"So, what? You think it's your fault? You've been an honorable man your entire life, Logan Dodge. You did what was right years ago, and you're still doing it now. He was in the wrong. Always has been. And one day, hopefully soon, he'll reap all the rest of what he's sown."

I kissed her cheek and thanked her for the pep talk. After doing the dishes, I stepped out to the balcony for a breather. Our stilted house was simple at around sixteen hundred square feet. But we liked it that way and loved the location, the green backyard ending right on a channel.

Ange followed me with two mojitos. She handed me one and I took a long pull, splashing down half the glass. The combination of lime juice, mint, and club soda tasted amazing, and the white rum felt even better, warming and relaxing me from the inside.

"We need to figure out what we're going to do about this," I said. "How we're going to find him and Vito."

Ange shrugged. "Not much we can do until the police find the getaway vehicle."

"You heard anything?"

She shook her head. "But the roadblock will be up until early morning—checking vehicles as they pass. I'm sure when Jane does discover something, mine won't be the first number she'll call."

I nodded. Though Ange and I weren't law enforcement, we'd worked closely alongside Key West Police, the Monroe County Sheriff's Office, the Coast Guard, and the Navy on many dangerous operations over the past three and a half years.

"He'll attack you again," Ange said.

"Yes. He and Vito both." I paused. "Hopefully, he does it soon, and he mans up and keeps it between us."

Ange fell silent, something clearly nagging at her mind.

"What is it, Ange?"

She took a sip, then cleared her throat. "Brier. He's different from the criminals you've faced off against before. And I'm sure he still has connections from Darkwater."

Darkwater was a private military group that had fully disbanded following the death of its leader, Carson Richmond, after she'd blown up in a helicopter accident while fleeing a corrupt oil rig operation in the Gulf. Brier had been a part of the mysterious and notoriously violent group and no doubt still had more than a few contacts from his old tribe. That made it all the more important to find the guy and take him down before he had yet another chance to regroup.

Ange leaned against the railing and peered out over the dark channel. "And even worse... he's not after money or power." She turned and looked me in the eyes intensely. "He's after revenge."

ELEVEN

Despite the lack of sleep and the events of the previous night, I woke up just before sunrise for a morning run. I needed to clear my head, and for me, that generally involved breaking a sweat.

After a quick conversation with the police officers staking out in their squad car at the end of the driveway, I broke into a slow warm up trot. My usual route was south to the waterfront, wrapping around the airport, then west past the southernmost point marker, through Old Town, then back around on the northern side of the island. But today I deviated, continuing on Bertha Street and swinging by the high school.

It was half past five, and the scene was quiet, a drastic change from the chaos that had enveloped the campus the previous night. I dialed back my pace to take in the scene but still kept to a steady jog as I rounded the front buildings, then skirted the main parking lot. The gates were locked and much of the campus was roped off. I slowed when I reached the auxiliary lot and, after not seeing anyone nearby, slipped between the tennis courts and the back of the gym.

I've always enjoyed the early-morning hours. While most of the world sleeps, you get time to yourself. To just think or observe things unencumbered by the presence of others. In the quiet, I relived the previous evening, tracing the path I'd taken from the football field up through the school, around the building, and up the ladder. I considered climbing up for a better look around but figured I'd be pushing my luck. I'd told the detectives about the scuffle, and they had the ladder taped off.

I glanced at the dumpsters where I'd relinquished my weapons, and then had later reclaimed them while describing to the officials what had happened. After looking around, I turned and followed the route that Brier and Vito had used to scurry off into the night. I picked up my pace, passing the tennis courts, then crossing the road and taking the side street to where the Porsche SUV had been parked. When I reached the spot, I noticed tire marks on the pavement. They were faint, but still visible. I pictured the vehicle peeling out, huffing smoke in its wake as they throttled like hell away from the crime scene.

Pulling out my phone, I snapped a few pictures of the markings. I wasn't a detective, but I had more than a little experience tracking down bad guys and figured the tire marks might come in handy. I'd still yet to hear any word on Brier or their getaway car.

After snapping the shots, I pocketed my phone, had one more look around, then decided that I'd taken a long enough breather. Pacing back into my usual rhythm, I jogged around the school, then south to the waterfront. I picked it up a notch after passing Martello Tower and Higgs Beach, returning to my usual route and cutting across the island after passing the ten-ton concrete buoy that marks the southernmost point. I swung by Key West Bight and the Conch Harbor Marina, where I'd kept my 48 Baia Flash moored since moving to the Keys, then made my way back east toward the other side of the island.

My lungs burning and heaving for air, I returned to our house and came to a stop in the driveway, planting my hands on my knees. A glance at my dive watch told me that I'd completed the final mile of the nine-mile workout in just under six minutes. Far from my best, but given my fatigue and bruises from the night's scuffles, I chalked it up as a win.

I wiped the layer of sweat from my brow, then marched under the house to our makeshift gym. With my warmup complete, I went straight into a circuit of kettlebells, battle ropes, and pull-ups. When my heart rate was jacked and my muscles weary, I pushed even harder, wrapping up by pulling on my boxing gloves and going a couple rounds on the heavy bag.

Sweat sprayed off me with every strike. I beat the bag with a series of various combinations, my anger from the previous night and seeing Brier and Vito get away driving me to a potent level of intensity. Wrapping up a combo with an elbow strike, a turning kick, and a flying haymaker, I lurched forward and collapsed onto my back.

"You trying to destroy that thing?" Ange said, catching me by surprise.

I snapped my head and noticed her standing barefoot at the edge of the rubber-matted workout area. She wore denim shorts and a tank top and had her hair down.

"Always," I gasped. "Maybe I will one of these days."

She brisked over and handed me a chilled coconut water.

"My hero," I said, popping the top and chugging half its contents. "You know, sometimes it scares me just how stealthy you are."

She chuckled. "You were a little distracted fighting that bag."

"Well, it's undefeated against me."

She handed me a small towel and I patted my face with it. "Got eggs ready if you want." She turned, glanced at my phone resting on a wooden chair, then stepped toward it and scooped up the device.

"What is it?" I said, dabbing my neck with the towel.

"You've got a missed call from Jane."

I jumped to my feet and she handed it to me. I saw that the chief of police had called five minutes earlier, right in the middle of my final barrage. I thumbed the screen right away to call her back.

"Please tell me you've got something, Jane," I said after she answered.

"Nothing concrete yet. But I'd like to meet up."

"At the station?"

"I was thinking coffee. Moondog at nine work?"

I agreed, and after cleaning up and eating breakfast, I gathered the family to head downtown.

"You sure you want us to come?" Ange said,

speaking mainly for Scarlett and Atticus.

"After what happened last night, the Dodge clan's sticking together." Atticus leapt onto the couch and connected with a slobbery tongue across my cheek. "Yes, that means you too, boy."

Before heading out, I grabbed a few items from the safe in our master closet. A spare Sig to keep in the truck as well as a plastic hardcase filled with various gadgets I'd accumulated over the years. Our lives were at risk every time we stepped out the door, and I wanted to be prepared as possible. I set the case on the floor behind the passenger seat and stowed the extra firearm in the center console.

Once everyone was loaded into the Tacoma, I drove us into the heart of the city. I'd been living in Key West for three and a half years and had also spent a four-year stint here as a boy. The island paradise had my kind of perfect blend of tourist spots, nightlife, and laid-back attitudes. It also served as a jumping-off point to some of the best diving and most beautiful scenery I'd found anywhere in the world. But the capitol of the Conch Republic felt different as we cruised its morning streets with the windows down.

It felt off.

People strolling the sidewalks usually floated casually along, fully engrossed in island time and not needing to be anywhere or do anything that warranted a rush. Everyone just kind of went with the flow and the vibrations of the tropical vibes. But that morning, people stood more erect and walked faster. They weren't smiling as much and shot routine glances over their shoulders. It was like the entire island had been covered by a gray curtain of anxiety.

"I wasn't expecting everyone to be so on edge," Ange said.

With the internet and smartphones, not to mention the slew of echoing gunshots the previous night, word had spread fast about what had happened. An attack on one islander was an attack on the whole bunch, and the people clearly weren't taking the news lightly.

I managed to achieve nothing short of a miracle by locating an empty parking spot along Whitehead Street. After hopping out and paying the meter, we strolled two blocks, passing right by the Hemingway House before turning into Moondog Café. The small, charming local spot had a cozy dining area as well as an ample patio parallel to the sidewalk.

I spotted Jane sitting at an outside corner table and we pushed open a gate in the white picket fence. She was sitting across from a man I recognized as Ezra Nix, the recently elected mayor of Key West, though I'd never met him before. To the mayor's right sat a powerfully built black man who wore a crisp gray button-down shirt with the sleeves rolled up and dark slacks. Jane introduced the stranger as Darius Maddox, a Homeland Security agent who was heading up the investigation. The strong middle-aged man didn't say a word as I shook his hand, but his expression and body language told me that this guy was a force to be reckoned with.

After introductions, we sat, and Atticus plopped down under the shade of a thatch palm beside us.

"It's good to meet you," Mayor Nix led off in a somewhat condescending tone. I'd seen the man's face in the news but knew very little about him other than that he'd worked as a lawyer in Key West for years before running for public office. "I wish it were under different circumstances."

Scarlett ordered a smoothie while Ange and I got coffee. The warm beverage felt good going down, and the caffeine felt even better as it coursed through my veins.

"You called us here for a reason, I assume?" I said after a few minutes of chatter.

The mayor glanced at Scarlett, and when I followed suit, our daughter got the message. "I'll take Atty for a walk," she said, jumping to her feet with his leash and whistling for the Lab to follow her.

"Steer clear of the cats," Ange said.

Scarlett shot us a wink as she bounded through the gate and headed inland along Whitehead. One of Atticus's many favorite pastimes included chasing down felines, and the famous six-toed variety that inhabited Papa's old abode proved to be his favorite quarry.

"And stay in sight," I added as she headed down the sidewalk.

From my position, I could see clear down to the intersection at Petronia. I doubted that Brier would make any kind of move so soon after his colossal failure the night before, but I preferred to err on the side of caution.

I turned my attention back to Jane and Mayor Nix, wondering who'd speak up first. Agent Maddox hadn't uttered more than a word or two since we'd arrived, seeming to be far more interested in his brioche French toast and iced coffee than our conversation.

Jane cleared her throat. "I don't have much time, so I'll get right to it. The results from the bomb squad verified that they were blocks of C-4, and relatively new. They believe that they could have been part of Darkwater's stock following the organization's fall. That's all I know as I'm not a bomb expert, but I can send you the full report if you want. Bottom line, we can't track where they came from. Second, the initial autopsy reports have confirmed that the men who died last night had rap sheets and were connected with Vito Bonetti's drug operation. His connection makes this even more alarming since many of his group are still unaccounted for, missing since the day you two took down the restaurant in Coral Gables."

"What about the getaway car?" I said. "Any headway?"

Jane shook her head. "Not much yet. There was nothing in the DMV database on the plate number, so it's clear that they replaced it with a fake. But a black Porsche Cayenne was reported stolen near Miami two days ago." She paused a moment, then added, "They must've hidden it good. If they'd tried to leave the islands by land, we'd have found them. The roadblock stopped every vehicle, and all police from here to Orlando are on the lookout for the vehicle. All private flights out of Key West were grounded minutes after the incident ended, now requiring full inspections and ID checks prior to takeoffs. And all commercial airlines are keeping a sharp eye out for the criminals and connected persons. At sea, the Coast Guard is in full swing, along with other police boats up the island chain. Long story short, I'd bet my life savings that these guys are still in the Lower Keys."

I paused, took a sip of coffee. "We'll find him, then."

Mayor Nix cleared his throat. "The authorities will find him." He waited a moment to let his words resonate, then added, "Frankly, I think that you two have done more than enough already."

I studied the man. "Clearly there's more that you want to say, Mayor. So, floor's yours."

The man exchanged glances with Jane. "You must understand the extremely serious debacle that this recent incident, and the following threat, presents to our islands."

"Following threat?" I said, raising my eyebrows.

He nodded toward Jane, and the chief of police withdrew a manilla envelope. She slid out a piece of paper that had words written using cutout letters from a magazine.

"This is just the beginning," was all it said.

"It was in the mailbox at the police station. We checked the security tapes, and it was dropped by a hooded man at three o'clock this morning."

"These threats are serious," Nix said. "This Nathan Brier maniac is putting all of our citizens at risk. And, given that he murdered the last man to hold my political position, I feel particularly uneasy."

"Before proceeding any further," Ange said, "it should be noted that we'd be dealing with hundreds, perhaps thousands of dead bodies right now were it not for the actions of my husband."

"And Ange," I said. "She's the one who disabled the bombs, for goodness' sake."

Nix held up his hands. "Yes, I know. And I thank you for all that you did to prevent a catastrophe. But I wonder if the incident would've occurred at all were it not for Logan and his history with this domestic terrorist."

The words cut deeper given that they reminded me of the ones I'd spoken to Ange just hours earlier, acting as a painful echo of my own difficult questions.

"What do you want from me?" I said, tired of going in circles. "You called me here for a reason, right? Why don't we get to that?"

The mayor adjusted his glasses. "I'd heard you weren't a fan of red tape."

"More like I don't have time for it. You failed to mention that my family is center stage in the line of fire here."

The man sighed. "All right, Logan. We want you to leave Key West." He paused a moment to let the statement settle. "It's clear that this man has a personal vendetta against you, and we feel like it will be what's best for the people. You and your family would be kept hidden in a government safe house until Brier is dealt with."

I shook my head. "I'm not sure what you've heard or read about me, but I'm not the kind of person who runs away from my problems."

"With all due respect, it's evident that, in this case, your mere presence is responsible for the problem."

"Are you saying that it's Logan's fault this happened?" Ange leaned forward. "'Cause from where I'm sitting, the only thing he's guilty of is standing up for what's right."

"Are you saying, Mrs. Dodge, that you believe this Nathan Brier would be attacking our citizens were it not for your husband?"

My wife fell silent. She knew the answer. We all did, but she dared not utter it.

"I'm going to take Brier down," I declared. "I'm gonna deal with this."

"And how many innocents will be caught in the crossfire?" Nix said. "We have good people whose job is to keep law and order on the island. They will deal with this madman. You and your family will stay out of it."

"With all due respect," I said, "there's no one alive who's better equipped to take Brier down. No one who knows him better."

"And yet... he's still alive and at large." Nix sighed and steepled his fingers. "Look, I didn't call you here to argue, Logan. And I'm not forcing you to leave. But I believe it's what's in the best interest of not only Key West, but you and your family as well."

TWELVE

Mayor Nix leaned back and looked to the two at his flanks for support. Jane replied only by checking her watch, signaling loud and clear that she needed to get a move on. She didn't have time for this, not with a band of killers at large in the islands.

Turning to his right, Nix said, "Agent Maddox, don't you agree?"

The man casually sipped down the rest of his iced coffee, then eyed the mayor through a pair of sunglasses. "Agree with what?"

Nix threw his hands in the air in frustration. "With everything I just said."

"Oh," the Homeland agent replied calmly, wiping his lips with a napkin. "No. I don't agree."

Nix glared at him. "You told me on the phone that—"

"That civilian interference rarely goes well," Maddox said, finishing the sentence for him. "But you'd asked me open-endedly. Then I read Logan's file, heard the man speak, and now… now I couldn't disagree with you more." He set his drink down and looked back and forth between Ange and me. "I'll feel better going after this maniac with these two on our side. Civilian, police officer, agent, I don't care. Bullets don't discriminate, and neither do I."

Nix sighed and his nostrils flared a little. "Excuse me," he said, pushing his chair back, "but I've got a lot of work to attend to, as do you both." He glanced at the chief and Homeland agent, then headed toward the gate. Just as he reached it, he turned back and stared at me. "Regardless of Homeland's opinion, one more incident and I won't be asking you to leave, Logan. I'll be ordering you to." He pushed out the gate and strode down Whitehead toward a parked Mercedes.

"Don't judge him on this interaction alone," Jane said, rising as well. "He's just scared. As we all should be. But I've got your backs, you both know that."

I nodded to her, then she turned to Maddox. "We'll be in touch."

"Yes, we will," the man said, staying put as Jane marched toward her squad car just down the street.

The three of us sat in silence for a moment, then Ange said, "Thanks for backing us up."

Maddox shrugged. "It's selfish, really. The sooner I find this asshole and take him down, the sooner I can get out of this heat."

"It's more enjoyable in shorts and a T-shirt," I said.

He laughed. "I'll pitch the lax dress code to Homeland."

83

I gave the man a second quick glance up and down, then said, "What battalion were you in?"

I gestured toward the tattoo on his left forearm. It was a shield with a radiant sun in the upper left quadrant, a star in the lower right, and a lightning flash through the middle. It was the crest of the 75th Army Ranger Regiment, one of our nation's most elite special operations forces.

Maddox eyed his tattoo, then said, "Third. Out of Fort Benning. Served twenty-six years, starting with operation Urgent Fury and ending with Iraqi Freedom."

"And you went straight into work with Homeland?" Ange said.

Maddox nodded. "In a way, I'm still doing the same thing I did back in the Army. Now I'm just doing it on US soil. And wearing dress clothes instead of a uniform."

I wasn't surprised by his resume. I'd noticed the rarity of his persona the second I'd laid eyes on him. The Homeland agent was cool as ice. He had that unique brand of composure that was typical among combat veterans. Once you've been holed up in the mud, going days without sleep, wet, hungry, and with enemy fire whizzing by right over your head, everything else becomes infinitely less stressful.

I spotted Scarlett walking with Atticus on the other side of Whitehead, coming our way.

Maddox wiped his lips with a napkin, then rose. "Like I said, I read your file and I disagree with the mayor. I try hard to get Homeland to entice more former special forces guys, but it's not easy to recruit talent. I'd be honored to have a SEAL helping us out

84

down here. And Ange… let's just say I know the goods when I see it. These local law enforcements are damn good at what they do. But this guy Nathan Brier is different. He's a special breed of man, and it's gonna take the same types to take him down. People like us. My job is to take this guy out. I could care less if it's my weapon or yours that does it."

He told us that he'd be keeping us in the loop regarding updates on the investigation, then strode away from the restaurant and climbed into a blacked-out BMW.

Despite the rather intense conversation with the mayor, I couldn't help but smile as Maddox drove off, as I was unable to imagine a more capable force being sent down to the islands to help take down Brier.

The three of us strode back down the sidewalk and climbed into the Tacoma. I started the engine and blasted the AC. First things first, I wanted to make absolutely sure that Maddox was who he said he was. He'd been very convincing, but if we were going to fight alongside him, I needed to be certain, so I called Elliot Murphy, a brilliant hacker friend of ours who'd helped us out on more than one occasion. The computer whiz had a relentless work ethic and busy schedule, so I was surprised when he picked up; usually I had to leave a message.

Murph was like a ghost, always bouncing around the globe from one strong internet connection to another, working odd internet jobs and always concealing his location and identity.

I requested for him to run a thorough background check for me.

"Too easy," he replied, his voice altered to sound low and robotic. "Send over the info."

I gave him the name and told him that he worked for Homeland.

"I'll get this back as soon as I can, but I'm running on two hours of sleep and already emptied three Red Bulls."

"Scott keeping you busy?"

"Bit of an understatement. He and Jason are in Iceland and..." The guy stopped and I heard frantic clicks on a keyboard. "Got to go."

The line went dead. I hoped that everything was all right, but I knew that both Scott Cooper and Jason Wake were as up to the task of dealing with dangerous encounters as anyone.

Ange turned to me and went into a rant as I pulled out onto Whitehead. "If Mayor Nix honestly thinks that Brier will just kick back and set his weapons on the table if you leave the islands, he's not only stupid but borderline crazy."

"He's just doing what he thinks is best for the people here," I said, trying to play devil's advocate.

It wasn't easy. Our conversation, and the mayor's opinion regarding how things should play out, illustrated a perfect example of what's wrong with our government. When men who know nothing beyond the office and boardrooms and meetings try and tell seasoned warriors how to go about their business.

Mayor Nix didn't know Nathan Brier. He didn't know what the man was capable of. If he did, he'd be a hell of a lot more scared than he already was. He'd probably call in and request the National Guard, which, in all honesty, wouldn't be such a bad idea.

"Yeah, well, he's dead wrong," Ange continued. "And it's a dangerous thing when people are wrong and think that they're right."

We swung by the Lower Keys Medical Center on the way home to check up on Scarlett's friend. Scarlett had been texting her nonstop since the incident and had been informed that she was getting an MRI that morning. Needless to say, her parents weren't exactly excited to see us coming through the doors into the small radiology waiting area. I had to stand between the girl's father and Scarlett as he chastised her for being so reckless.

"Easy now," I said, holding up my hands. "Scarlett took down a man who was about to open fire."

I tried my best to be calm and understanding, knowing that if my daughter had been injured, I'd no doubt feel the same way. After letting the father blow off some steam, we managed to talk through it and still be on good terms. It would've been easy and a natural reaction for me to throw the guy's anger back into his face, but where would that have left us? We lived on a small island and she was Scarlett's friend's dad—the last thing I wanted was for us to be cold toward each other.

Fortunately, Dr. Patel informed us that Kate had only suffered a mild concussion. She'd need to stay home and rest for a few days, and avoid strenuous activity for a week or two, but she wouldn't suffer long-term effects.

After getting the news, Ange offered to have them over for dinner after the mess with Brier was over, then we strolled out. Though it'd ended well enough, my talk with the man was the second not-so-pleasant conversation I'd had that day, and it wasn't even noon yet.

"Well, we're just becoming the most popular family in Key West, aren't we?" Ange said as we climbed into the Tacoma and drove home.

Scarlett leaned forward from the backseat. "Yeah, I've never seen Kate's dad act like that before."

"He's a father," I said. "He's scared for his daughter. You don't think I'd walk barefoot through fire to protect you, Scar?"

"Yeah, I remember Cuba," she said, referring to the time when sex traffickers had abducted her in order to sell her into a life of servitude. "And I wasn't even your daughter yet."

THIRTEEN

We spent most of the following two days at home. We worked out, relaxed in the yard, and played with the dog, and I took care of a few long-overdue household tasks. It felt like every hour I was contacting either Jane or Maddox, hoping for any word of progress in tracking down Brier. But there was none to be had. Nearly sixty hours following the incident, there was still no sign of Brier, Vito, or the getaway vehicle. It was like they'd vanished into thin air.

Murph had gotten back to me pretty quick considering how busy the guy kept himself. He sent me pages of info on Maddox that backed up everything the man had said and then some. Darius Maddox had retired as a sergeant major, the highest enlisted rank in the United States Army, and had earned two Purple Hearts and a Silver Star. The man had a nearly spotless military and civilian record. He was a hero, and after a career in Special Forces, he'd chosen to continue his service by taking a senior field position at Homeland, putting his skills, experience, and training to use against terrorists like Brier.

That afternoon, while lounging in the shade in the backyard and tossing a tennis ball to wear out an energetic Atticus, I got a call from Jack. I answered, clicking the device on speakerphone before taking a swig of coconut water.

"We've got bombers incoming!" my friend exclaimed. If anyone else had called and said that, I might have shielded my eyes from the sun and squinted skyward in worry. But I knew what my friend meant. "Cali just called and told me that there's about a dozen skirting southwest along the reef. You guys up for some ocean excitement?"

Atticus dropped the slobber-covered orb in front of me, and I fired it across the lawn.

"Look, I understand if you're not up for it," Jack said. "Given everything that's going on. We can blow bubbles some other time."

Scarlett, who swayed in a hammock, waved at me with both hands, fighting for my attention. I raised my eyebrows at my daughter, but she didn't need the encouragement.

"We should go," she said. "Diving with Jack. It'll be fun and... we haven't had a lot of that lately."

"There's too much going on to go off playing around," I said. "I've never clung to the notion of ignoring your problems to make them go away."

"It's just for the afternoon."

"Scar makes a good point," Ange chimed in, peeking over the pages of an old copy of John D. MacDonald's *The Deep Blue Good-by*. "You need to relax a bit. This whole thing has got you too high-strung. Not like there's been much progress the past few days. Besides, I like our chances if Brier's stupid enough to try something against us on open water."

They both made good points. With cabin fever already beginning to set in, we needed to get out and soak up some life. And I couldn't imagine anyone accusing me of being a reckless vigilante while enjoying a day of diving.

"So, you guys in?" Jack said.

I leaned toward the phone. "We'll meet you at the marina."

I locked up the house, powered on the security system, and drove us over to Conch Harbor Marina. After parking, we made our way down to the dock, passing by a bronze statue of Gus Henderson. Though I was glad that Jack had seen fit to memorialize the former marina owner, the sight gave me a sick feeling. The former mayor, Elijah Crawford, hadn't been the only one to perish at Brier's merciless hands. Six months ago, Brier had murdered Gus right there on the dock. Atticus had been with him and had pounced, trying to protect the local, and had been lucky to get away with just a stab to the shoulder. Our courageous Lab still walked with a slight hitch, though it was barely noticeable.

Brier's done too much to this community already, I thought as we strode down the planks. *And he won't slip through our fingers this time.*

Jack was loading up a cart of dive gear from his forty-five-foot Sea Ray, dubbed *Calypso*. I'd told him over the phone that I preferred to take my boat out. Though she had less deck space and wasn't quite the scuba diver's dream that his charter boat was, the Baia was more than adequate and would give us much more speed in case we needed to get somewhere in a hurry.

"Glad you agreed to come," Jack said, patting me on the back. His curly blond hair danced in the ocean breeze. The tanned, wiry conch wore nothing but a pair of board shorts and sunglasses. My old beach bum friend was fully in his element. "I think the fresh air and time beneath the waves will do you all some good."

"That's what I said," Scarlett pronounced, helping Jack with the tanks.

"It'll just be a few hours anyway," Jack said. "Lauren wants to be back for her early snorkel trip."

"The curfew makes evening cruises interesting, that's for sure," Jack's girlfriend said, popping out from the saloon with a bag over her shoulder.

Lauren Sweetin had grown up in Tennessee, migrated south after a divorce, and founded her own snorkel and sunset charter business on her catamaran *Sweet Dreams*. She was pretty, her long auburn hair gusting in the ocean breeze and her skin tanned from hours on the water each day. Like Jack, her demeanor was generally relaxed, but she had a stern side that acted as a good counterweight for the two to keep the relationship balanced.

"Any news on when it'll be lifted?" Ange said.

Lauren shrugged. "None yet. But hopefully it's soon. Thirty minutes after sunset. That's not a lot of time for the evening Mallory Square spectators to scramble to their homes and hotels."

The curfew had been put into place two days

earlier by Mayor Nix, beginning the evening after the incident at the high school had taken place. But keeping islanders in their houses after dark was proving to be a task nearly as difficult as locating Brier.

We loaded everything onto the Baia, then tossed the lines. The sleek, blue-hulled craft I'd christened *Dodging Bullets II* after the first one had been blown to pieces was like a sports car on the water. With ample space below deck, a topside dinette, a sunbed, and a large swim platform, the boat offered a perfect combination of speed and comfort.

I rumbled the twin 600-horsepower engines to life and motored us out of the harbor. Once beyond the bight, I shoved the throttle forward, accelerating us to thirty knots as we cut alongside the downtown waterfront. The sky was mostly clear, and the air was already eighty degrees despite it still being a few hours until midday.

I breathed in the fresh ocean air and smiled broadly for the first time in days. Jack and my family had been right. I needed this. Whipping us around Fort Zachary Taylor, I cut the distance to our dive site in just under half an hour.

Calihan Brooks, a dive charter captain based out of Boot Key, had informed Jack that a group of eagle rays was swimming along the reef. The fellow islander had spotted the rare sight up near Molasses Reef off Key Largo earlier that day and helped us predict where they might be by the time we got out there. We agreed on the Thunderbolt wreck, figuring that even if we missed the fish swimming by, we'd at least have a great dive site to explore.

"Why does it seem like this baby gets faster every time I'm on it?" Jack said, beaming as I eased toward a dive buoy.

Scarlett, having taken to the boating lifestyle better and faster than anyone I'd ever met, sprang up to the bow and quickly tied us off.

"All set," she said, throwing me a thumbs-up.

I waved, grabbed a dive flag and coil of rope from the cockpit locker, and tossed it over the side. Shielding my eyes from the sun, I took in our surroundings, then peered down into the blue.

"Great day," Jack said. "I'd say a seventy-foot viz easy."

"Let's just hope some majestic fish show their faces," Lauren said, divvying out the gear they'd prepped on the trip over.

I climbed up onto the bow with a pair of binoculars and scanned the horizon. No boats caught my attention as being suspicious, and there was only one within a quarter mile of us. That was one of the many things I loved about the Keys. Though there are more boat owners per capita than just about anywhere in the States, the vast number of dive sites, great fishing spots, and quiet coves still allows relative seclusion, depending on the location and time of year.

Everyone but me donned wetsuits and BCDs. One at a time, they slid into fins, positioned their masks, and stepped out into paradise. I stayed up for the first half hour, wanting to make sure that someone other than just Atty watched the boat. When Jack surfaced, we switched places.

"You're not gonna believe it, bro," Jack beamed as he popped up near the stern.

I offered a hand and helped my friend up onto the swim platform.

"You spot a few rays?" I asked.

He chuckled. "More like a few dozen."

"You're kidding."

He gestured toward the water. "Drop on in and see for yourself." He shook his head in bewilderment. "I thought they were no-shows at first. But they just soared into view. One of the coolest things I've seen in the Keys, and that's saying something."

It was saying more than something. The son of a charter captain, Jack had lived his whole life in the islands and had taken the reins of the operation at just twenty-two. The fourth-generation conch had logged over five thousand dives, most of them in the Florida archipelago.

Excited, I quickly strapped on my BCD and splashed down. The rush of the tropical underwater world revealing itself through a cluster of tiny white bubbles is a sensation that never gets old. I peered through the translucent water, my eyes adjusting as I focused deeper through the turquoise, toward the dark blue below. The Thunderbolt wreck was a relic frozen in time in a hundred and twenty feet of water, claimed by the ocean and all its creatures.

I spotted the girls just off the bow of the sunken vessel, their bubble trails dancing toward the surface.

Scarlett, who wore her favorite black-and-pink wetsuit, noticed me first and waved me over as I descended. She had her underwater camera in one hand and kept the lens trained forward.

I finned toward the bottom, breathing calmly in and out of my regulator. The underwater world was teeming with colorful marine life, but as I closed in on the group, I gazed upon a sight so spectacular, everything else paled in comparison. Just off the reef line was a pack of at least two dozen spotted eagle rays, resembling a cluster of B-2 Stealth Bombers as they glided leisurely along. The massive, majestic creatures passed by in a long, spread-out line, heading southwest. I leveled my buoyancy at ninety feet down, hovering just above the deck of the sunken ship as we took in the amazing show.

When the pack eventually moved on, the girls each looked at me with wide eyes and we exchanged a thumbs-up. Scarlett held up her camera, then removed her regulator to give me a big toothy smile. I shook my head and she quickly pushed it back into place. Though she was just playing, I didn't like her removing it during a dive, especially that deep.

We spent another fifteen minutes beneath the waves, exploring the wreck and taking in the colors and sea life. A school of thousands of silver spades greeted us near the main deck, along with a tucked-away green eel and a barracuda. As we were about to ascend, I noticed a few colorful spines sticking out from under the ship's cable reel on the bow and made a mental note of their positions. The three of us kicked smoothly for the surface and, after a five-minute safety stop, broke out into the warm twenty-fourth parallel sunshine.

"Okay, that was amazing," Scarlett exclaimed, smiling from ear to ear.

"Unbelievable," Ange added.

We ate lunch on the boat, sandwiching leftover lobster between warmed baguettes from Old Town

Bakery. While digesting and letting the excess nitrogen bleed from our bodies, I climbed up onto the bow with Ange and lay on a towel. The sun glistened off her tanned skin, and she dazzled like a supermodel as she curled up next to me in her purple bikini. Just as I'd hit a point of relaxation I hadn't approached in nearly a week, Jack brought me back to reality.

"Hey, hate to ruin this moment," he said, climbing up to us, "but you've got a message and it looks important. Some guy named Maddox."

He handed me my phone and I blocked the sun to read the text.

Logan, we got a lead. It's not much, but I was wondering if you could watch some footage we caught of Brier and let me know what you think.

I replied right away, giving him my secure email address.

While waiting for Maddox to get back to me, I asked Jack if he was interested in joining me in a little pest control.

Having removed our wetsuits, Jack and I both grabbed a pole spear and mask, as well as freediving fins, and jumped back into the water.

"We'll be right back," I said.

"Can I come?" Scarlett pleaded. "Remember how many I speared during the tournament?"

I smiled. "You're an Ama in the making for sure. But it's a little too deep, kiddo."

"Ama?" she said, squinting at me.

Ange replied, "The famous sea women of Japan. They've been freediving for pearls for over a thousand years."

"And some are over eighty years old," I said as I

squeezed into my long fins, then I nodded to Jack.

"I'll be harnessing my inner Ama," Jack said. "I've been craving some fresh lion lately."

We each sucked in a breath, then duck dove into the water. Keeping our bodies flat, we descended straight down with big, smooth cycles of our fins. The specialty flippers allowed us to reach the bottom with relative ease, and I led my friend to the spot at the bow of the ship where I'd spotted the lionfish.

Lionfish are an invasive species and threat to the ecosystem, so I tried to skewer every one I found. And, if you can fillet them without getting poked by their long venomous spines, they make a delicious meal. I pulled back on the spear, tensioning the tubing, and closed in first. When the tip was just a few feet away from the closest colorful fish, I let go, the rubber snapping and launching the spearhead through its body. It shook, then went rigid.

Jack took down a second, killing his quarry instantly with a headshot. We finned our kills to the surface, dropped them into a plastic bucket Lauren had set on the swim platform, then relaxed for a minute before heading down for another go.

We managed to remove all five of the scattered lionfish in three trips, then scoured the rest of the wreck for stragglers. Jack and I were both experienced freedivers and could stay down for nearly three minutes if we needed to. Breaking the surface after our final dive, we both exhaled forcefully twice, then calmed our breathing and leaned against the swim platform.

"Sometimes, it's a real pleasure doing one's civic duty," Jack said, carefully removing the last lionfish from his spear and plopping it with the others in the bucket.

Atticus, worked up by all the excitement, wagged his tail and pattered toward us. But one look at the tropical fish and he whirled around and dashed below deck with his tail between his legs.

I laughed. "All it took was him being poked once."

"That's all it takes for anyone," Lauren said. "It's like a bee sting times a hundred."

Lauren kept her arms extended, ensuring that the fish were far away from her as she grabbed the bucket and carried it over to a cooler. Ange sat at the dinette, staring at my phone. She stood and stepped across the deck as I pulled myself up the swim ladder.

"You just got a reply from Maddox," she said. "He says he just sent the footage."

I toweled off and gestured toward the hatch. "The onboard laptop will do nicely."

After drying and throwing on a shirt, Ange and I huddled with Atticus down in the saloon. I didn't want the others to watch at first, more out of respect than anything else. Agent Maddox was trusting me and going out on a bit of a limb by sending it to me in the first place. I wanted to keep information sent to me on the down-low unless I needed other opinions.

I cracked open the laptop, then opened my email and read a message from Maddox.

"This was caught by a camera at the Shell gas station on Cudjoe on the night of Brier's escape."

I clicked on and downloaded the attached file. It was a fifty-eight-second video. When I pressed play, I realized that it was from a security camera at a gas station.

"Look," Ange said, pointing at a time stamp in the bottom right corner. "That's just minutes after you appeared in the high school parking lot beside Scarlett's Bronco."

Ange was right. It displayed nine fifty-two in the evening. Five seconds into the clip, headlights shined into the camera as a vehicle pulled up to one of the pumps. It was a black Porsche Cayenne, the getaway car that Brier and Vito had used. The headlights went out as the SUV stopped, the driver's-side door hinged open, and Brier stepped out.

He wasn't even trying to conceal himself. No hat or hood, just the same T-shirt he'd been wearing back at the school. He strode into the gas station, then returned just under half a minute later with a plastic bag of items. Pulling open the driver's-side door, he set the bag on the seat then leaned inside. Roughly ten seconds later, he re-emerged holding a notebook. Shifting his body, he stared straight at the camera and held up the bound sheets of paper, revealing words written in black sharpie.

"This is just the beginning."

He shot the camera a cocky smile, then climbed back into the Porsche and drove out of the lot.

Ange glanced at me with raised eyebrows. "Okay, I'm officially confused."

"Wait," I said, peering carefully at the screen. I watched as the SUV appeared back into frame, cruising west down what appeared to be US-1. Just as the vehicle was about to vanish from view, I saw a brief glimpse of red, then it was beyond the corner of the frame.

"Sure looks like he headed back into town," Ange

said.

"Yeah, it does look that way."

"But why in the hell would he stop in the first place? And so calmly. He looked like he was just dropping by to pick up a few items on his way home from work. At least the message is more in line with his character, but do you really think he'd stop just to give another warning?"

I thought over the footage and agreed with her completely. I couldn't think of anything dumber than stopping in the middle of a getaway.

I rewound the footage and paused as Brier stepped out from the gas station.

"Only thing I can make out is the notebook and a magazine," Ange said, leaning in for a better look.

I leaned back into the cushion and rubbed my chin. "A magazine to cut out letters and send a threat, perhaps?" I said, referring to the warning that Jane had shown us two days earlier at Moondog. A warning that had said the exact same thing as Brier had written on the notebook.

Ange shook her head. "There's more than one thing not right here. Brier's smarter than this. Much smarter."

"Yes. He is."

"Then why did he do it?"

"Could very well be hubris. Maybe he was just showing off. Flaunting the fact that he knew he had some time to play with before word got out and police closed in. Trying to send us a clear message that even though he'd failed, he's still in control."

Ange shook her head. "I guess I could buy that. But why drive all the way there and then turn around?

If he just wanted to buy a few things and show off, why not stop at a gas station sooner? It's like he's just trying to confuse the hell out of everyone."

"It's working."

I played the clip from the beginning again, and Ange and I paid close attention to details and areas that we hadn't looked at the first time around. Jack appeared, striding into the galley.

"We need to head out soon?" I said, assuming that he'd stepped down to remind us that Lauren had a charter later that afternoon.

"Just need some more hydration," he said, opening the fridge and grabbing three chilled cans of coconut water. "The people scheduled to go out on *Sweet Dreams* called and canceled. Said they were taking a vacation elsewhere because of the bomb scare and criminals still on the loose." Jack shut the fridge and added, "And Pete called inviting all of us to have dinner with him tonight. Would seven work for you guys?"

Pete Jameson was a local friend of ours and the owner of Salty Pete's Bar, Grill, and Museum, a popular island hangout just a few blocks inland from the bustling Duval.

"He's not worried about the curfew?" Ange said.

"Doesn't sound like it. But the place will be closed. So close friends only."

I told Jack that dinner at Pete's sounded good, and he headed for the stairs. Peering back over his shoulder, he froze mid-step as he focused on the computer screen. "That looks like the Shell station over on Cudjoe."

It didn't surprise me that Jack was able to locate

the place with just one quick look. Few people knew the islands as well as he did, especially the Lower Keys. I motioned for him to come closer, figuring a third pair of eyes could only help as I played the clip again.

"That the guy?" Jack said as Brier climbed out of the Porsche and headed inside.

"That's him all right."

"Jeez, he looks like, you bro. Same height and build, and similar facial features."

"And he's just a few years older than me," I said.

Jack gasped dramatically. "It's like you're facing off against your opposite. Fighting a twisted version of yourself."

Jack's words resonated in my mind as we observed the rest of the clip. My good friend didn't possess any prestigious degrees or extensive book knowledge, but when it came to good old-fashioned common sense, he had it in spades. Jack was right. Brier and I shared far more similarities than we did differences and, as Ange had said a few nights earlier, he was unlike any adversary I'd drawn swords against.

Jack leaned forward as the clip neared the end. Just as the video stopped, he stabbed a finger at the screen.

"Rewind it," he said. "Just the last five seconds."

Curious what he'd noticed, I did as he said, playing the feed again.

"What is it, Jack?" Ange said.

Jack kept his focus on the screen, his mouth agape. "Pause it… now," he said, and I rapidly clicked the trackpad. "Right there." He pressed a finger against the tiny, distant image of the Porsche in the top left corner of the screen as it drove away.

Still not catching on, I was about to ask what was going on in that conch head of his when he said, "Brake lights."

I focused closer and noticed two tiny glows of red at the back of the SUV.

"So he's slowing down," Ange said. "What's so weird about that?"

"That's the Overseas Highway," Jack explained. "He pulled out of the station, turned right to drive back southwest, then braked right after merging. There aren't any stop lights or signs there, and the speed limit's forty-five all the way across the island. And there aren't any other cars ahead of him that I saw. No reason for him to brake."

I shook my head. "What are you thinking?"

He paused a moment, picking at his teeth. "I'm thinking that he must've turned. But... there's no cross street there. Not even a store. So he must've done a U-turn right after leaving the camera's field of view. He would've had to drive over double yellows, but it sure wouldn't be the first time someone did that."

We fell silent a moment.

"So, Brier flees the islands, stops to buy a few things and send a quick message," Ange said, running through the series of events. "All right after the school incident. Then he drives back in the direction he'd come for a moment before doing a U-turn." My wife thought it over for a split second before coming to the same conclusion that popped into my head. "He was trying to make detectives think that he'd gone back toward Key West."

I smiled. "Makes sense. Throw them off his

scent."

To test the theory, I slipped out my phone and called Maddox.

"I'm willing to bet that this Shell station isn't the only place with a camera that catches US-1 in it's frame," I said after he answered, getting straight to the point.

"One of the first orders I made that night was to check all cameras along US-1," Maddox replied. "But there's a lot. And we started in Key West and worked our way toward the roadblock. Early this morning we spotted a glimpse of the getaway Porsche on one of the cameras outside of the sheriff's office on Cudjoe. I'd read up on this Brier guy and heard he was bold, but I never expected him to drive so close to the roadblock."

"The man often does the unexpected and seemingly stupid thing."

"Right. Well, we checked the gas station soon after. Fortunately, they keep footage for a week before deleting it. Attendant said that Brier paid cash and bought a magazine, notebook, and sharpie." He cleared his throat. "What did you think of the clip?"

"I think it looks like Brier headed back to Key West. Were you able to catch the vehicle on the sheriff's office camera heading back?"

"That's a negative. But a line of semi-trucks drove by that could've blocked it."

"How about any other cameras?"

"No. The vehicle seems to have vanished off the face of the earth after that." I paused a moment, thinking everything over. "Still there, Logan?"

I told him our theory about Brier turning around,

but said that we'd dig deeper into it.

Jack ran his fingers through his messy hair after I hung up. "With the roadblock set up at the Kemp Channel Bridge, that wouldn't give him much space to work with. Just a few streets on Cudjoe and a relatively small area to hide the getaway car."

I grabbed a cardboard tube from under my seat, unfurled a chart of the Lower Keys, and pinned it to the dinette with mugs and a can of coconut water. The three of us huddled over the chart and Jack pointed straight at the location of the gas station.

"Here's the Shell," he said. He tracked his finger along US-1, stopping at the spot where the roadblock had been set. "So, if he did turn around, then he must've gone somewhere in this area. My money would be on either Blimp Road, Henry Morgan, or one of the other streets heading into the north side of the island. The south side is too packed with houses and would risk being spotted."

Ange said, "And if he didn't manage to sneak away from the islands somehow, my guess is he's still nearby. Regardless, that Porsche has to be there somewhere. There's no way he drove it out of the islands without being stopped."

"That part of Cudjoe is pretty sparse," Jack said. "Not a lot of houses, and they're spread out. Lots of people who like to keep to themselves. And it's thick with groves. It would take us a while to drive every back road and search the place."

An idea popped into my head. "Unless we conducted our search by air." I turned and looked toward the guest cabin. Striding across the saloon, I pulled open the door, reached under the guest bed, and slid out a plastic hardcase containing my top-of-the-line remote controlled aircraft. "You guys mind if we take a little detour on the trip back?"

FOURTEEN

When everyone was ready and Jack had unclipped the line from the buoy, I fired up the engines and accelerated us away from the site. It had been an enjoyable day out on the water. An unforgettable dive, relaxing times topside, and a little spearfishing to ice the cake.

But now it was time to get back to business.

We knew that the theory was a stretch and that, in reality, Brier could be anywhere by this point, but the only way to know for sure was to motor over and take a look around. After all, it was the only thing resembling a lead that we had. I'd called Maddox and informed him of my initial thoughts. He too had believed it odd that Brier would stop in the first place, and confirmed that most of the other Homeland agents and local detectives had concluded that Brier must've headed back down the island chain, away from the roadblock.

I motored us up along Sugarloaf Key, then cut

north into Pirates Cove and under the Bow Channel Bridge between Upper Sugarloaf and Cudjoe. It was a normal, busy day, with boats passing in all directions, jet skis zipping by, and paddleboarders hugging the shorelines.

We skirted along the western side of Cudjoe and eased into a small, relatively secluded inlet.

"As good a spot as any to let it fly," I said, easing back to an idle, then killing the engines after dropping and setting the anchor.

I heaved the hardcase up onto the sunbed and cracked it open.

"Man, you guys sure are prepared for this kind of thing," Lauren said, gasping at the sight of the advanced little drone.

It wasn't the kind that was available from normal consumer outlets. Over the years, Ange and I had forged connections all over the world. One of them, a good friend of mine named Scott Cooper who was presently leading a covert group he'd formed nearly a year earlier, was one such connection. The former senator had acquired the little drone years earlier and had given it to me during one of our many adventures together. The quadcopter could fly up to seventy miles per hour and had a twenty-mile range and two hours of battery life. It could also soar to over two miles up and had a high-end camera with zoom capabilities.

I set up the device, powered it on, and zipped the rotors to life. Within seconds, the little recon machine was up in the air, whirring high into the crisp blue sky. I watched where I was going via an eight-inch screen built into the remote control. Once at a thousand feet, I piloted east over the land.

"Just watch out for Fat Albert," Jack said, referring to the massive tethered blimp that flew above the northern tip of Cudjoe.

Fat Albert had been used by the Air Force for radar purposes since the program had begun on Cudjoe in 1980. Like many things in Florida, the blimp had a strange and somewhat unbelievable history. The craziest story I'd ever heard had been told one night at Salty Pete's, when the animated proprietor regaled us about the time the blimp had broken free and a group of locals out catching lobsters had raced it down. The islanders tied the line off to their twenty-three-foot fishing boat, and the blimp lifted the vessel clear out of the water before finally dumping it in the Mud Keys.

Only in Florida, I thought with a grin.

Jack was joking around about warning me to watch out for the balloon, but it was sound advice. Though unlikely, it would be a bad day if I accidentally crashed into the blimp's line.

I flew over the island, zooming in with the camera and carefully observing the roads. Jack hadn't been kidding about the place being sparse. In the land between the Shell station and where the roadblock had been set, there were only two dozen houses at most on the northern half of the island. We checked them over one by one, focusing on the driveways and hoping to catch sight of Brier's getaway car. Some of the houses had carports and a few had garages, but most were open and allowed us to inspect each of the parked vehicles in turn. After half an hour, I reached the other side of the island, having scanned over them all.

"No sign of the black Porsche," Jack said, leaning over and observing the screen.

"What about that place on the point?" Scarlett said, pointing toward a cluster of structures on the northern edge of the island.

"That's the Air Force station," Jack said. "You'd have to be a special kind of dumb to run there. It's gated off anyway. Just a bunch of military and pocket protector types making sure we don't get bombed and keeping their eyes out for smugglers. Cool place, though. And they've got their own dock."

Knowing that my daughter's intuition was often spot-on, and with our other options exhausted, I followed Blimp Road with the drone, cruising about a thousand feet directly above the pavement. I reached the spot where the road forked, one part branching right to a public boat ramp and the other left to the Air Force compound.

"Punk kids street racing," Jack said as I piloted the drone over the fork.

"Hey, you used to be one of those punk kids, I'm sure," Lauren said.

"I was more of a boat racing type. Right, Logan?"

The mention of my name snapped me from my thoughts as I turned the aircraft around, not wanting to fly too close to the government facility.

"Punk kids?" Ange said, as confused as I was.

"Yeah, what are you talking about?" I added. Lauren pointed at the screen. "Oh, just tire marks on the road. Kids having fun."

"Where?" I asked, having missed them entirely.

"Back near the fork," Jack said.

I turned the drone around, accelerated back north, then zoomed the camera where the road split. There were two black lines roughly thirty feet long.

Not sure how I missed that, I thought as I cruised in for a better look.

Staring at the rubber burn marks, I cocked my head, then blinked.

Could it really be? I thought, my heart rate cranking up a peg.

I reached into my pocket and slid out my cellphone. Thumbing to the pictures, I found the ones that I'd snapped two days earlier during my run. I kept the drone stable, the camera focused on the markings as I held up my phone.

"Where'd you take those?" Ange said, staring at my smartphone.

"The southern end of Fifth Street."

"Right by the high school?" Scarlett said.

I nodded. "They're the ones left behind by the Porsche Brier and Vito drove away in."

"They sure look the same," Scarlett said, looking back and forth between the two.

My daughter was right. There were the same grooves and number of lines, and it was hard to tell, but the width appeared the same too, as well as the tires' amount of tread.

I snapped a few photos using the drone's camera, then sent both them and the ones I'd taken near the school to Maddox. Sure, they looked the same to untrained crime scene eyes like mine, but Homeland would have forensic and crime scene investigation agents who'd be better at comparing the two.

Maddox replied right away, letting me know that

he'd get back to me. I performed another sweep of the northern part of Cudjoe, then back up to the tip, not discovering anything else that looked promising. Thirty minutes later, as I landed the drone back onto the sunbed, Maddox called back.

"I sent the photos to a forensics engineer who specializes in traffic-crash reconstruction," he said. "He confirmed that the skids are both acceleration marks, that they were left by tires of the same width, and that they're likely both relatively fresh. Less than a week, he guessed, but a lot of that depends on things like weather and how often a road is driven on. He also put them into a program to be analyzed, and says that they're likely the same type of vehicle given the length of the skids and spacing of the wheels, but he couldn't be certain without checking them out in person."

Just because the marks were left by the same kind of vehicle and tires, that didn't guarantee that they'd been left by the getaway car. Regardless, I knew that it was time to put boots on the ground and have a closer look around.

FIFTEEN

We motored around the northern tip of Cudjoe, cut into Kemp Channel, then pulled up to the boat ramp at the end of Blimp Road. I'd considered stopping by the dock jutting out from the Air Force station but figured I could get a little snooping in beforehand and then ask them if they'd seen anything suspicious later on.

The girls climbed up to the bow and surveyed the water near the base of the ramp. On the trip around the island, we'd reasoned that Brier could very well have accelerated quickly down Blimp Road in order to drown the Porsche in the channel, hiding it from view. Though it sounded like a decent idea in theory, I doubted that a submerged vehicle would go more than twelve hours before being spotted by someone backing their boat down the ramp. Still, we figured it couldn't hurt for them to keep their eyes out.

"Anything?" I said, calling up to the three women.

As Ange and Lauren shook their heads in unison,

Scarlett turned back and said, "A Jaguar but no Porsche."

She giggled, and I idled the engines.

"Stays pretty deep along the left side of the ramp on approach, bro," Jack said, pointing over the bow. "No less than five feet."

I kept us slow and my eyes locked onto the depth gauge. When I had us as close as I felt comfortable motoring to the shore, I spun the Baia around, then offered Jack the helm. I grabbed my sat phone from a nearby locker, knowing that service could be poor in that part of the islands, and shoved my Sig into the back of my waistband.

"Want me to come with?" Ange said while I laced up my running shoes.

I waved her off. "Just gonna take a quick look around. You guys stick together and keep on the lookout for anything suspicious."

"Be careful, Dad," Scarlett said. "With my Bronco in the shop, I can't ram into any more bad guys."

I smiled, then threw a wave and splashed into the shallows off the swim platform. Sloshing up onto the boat ramp, I quickly reached the shore. Jack chugged the Baia out into deeper water as I trekked up the road, scanning up and down the shoulders. A line of two trucks and a van, each with a trailer in tow, were parked in the shade of the encroaching mangroves to my right.

With no one around, I picked up to a steady jog and soon reached the fork. It was hotter there than on the open water, and I worked up a sweat by the time I stopped beside the tire marks.

I inspected them, kneeling down and observing the

dark traces carefully. They started about fifty yards back from the fork and, inspecting the trajectory from low on the pavement, I noticed that they appeared to head toward the ramp. From the angle I'd caught with the drone, it'd appeared the opposite—that they'd cut left to the military installation.

"Strange," I said to myself as I stood and scratched the back of my head. "Why would they book it straight to the water if they weren't trying to hide the getaway car?"

The slab of concrete that stretched the entirety of the road to the boat ramp was only about two football fields long. A floored vehicle of any kind would need a vigilant driver with a quick brake foot to avoid running out of road quick. I backtracked but kept to a walk, carefully observing the foliage on both sides. Nothing seemed even remotely disturbed, let alone broken enough to indicate a vehicle had driven through. There wasn't even a footpath, and by the time I made it back to the boat ramp, I was left scratching my head again.

Maybe it's just a coincidence? Maybe some other vehicle made those marks. Local kids out having fun, like Jack had originally assumed.

But Agent Maddox had said that they were somewhat fresh. Less than a week. He'd said that time and rain and sun combine to fade the marks away, even if they aren't pressure washed.

If the marks were made by Brier's getaway vehicle, where did it go?

My gut told me that perhaps Brier had stopped there to board a boat, or maybe he'd turned around and cut into one of the half dozen dirt roads that branched off from Blimp Road.

After scanning over the area yet again, I hailed Jack on the Baia. Since there was a steady current in the channel, he'd kept the engines running to stay in one place while I played Sherlock Holmes.

"Anything?" Ange asked from up on the bow as they motored toward me.

"If there is, I didn't catch it. But the car that left the marks definitely headed toward the ramp."

I sloshed back into the water as the Baia approached. Jack piloted it to the same area where I'd hopped out, but the current pulled him a little closer to the murky water along the wall of mangroves. I kept in knee-deep water as he turned the vessel around. Just as the swim platform was about to face me, the craft shuddered as the hull struck bottom.

"What the hell?" Jack said, idling the throttles immediately and turning back the opposite way.

"I thought you said it was no shallower than five here," I said, splashing deeper.

"It is," Jack said. "I'd bet my life it is." He shifted over to the starboard gunwale after pulling back from where he'd hit something. "I've been boating and swimming here since—" He cut himself off as he peered into the water, sliding his sunglasses up to his forehead.

"What's that?" Scarlett asked, leaning over beside him and staring as well.

"That's a good question," Jack said, squinting and cocking his head. "Looks pretty big, though." He grinned and added, "What are the chances that's Brier's Porsche?"

Scarlett looked back and forth between the blurry

submerged object and the side of the boat ramp a good distance away. "But how could it have gotten all the way over here?"

"Toss me my mask and light, will you, Ange?" I said, splashing up to my waist.

Lauren was closer to the locker beside the sunbed. She snatched up my mask and dive light and lobbed them my way. Once the mask was secure over my face, I removed my shoes and tossed them onto the swim platform, then clicked on the flashlight.

"Let's just hope it's not a dishwasher or some other piece of old junk," Jack said, shaking his head. "That would sure be anticlimactic. And careful not to disturb the bottom. You think the viz is bad now, but you churn it up and you won't see your hand in front of your face." He took another look, then glanced at the depth gauge. "We're twelve feet here, bro."

I nodded, took in a breath, then flattened my body. Taking my friend's advice, I swam with slow, mindful strokes and was soon directly over the object. It appeared flat and large, but it was far down and the water murky. Shoving my upper body down, I kicked toward the bottom and the object rapidly came into focus in the beam of my dive light.

I gasped a few bubbles and my eyes bulged as I realized that I was looking at a vehicle—and not just any vehicle, the same Porsche Cayenne that Brier had used to flee the scene.

Kicking deeper, I grabbed onto the roof, then hooked my body around the driver's side. All four windows were open, allowing me to peek inside. It was dark and cloudy, but I could make out that the interior was empty. Pushing myself back out the driver window, I checked the rear plate just to make sure. It was a match. I looked up and swam for the surface. I caught my breath, lowered my mask, and wiped the dripping water from my hair.

"Well?" Scarlett said, eyeing me expectantly.

"Well, it isn't a dishwasher."

"Washing machine?" Scarlett guessed again.

I kicked to the swim platform and slid up onto the edge. "It's Brier's getaway car."

"Please tell me the guy's in there," Jack said, leaning over the side and peering toward the water again. "That would make this whole thing easy, and we can get back to the things that are truly important—like scouring for lobster to replenish my supply."

"It's empty," I said. "Aside from a few curious blue crabs."

"I'm guessing they didn't swim for it?" Lauren said with a chuckle, gazing out over the waterway, which was nearly a mile wide at parts.

Jack traced a line to the boat ramp with his eyes. "We've gotta be at least fifty feet from the ramp."

"And perpendicular to it," Lauren added.

Ange shielded the sun from her eyes as she gazed toward the shore. "There are no damaged branches to indicate a vehicle veering off the road and plowing through. It must've been pulled over here from the base of the ramp."

I smiled. My family and friends had worked through the problem in under a minute. They say that you're only as good as the people you surround yourself with. And I had about as first-rate a support system as anyone could ask for.

"I was thinking the same thing," I said. "The transmission was left in neutral, and all the windows were open."

"So, they hopped out, let the car roll into the water, then dragged it into this deep, murky area to hide it?" Scarlett said.

I nodded. "Looks that way."

"There anything else useful left in the car, bro?" Jack said.

"Go ahead and take a look," I said, coming to my feet and handing him the dive light. "I'm gonna call Agent Maddox."

"Want me to go down too?" Scarlett said, ever eager to play as much of a role as she could in our escapades.

"Let's let Jack take this one. But you can watch from above. It's easy to get stuck or tangled on something in a sunken vehicle."

"Logan's right," Jack said, slipping on his mask. "Especially when the water's this mucky."

I dropped down to the saloon and placed the call.

"We found the getaway car," I said, getting straight to the point.

Or more like it found us, I thought.

"Where?" Maddox replied.

"Submerged on the northern tip of Blimp Road on Cudjoe. It's devoid of bodies and was clearly pulled out deep into the water along the shore."

"I'll have some of my guys head over and check it out right away."

"We'll tie a buoy to it just before we leave."

The Homeland agent fell quiet a moment, then said, "Brier getting away on a boat ties into

120

something else I discovered this afternoon."

I waited, giving him a chance to elaborate. When he didn't, I said, "You're just gonna leave it at that?"

"Let's meet up this evening to discuss it. Moondog sound good? That iced coffee is calling my name."

Most all the restaurants in Key West are incredible. It's a wonder any of the locals are able to keep the gut at bay. I remembered the plans I'd made earlier that day.

"I'm meeting friends at a different local spot tonight. I'll send you the address. Seven work?"

"That's cutting it a little close to the mayor's curfew."

"You gonna arrest me?"

The hardened military man chuckled. "I'll see you then."

We ended the call. I liked Agent Maddox. He didn't beat around the bush. The man didn't have the time or the patience for that.

After messaging him the address for Salty Pete's, I set my phone on the dinette and headed back topside when I heard splashing aft of the stern. I poked my head up just in time to see Jack slide down his mask and climb onto the swim platform.

"Find anything?" Scarlett was the first to ask as she watched him closely.

"A long metal chain attached to the front axle. So we were right about it being pulled." He paused, then added, "It would've taken a lot of muscle to get that thing so deep. At last two hundred horsepower, probably far more, and a good-sized boat."

I grabbed an old crab pot buoy from a storage locker in the guest cabin, cut a fifteen-foot piece of rope, then splashed in and tied it around one of the wheel's spokes.

Once back on the Baia, I stared out over the horizon as the sun made its arc toward the Gulf. Glancing at my watch, I saw that it was half past five. Part of me wanted to scour the area for any sign of Brier's boat, maybe take the drone up for another round. But I wanted to check up on Pete and a few of the locals, and Maddox's new info had me intrigued. I plopped into the pilot's seat, fired up the twin 600s, and accelerated us back to Key West.

SIXTEEN

We motored into Conch Harbor forty-five-minutes later and tied off the Baia at slip twenty-four. I'd rinsed the grime off in the main cabin shower on the trip back and changed into a pair of cargo shorts, a T-shirt, and my Converse low tops.

After tidying up, the Dodge clan loaded into the Tacoma, and Jack and Lauren climbed into his blue Wrangler, then we drove over to Salty Pete's. Just a few minutes' drive from the marina, Pete's looked like a normal old two-story house. Were it not for a small painted sign out front indicating the place's name, you'd never guess that it was one of the most happening establishments in town.

When I'd moved back to Key West, I'd strolled into the local joint on Jack's recommendation, looking to pick the proprietor's brain regarding searching for and salvaging a Spanish galleon. Pete's had been on its wobbly last legs, rundown and devoid of many patrons aside from cats and the chickens in the backyard. But I'd used part of my finder's fee to spruce up the place, and it'd regained its former glory, turning into one of the most popular restaurants in the islands, especially when the mic was hot with one of the many local artists Pete booked.

But tonight, thanks to the curfew, the small lot was nearly empty. I parked against a railroad tie near the front porch, and Jack pulled in beside me. After hopping out, I pointed toward Atticus's favorite patch of grass in the islands beside a flowerbed and under a gumbo-limbo tree. Atticus had spent hours there, keeping his eyes and ears alert and greeting everyone who came and went into the restaurant.

"Good boy," I said as he did a few tiny circles, then plopped down and watched us with his tongue out.

Pete's was like a tomb on the inside, the high-pitched bell echoing across the dining area as the five of us entered. The place was empty aside from two local fishermen at the bar across the room and a waitress sweeping the floors. Osmond leaned out through the kitchen order window, the tall, wide-shouldered Scandinavian barely fitting through.

"Pete's upstairs," he said, pointing a metal spatula to the staircase.

"Thanks, Oz," I said, throwing him a wave.

"You guys eat yet?" he said. "Slow night, so I've got a lot of fresh grouper left. I could grill up a few plates with sweet potato fries. And conch fritters for you, Scar."

My daughter beamed as he mentioned her favorite island dish.

"Sounds great," I said, then thanked him as we

strode to the back of the dining room.

The wide wooden staircase creaked as we headed up to the second floor. Rows of glass cases of various artifacts greeted us. Nearly the entire second level was filled with exhibits displaying and describing finds from across the archipelago, some of the artifacts dating all the way back to the 1600s. A sliding glass door led out to the large balcony, which had a peekaboo view of the ocean through nearby structures and palm trees, along with a tiny satellite bar and a stage. In the opposite corner of the museum area was a door leading into Pete's office.

We spotted a group outside and slid open the door. Pete Jameson sat beside Jack's nephew and across from Agent Maddox and Harper Ridley, a good friend and reporter for the Keynoter. Recently, Ange and I had gone after the men who'd murdered her uncle after he'd discovered a Civil War Confederate belt buckle in Jones Lagoon in the Upper Keys.

"I was just keeping Agent Maddox here company until you arrived," Pete said in his gravelly but friendly voice. The short, sprightly sixty-year-old with an impressive beer gut and a tanned bald head bounced over to greet us.

"Some of the best sea stories I've ever heard," Maddox said, sitting as casually as ever and sipping a Key limeade. "Especially the one about your lost right arm."

I couldn't help but grin as I wondered which one of the stories Pete had chosen that evening to explain how the limb had been swiped.

"You mind if we talk in your office?" I said.

Isaac, Jack's nephew, sat at the end of the table, a

textbook opened and his laptop beside it. The scrawny sixteen-year-old was already taking classes at the local college and loved working with computers.

Despite her protestations, I told Scarlett to stay there on the balcony with Isaac and Jack.

"I'll stay out here too," Lauren said. "I've got a lot of emails to send out."

"You want me to stay as well?" Harper added.

"Please join us," I said, knowing that Harper had a unique perspective on the islands and could very well be of help. "Off the record, of course."

Leaving Scarlett, Isaac, Jack, and Lauren on the balcony, we shuffled back inside and across to Pete's corner office. The space had newspaper clippings and photographs on the walls, shelves of books, and various artifacts from gold coins to a six-pound cannonball resting on a stand on his worn desk. You could spend hours poking around the room and not examine everything. A small window provided a faded glimpse out to the palm trees and Pete's shop out back, where he kept his restored '69 Camaro.

We left the door cracked open behind us. Ange and I plopped onto the old leather couch, while Maddox and Harper dropped into chairs, and Pete sat behind his desk.

"Your guys find the Porsche?" I led off.

Maddox nodded. "Some of my guys enlisted local help and they just cranked it out of the water with a tow truck. They've yet to find anything that you didn't notice already, though."

"It was hauled out into that deep water," Ange said. "No question about that."

126

"And you mentioned that you had new intel?" I said.

"I received word from a Coast Guard officer. He said that they spotted a boat heading east in that area near Cudjoe. Initially, we'd been focusing our attention on Key West and Stock Island, so we didn't give it much thought. But with this new info regarding the abandoned getaway car, I'd wager that this was our boat. I spoke to the radar man who saw it. He said it was flying fast. Upwards of forty knots. And he said it looked like they were trying to skirt their radar. They got no reply when they hailed the mystery craft."

"You have the trajectory?" I said.

"Mr. Jameson," Maddox said, "do you have a—"

"Pete," the conch said as he spun his chair around and opened an old chest, revealing stacks of cardboard tubes.

Fingering through the bushel for half a second, he slid one out, unfurled a chart, and pinned it to his desk. It showed the Lower Keys, from Sugarloaf to Bahia Honda.

We all rose to our feet, and Maddox pointed at the map. "The radar man said that it was here," he said, stabbing a finger just south of Toptree Hammock Key. "And that it was heading east before vanishing south here."

We observed the map carefully.

"Where was the patrol boat?" Pete said.

"Here." Maddox pointed just north near Big Torch. "Also heading east apparently. The boat hopped off their radar and they never saw it again after that."

"They couldn't have jumped back into the Gulf, then," Ange said. "They would've been spotted for sure."

"And with the other patrol boats, it's unlikely they'd motor down into the Atlantic," Pete said.

"Which means they likely stopped somewhere in here," I said, pointing at Niles Channel.

We stood in silence for a moment, mulling over the info.

Harper perked up. "There's a string of rental houses here," she said, pointing at the eastern shore of Summerland Key, which ran right along the channel. "They pop up in our classifieds section all the time, and on our website for ads."

Maddox smiled. "You have their info?"

She nodded and slipped out her phone. "I know the property manager. We could ask about any recent occupancy."

I narrowed my gaze as I eyed the map. After three days, it felt good to finally be making solid headway. Having found the sunken getaway car and narrowed down the search area, I could feel us closing in on Brier. It was very possible that he'd merely used the boat to skip around the roadblock, then driven out of the Keys. Or that he'd sat tight, then motored out on the boat later on, once everything had died down. But my gut told me that he was still in the islands, hiding out and waiting for the right time to take another swing at me. If he was still here, he wouldn't be able to hide from us for much longer, and when—

My thoughts were interrupted by a shriek coming from the dining area beneath our feet. It was followed by a loud thud and heavy footsteps hustling up the creaky staircase. I snatched my Sig and, peeking through the crack in Pete's office door, spotted three men stomp into view, their pistols at the ready.

SEVENTEEN

Sick and tired of sitting around and waiting for Brier to come up with his next plan of attack, Vito Bonetti and three of his men snuck away from the compound without a word to Brier, heading toward Key West.

They pulled up along Mangrove Street, and one of Vito's men who'd followed Logan from the marina strode over to the vehicle and climbed into the back.

"He's in there," the man said, pointing toward the side of the unassuming restaurant. "Went in twenty minutes ago."

"Who else is in there?" Vito growled, eyeing the mostly empty lot. "Place looks deserted."

"With the curfew in effect, most of the locals are home."

Vito leaned forward and glanced through the window at the dimming red sky. The sun had already set, and they had another fifteen minutes at most before their vehicle would be pulled over just for being out past the set curfew. He'd wanted to attack

Dodge at the man's house, but deep down, he knew that it was now or never.

He had three missed calls from Brier on his phone. The former soldier would be furious that they'd snuck away and attacked without him, but Vito didn't care. He was there for one reason and one reason alone: getting revenge against Logan Dodge. Once the local was dead at his feet, Vito would disappear—run away to South America and change his identity as he had years before.

"Pull into the lot," Vito said. "Slowly."

The driver did as instructed, turning off the pavement, crunching the gravel, and coming to a stop beside a row of hedges. He killed the lights and engine, and they waited a moment in silence.

Vito snarled, then looked each of his men over in turn. The three hardened members of his criminal operation had just arrived in the islands the previous day. Aside from the two still back at the hideout, they were the last remaining members of his criminal operation. What had once been a lucrative multimillion-dollar business had been whittled down to a mere shadow of its former glory, all thanks to the man they were after.

"Five hundred thousand to the man who kills Logan Dodge," he said. "The rest will receive their cut as well. This ends tonight."

The men each nodded. They were tough, experienced criminals. None of them strangers to taking lives. Following Vito's lead, they opened their doors and strode to the front of Salty Pete's.

A yellow Lab eyed them from a patch of grass. His tail wagged at first, then he began to growl as they stomped up the porch steps.

"Shut up, you stupid dog," Vito said, eyeing the canine and threatening to withdraw his pistol.

Vito stopped and let his men go first. They threw open the door, and the four of them pushed inside.

"We're closed," a woman said as she swept along a row of booths.

The men didn't break stride. They stomped toward the center of the dining room, each of them scanning over every inch of the place.

"We're not here for the food," Vito said in his pompous Italian accent. "We're here for Logan Dodge."

The woman turned ghostly pale as Vito withdrew his pistol. The three other men followed suit.

"Don't even think about it, local," Vito snapped, aiming his weapon at the two fishermen at the bar, who'd turned and slid off the stools to their feet.

The islanders froze and swallowed hard as they stared back at the barrel.

Vito stormed over to the hostess, grabbed a fistful of her hair, and yanked her back. The woman squealed and nearly toppled over.

"Where is he?" Vito spat.

The sounds of shuffling feet resonated from the second floor.

"Boss," one of Vito's men said, motioning toward the stairs.

Vito tossed the woman aside and cut toward the base of the steps. A hulking Scandinavian man wearing an apron stormed out from the kitchen, cutting Vito off. The man was six and a half feet tall and two hundred and fifty pounds. He held a cleaver in one hand and began to tell Vito to get the hell out of the restaurant when one of the men kicked him in the gut. The colossal cook tumbled backward and slammed hard into the wall. Before he could retaliate, a second criminal punched him in the throat. The man fell to his knees, pressing his hands to his damaged trachea and wheezing desperately for air.

"Idiot," Vito hissed. He gestured toward the steps. "You three go up and get Dodge."

The men didn't hesitate, the large sum of a reward burning in their minds as they raced up the stairs to claim their prize. Vito stood over the injured man and kept his eyes on the others in the dining area, making sure they didn't try anything.

"Pitiful," he said, kicking the cleaver across the room and shaking his head at the chef.

When Vito's three men reached the top of the stairs, they raised their weapons and scanned the place. Hearing noises coming from the back corner, they took aim at a door just as their mark spotted them through the crack and then swiftly opened fire.

EIGHTEEN

I pulled the trigger, letting loose a single round at our attackers before lunging to my left. I crashed into Ange, and we dove for the opposite side of the office just as the three men rained hell upon us. Bullets tore into the small space, pelting the walls and splintering the door.

Maddox helped Harper, and they both took cover as well, narrowly flattening their bodies against the floor before they were filled with lead. Pete didn't hesitate. When the four of us had landed on the other side of the office, the fearless restaurant owner grabbed the edge of his mahogany desk and yelled as he flipped it forward. The heavy hardwood slammed into the floor, and I helped him shove it around, the desk acting as a shield as the three men continued their incessant barrage.

We were trapped. Pinned down.

It doesn't matter how well trained you are or how tough you are, a bullet will tear through your flesh just the same as any other person's.

Needing to tip the scales and retaliate, I glanced up at the back window.

"Cover me, guys!" I yelled as Pete, Ange, and Maddox grabbed their pistols.

The three of them opened fire, causing our attackers to pause and take cover themselves as I reached for the cannonball that had fallen and rolled against the wall. I gripped the heavy iron sphere and heaved it through the window. The object crashed through the glass, punching a hole through the middle and creating a spiderweb of cracks.

"Going for the flank!" I shouted as Ange and Maddox opened fire again.

I jolted forward from my kneeling position, launching my body across the gap and into the glass. I looked away and flew into the window shoulder first. The loud crash filled the air and shards broke loose around my body. Landing on the eave, I regained my balance and shuffled along the edge of the house.

A shriek cut through the night air, stabbing deep into my heart. It was Scarlett.

In all the chaos and confusion and surprise from the sudden attack, I'd forgotten about the others we'd left back out on the balcony. Gripping my Sig, I wasted no time sliding around the corner and taking aim toward the deck. It was empty, and they looked like they'd left in a hurry, with two of the chairs surrounding their table on their backs.

I heard shuffling bodies, then spotted four figures climbing down the support beams to the backyard. I heaved a short sigh of relief before the men opened fire yet again from the museum area, raining rounds upon Pete's office. From my vantage point on the eave, I could barely see part of the sliding glass door, and I caught glimpses of bright flashes from the exploding gunpowder.

With a six-foot gap between me and the balcony, I stowed my weapon, stepped back, and darted forward, launching my body through the air. I barely cleared the railing and landed between the stage and a table, rolling to slow my momentum before snatching my pistol and taking aim through the glass on one knee.

Training my sights inside, I locked onto the attacker closest to Pete's office and opened fire, popping two quick rounds from the chamber. Both hit the guy center mass, and he barreled sideways and slammed into the floor. The two other assailants were quick to respond, whirling around and directing their fire at me. I dropped out of sight to my left as they riddled the sliding glass door with holes, bullets zipping by into the evening air.

They ceased fire and I heard a yell as shots rang out from Pete's office. Peeking around with my weapon leveled, I watched as the two attackers dropped down behind display exhibits. Maddox appeared from the back doorway, his service weapon raised. Wanting to come at the men from both sides, I cut around the corner and dashed through a broken gap in the glass.

I reached the nearest criminal just as he was about to take aim at Maddox around the corner of a display. His eyes bulged when he saw me, but by that time it was too late. I fired a round into his forearm, causing him to yell in pain and drop his weapon. But the blow didn't finish him off. Enraged and bleeding, the guy came at me, throwing a fist my way like a madman. I sidestepped, threw a slide kick into his shin, and sent him flying facefirst into a glass display case.

Seeing Maddox engaging the third attacker, I closed in to finish my man when he gripped an old dagger from the spread of artifacts and spun, slashing it toward me. The blade nearly connected with my right arm. He was fast and strong. But he was no match for another bullet, and I hadn't the slightest inclination to fight fair. He'd already lost that right.

As his momentum forced him sideways, I fired a round into his gut. His body scrunched and he fell back, sprawling over the damaged display. I turned back in time to see Maddox holding the final guy in a rear naked choke. The Homeland agent gave me a quick nod when he saw that I'd taken the other guy down.

Squeezing the criminal tight, he said, "You're going to tell us where Brier and the others are hiding out."

The man cursed and managed to slip a hand free. He reached for something in his pocket, but before he grabbed it, Ange buried a bullet in his left foot from her position near the doorway. The man shook, moaned, and keeled over.

Maddox forced him down, shoving his face to the floor and pinning a knee between his shoulder blades. With the three men out of commission, I scanned the space with my Sig raised, knowing there could very well be more. As if my mind had summoned the act, I heard a commotion downstairs. A woman squealed and the front door was thrown open, punctuated by its creaking hinges and the ringing of a bell. I took off for the stairs. On the way down, I kept my weapon raised, ready to open fire again at a moment's notice.

"He ran out!" the hostess yelled, pointing toward the door. She was kneeling over Osmond's motionless body near the base of the stairs.

"Already calling 9-1-1," a local I recognized said as he held up a phone and raced from behind the counter with a first aid kit.

I bounded for the main entrance, hearing footsteps behind me thundering down the stairs and not having to glance back to know that it was Ange. I slipped through the door and back out into the humid air to the sound of growling. Atticus had left his perch and was biting the hands of a shadowy figure on the other side of the lot.

I sprinted toward the commotion, the thought of something happening to my dog tearing me up inside. His growls got more intense as I heard a door open, then slam shut. A silver sedan rumbled to life. I stopped and took aim as the driver put the vehicle into gear and peeled out, spraying rocks. I caught a brief glimpse of the driver by the glow of the streetlights and realized that it was Vito.

Atticus continued to bark as the Italian crime boss flew out of the lot and onto the main road. I briefly scanned over my dog for injuries, then patted him on the head when I saw Vito's familiar Colt pistol lying on the ground.

"Good boy," I said as I ran to my Tacoma.

I fished the keys from my pocket and jumped into the driver's seat. Ange climbed into the passenger side as I rumbled the engine to life.

"It's Vito," I said as I put it in gear and hit the gas.

I tore out of the lot and floored it when the tires hit the pavement. The truck accelerated up to fifty, then I slowed into a turn, following Vito a hundred yards back. Though rows of cars lined the curb as usual, the streets were nearly empty, the sun having vanished over half an hour earlier.

I managed to catch up to Vito when we hit Roosevelt Boulevard. We hit a straightaway as we raced along the northern edge of the island, and I whipped out my Sig.

"You shoot him, and then what?" Ange said, gripping her weapon as well while hanging on. "Brier's still missing."

My wife was right, and her logic snapped me out of my current objective. Vito Bonetti was ruthless and vile and dangerous, yes. But Nathan Brier was the real enemy—by far the most dangerous of the two.

I followed Vito through a red light, running Ange's words around in my mind. My heart rate was spiked from the sudden attack back at Pete's office and the resulting confrontation. Trying to focus and come up with a better plan than just chase down and destroy, I glanced back for a moment and spotted my hardcase still resting where I'd left it on the floor behind the passenger seat.

Still cruising down a straightaway and picking up speed, I slid my Sig into my custom holster built into the bottom of the dashboard.

"Take over," I said, releasing my right hand. Ange leaned over and seized the wheel with a strong grip.

I counted down, then shimmied right while Ange rose and slipped over me. In a blink, she plopped down into the driver's seat and took over while I climbed into the back. Gripping the handle, I pulled up the hardcase, pressed my thumb to the biometric scanner, and cracked it open, revealing a foam liner and hollowed-out portions with snug gadgets I'd accumulated over the years.

"Hold on!" Ange shouted. "Turning right."

The moment the words left her lips, I pressed one hand to the roof and the other to the seat as she spun the wheel, sending us screeching south, back inland. Even bracing for the maneuver, my back still slammed into the side door. She eased off the accelerator and turned the other way, flying into the Searstown Shopping Center parking lot right on the sedan's heels.

Regaining control, I swiped the item I was after, then closed the case and dropped it back to the floor.

"Heading out to the bed," I said, sliding open the rear window.

I didn't need to explain to her what was going on inside my head. I knew that her words and my grabbing the small magnetic tracking device from the case told her everything she needed to know. I forced myself through the tiny opening and landed in the bed. Ange tried to skid around a speed bump, but the rear tire hit the slab of pavement, jolting me skyward and nearly tossing me out of the truck.

"Sorry!" she shouted.

I shook out of the haze, grabbed the side rail with my left hand, then crouched down right behind the cab, warm wind whipping against my face. I watched as Vito's vehicle roared out from the opposite side of the lot, then plowed right over a hedge and screeched back onto Roosevelt. I held on as Ange followed suit, the 4x4 and off-road tires having a much easier time traversing the curbs and shrubs.

Holding on, I focused far ahead as we roared around the corner of the island, flying toward the US-1 intersection. There was little doubt in my mind which way Vito would turn, and it would be a sharp ninety-degree change in direction.

The piercing sound of sirens filled the air. I peeked over my shoulder and spotted a Key West Police cruiser. It was swiftly gaining on us, it's lights flashing.

"We need to catch him before the intersection!" I shouted to Ange through the back window.

"Hold on, then!" she fired back.

My wife went into full race car driver mode, confidently planting her heavy foot on the pedal and thundering the six-cylinder engine. The truck jolted and shook, and the engine protested, but Ange didn't let up for a second. I kept low to avoid the harsh breeze as she brought us up to eighty, ninety, then a hundred. I peered over the roof and watched as Vito's sedan got bigger and bigger ahead of us.

Soon, the bumper was within fifty feet. Then thirty.

When we neared the intersection, Vito let off the gas for the turn and we closed the gap. Still gripping the tracking device with my right hand, I zeroed in on the vehicle, knowing that we'd only have one chance at this.

The sedan's tires screeched as Vito turned sharply. Ange altered our trajectory just barely as we cut right alongside him in the intersection. Clasping the rail to stabilize myself, I leaned over the left side of the bed, reached as far as I could, and was nearly able to press the tracker to the back. Letting go of it, I watched as the little gadget soared the five-foot gap and struck home on the bottom right corner of the rear paneling. The magnet did its job, keeping the device stuck to the car as Vito roared the gas once more, accelerating east.

Ange let off the accelerator, softly pressed the brake, and spun the wheel once our speed had slowed. We rotated twice, tires crying out as the truck shook wildly. I tried to hold on, but the sudden jostle threw me to the bed, and I slid against the tailgate as the truck finally came to a stop. By outward appearances, I knew that it would've looked like Ange had misjudged the turn and lost control of the vehicle. But I knew she hadn't—that she'd done it intentionally to make Vito think that he'd gotten away.

Shaking the daze from my mind, I hopped out of the bed as the police cruiser whined through the intersection. It slowed for a moment, then continued, chasing down Vito. A black BMW roared into view behind it and braked right beside us. Agent Maddox jumped out.

"What the hell happened?" he said, seeing our truck halfway on a sidewalk.

"Call them off," I said, gesturing toward the cop car. "Call off all the police. Tell them to leave the car alone."

Maddox's face scrunched. Before he could ask why, I said, "I placed a tracker on his car." Based on his understanding expression, that seemed to do the trick. He thought for half a second, then said, "He can lead us to—"

"Brier," Ange said, finishing his train of thought. "Exactly."

Maddox nodded. He slipped out his radio and called in to Jane, who was already calling in to squad cars east along the island chain to intercept Vito.

"This had better work," Maddox said. "Or we just let a wanted fugitive get away for nothing."

"It'll work," I said, turning and heading back toward the truck. "I'll send you his location when he stops."

"Where are you going?" he said, rushing to catch up with me.

"To prepare for a showdown."

"Remember what Mayor Nix said? One more incident and you're out of here."

"Why do you think I'm in such a hurry?"

Ange jumped into the passenger seat. "My daughter and friends will be at Jack Rubio's house. I'll send the address. Make sure officers are stationed there just in case."

He gave me a nod. "Will do. Make sure you leave some bad guys for me."

NINETEEN

Vito Bonetti stomped the gas, his back clapping against the seat as he accelerated east over Cow Key Channel. His heart pounded and he squeezed the wheel with a viselike grip. He glanced at the rearview mirror and watched as his pursuers lost control in the intersection, the truck spinning twice before shaking to a stop.

He gave a short sigh of relief as he brought the sedan over eighty miles per hour. He cruised across Stock Island, then Boca Chica Channel. He was flying across the islands and had lost the truck, but he still had the police to contend with. He knew that if he didn't pull a hell of a maneuver and fast, he'd be facedown on the pavement with cuffs around his wrists in minutes.

He cursed his men—cursed their inability to take down the man and finish the job. He was through. He vowed that, if by some lucky stroke of fate, he got away again, he'd cut his losses and get the hell out of

144

the country.

A drop of blood splattered onto his pant leg and he remembered that he was bleeding.

That damn stupid dog, he thought, eyeing the bite marks and trails of deep red sliding down his right hand.

With the police lights still at his back and the sirens growing louder, he kept his attention forward and accelerated all the way up to a hundred and twenty, blurring past Boca Chica and Big Coppitt. Approaching Shark Key Bridge, he gave it everything it had on the straightaway, nearly skidding out of control when he had to pass a vehicle. He did his best to keep the car steady, but he was driving so fast that he nearly plowed into the rail and flew out into the channel.

The crime boss caught his breath as he floored it straight across the other side of the bridge. His face contorted with rage when he saw the police lights appear once more at his back. He knew that it was only a matter of time before more cop cars arrived to block off his escape. He'd never reach the safe house in time.

How did it come to this? He shook his head, unable to believe how far he'd fallen.

Once the proud, rich owner of a successful restaurant chain and the leader of a lucrative drug-smuggling operation, Vito Bonetti was down to his last hope. He kept driving at full speed regardless, giving himself the best chance as he roared across the Saddlebunch Keys.

Just when all hope seemed lost, Vito rounded the turn near Harris Gap, and when he straightened out of it, the police car was no longer on his tail. Vito swallowed hard, the wind whipping past, the dark tropical world whirring by in a blur.

He glanced intermittently at the rearview but caught no sight of the lights. He cut across Upper Sugarloaf, then Cudjoe before eventually slowing and turning onto Niles Road on Summerland. He felt sure that police would pop out at any second and overtake him, but none did. Cruising across the northern part of the island, he knew that he could no longer afford to test his luck. The game was over, and he'd leave, regardless of what Brier wanted.

He skidded into a difficult-to-spot driveway, wound fifty yards toward the shoreline, then stopped under a covered parking space beside a stilted house. Vito rushed inside and barged through the front door.

"Boss?" a man seated at a couch said, startled by the man's sudden appearance. "Where the hell have you—"

"Where's Brier?"

The other of Vito's two remaining men stepped into the living room with his hands on his hips. He pointed out a rear-facing window toward a mangrove-infested shore and a long wooden dock.

"Get ready," Vito ordered as he stomped across the room and grabbed the back doorknob. "We're leaving right away."

Vito's men didn't say a word but followed close behind as the crime boss hustled onto the porch and down onto the dock. The sixty-year-old was in good shape for his age but had grown weary from the long night, the rushed escape, and the injury to his hand. His white button-up shirt was coated in patches of

146

sweat, and he wiped a layer of perspiration from his brow.

"Brier!" Vito said, pounding down the planks toward the man's shadowy figure.

Brier stood at the end of the dock, right in front of the covered boat area where their big stolen fishing boat was tied off. He didn't say a word as the angry Italian stormed toward him.

"We need to get out of here," Vito said, heaving as he reached the end of the dock. Stopping right behind Brier, he added, "Are you hearing me?"

Brier stood stoically, facing the water with his back to Vito. He brought a half-burned cigarette to his lips, took a calm inhale, then breezed out the fumes.

"You're a damn fool," Brier said, his tone relaxed but his words coated in poison. "What the hell were you thinking going after Dodge on your own? Did you kill him?"

"It was me and my men," Vito retorted. "And, no... the man's still alive."

Brier whirled his tongue around the inside of his mouth. "Of course he is. A man like you is incapable of bringing down a man like that."

Vito snarled. "And you are? You failed as well, remember? Dodge bested you. And I did what I had to do because I was sick of sitting around, waiting for you to make up your mind."

Brier took another long drag, then flicked the butt into the water, its embers dancing in the air like fireflies before going out in an instant.

"You made a very big mistake," Brier said, turning around to face Vito for the first time.

"We both did," Vito spat. "This is useless. I barely

managed to slip away with my life and freedom, and I'm not risking either anymore." He glanced back at his two men, who were standing right behind him. "Me and my men are through. We're leaving."

Vito turned on his heel, not bothering to listen to what Brier had to say about it. He took two steps and motioned for his men to go, but they stood tall. Locked in place.

"You sure about that?" Brier said, striding toward Vito.

The crime boss paused and looked back and forth between his two men. Both had stone-cold expressions on their faces.

"I said, let's go!" Vito grumbled.

Again, the two men stayed put.

Vito clenched his teeth. "You pathetic excuses for... what about blood? What about all that I've done for you?"

"The past, Vito," Brier said. "That's all the past. You're a has-been. Nothing more. Your remaining men, like me, look to the future." Vito turned to look over his shoulder as Brier added, "Your role in this operation has run its course. I'm no longer in need of your services."

Vito wasn't used to being talked to that way. The crime boss was used to being the one pointing fingers and criticizing subordinates. He was used to being in control.

Vito's face contorted with pure rage and his right hand squeezed to form a fist. He spun around and lunged toward Brier, but before he'd made it a full step, his two men closed in and grabbed him from behind. They quickly manhandled the crime boss into submission, holding him in place.

"You bastard, Brier!" Vito yelled.

Sick and tired of hearing the man talk, Brier signaled for the two men to bring him closer. Gripping Vito tight by the shoulders, they forced him over to the former soldier. Once the crime boss was before him, Brier gripped the man by the throat.

"Thus ends the Bonetti crime ring," he whispered into Vito's ear.

Letting go, Brier slid his hand to the man's upper back and pulled him forward while stomping his right boot into Vito's kneecap. The bones popped and cracked, and Vito let out a loud, agonizing cry.

The two men kept him on his feet and, upon Brier's order, dragged him to the end of the dock. Brier grabbed a coiled-up chain and wrapped the end around Vito's ankles. The crime boss continued to moan and curse as Brier wound loop after loop up his legs, then knotted the chain in place. At Brier's word, the two men held him on the edge of the planks.

Brier gave Vito one final smug look before rearing back and kicking him over the side. Still shaking from the pain to his knee, Vito flailed backward and splashed into the dark waters of Niles Channel, his sounds muffled, then vanishing altogether. Brier stepped to the edge and peered into the water. Slipping out a flashlight, he clicked on the beam. The water was murky by Florida standards, but it was only ten feet deep, and the glowing light illuminated the crime boss as he struggled and panicked, bubbles trailing from his lips. Brier watched with a cruel smile as the man met his end.

His shaking subsided, the final gasps of life

danced to the surface, and his body went limp.

Brier stared a moment longer, then clicked off the light.

"The old-timer was right about one thing," Brier said. "We need to move. Now."

He hustled down the dock with the two men at his flanks. After grabbing a pair of duffel bags from inside, they headed for the carport. One thing Brier hadn't been able to understand was how Vito had gotten away. Brier had heard the police sirens. He'd stood at the end of the dock and listened as they'd echoed across the archipelago.

How in the hell did Vito escape them?

Beating police in a chase is a daunting task anywhere, but especially in the Keys, with only one road in and out. He stomped for the back of the silver sedan, and when he reached to open the trunk, he spotted a small black object attached to the bottom right side of the rear panel. Dropping one of the bags onto the ground, the former Special Forces operative knelt and inspected the device. It only took him half a second to realize what it was.

"The idiot," he said, snarling as he eyed the tracking device.

That's how he escaped. They let him go so he'd lead them right to our hideout.

A chilling sense of urgency washed over his body, and he reached for his tactical knife. He was about to remove and destroy the device when an idea popped into his head.

TWENTY

Tossing the lines, I started the Baia's engines and motored us out of the harbor. Ange sat at the topside dinette with our laptop cracked open in front of her, watching a GPS image of the tracker I'd attached to Vito's getaway car.

"He's driving over Shark Channel," she said.

I nodded and accelerated us out through the opening in the bight. I'd called Jack on our rushed drive across the island to the marina. Of course, my old friend had offered to come with us and lend a hand.

"Right now I need you to watch over Scarlett and Atticus. He all right? I didn't have time to get a good look at him."

"He's fine. He's a Dodge too, after all."

I'd thanked him after he'd said they were on the way to his house just down the street from mine, and we'd ended the call.

Chugging past the city, I stretched the Baia's legs

to the max, gunning around the island and flying northeast on the Atlantic side. I quickly had us up on plane and cruising at her max speed of fifty knots. I wasn't concerned about burning too much fuel. I had both tanks topped off and a small window to catch Brier before he slipped through our fingers yet again.

When we blurred past the dark silhouettes of the Saddlebunch Keys, Ange perked up. "He's pulling into a short driveway on Summerland," she said. Sliding her fingers over the touchpad, she zoomed in on the map and leaned forward. "He's stopping, Logan. At a waterfront house off Niles Road."

I leaned over and glanced at the screen. "That's the area Harper was talking about. Where those rental houses were."

Ange nodded. She popped open another internet browser and swiftly discovered the address for the house. I pulled out my phone and placed a quick call to Maddox.

I gave him the address just as he answered, practically yelling over the roar of the twin inboard engines.

"Roger that. What's your pos?"

"Half a mile south of Sugarloaf." I didn't need to check my digital chart to add, "We're ten minutes out."

Maddox relayed the address to men beside him, then said, "Ten minutes is a long time with a man of Nathan Brier's experience."

"I know. But if you and the police move in right now, it might spook him out into the Gulf. We're almost there. Just make sure he doesn't escape by land and call in the Guard to have them get a boat over that way. Once we're there, we've got him cornered. Unless that boat of theirs has a rocket strapped to its transom, there's no way in hell he's gonna outrun my Baia."

Maddox paused again. "All right. We're on the move and we'll cover the road. Ten minutes, Dodge. I don't hear from you by then, and we're moving in."

"Copy that."

I hung up and kept my eyes glued forward as we flew northeast along the Lower Keys, then roared up into Niles Channel.

"What's the plan once we get there?" Ange said, glancing away from the monitor.

"Working on it."

"My sniper's here in the master safe. FYI."

I gave a faint smile, then resumed my stern, focused gaze. The previous week, before the school bomb scare and Brier's sudden reappearance, we'd taken a trip past Dry Tortugas to a secret island for an overnight trip. Secluded and with no one around, we'd done some target practice, shooting bobbing coconuts from up on the unique island's cliffs.

Before settling with me in Key West, becoming my wife and the mother to our adopted daughter, Ange had been one of the most dangerous snipers in the world. And her skills hadn't waned in the laid-back paradise.

"You cover me, I'll swim?" I said, cruising under the Overseas Highway.

"Someone's got to watch your back."

We motored up along the right side of the channel. Once on a line with our destination, I turned to port and throttled back for the first time since leaving Key

153

West, slowing alongside the southern shore of the tiny, privately owned Howell Key. Ange disappeared below deck, then returned with a gun case in one hand and a night vision monocular in the other. Leaving the case on the half-moon seat, she climbed up onto the bow and focused on the shore opposite the waterway.

"See it?" I said after half a minute.

She held up a finger while continuing to concentrate. I checked my watch and saw that we had all of two minutes before the clock ran out and Maddox ordered his team to move in.

"Got it," Ange said, pointing off the port bow. "Ease up along that point," she added. "If the water's deep enough, that'll be the best vantage point."

Throttling to just five knots, I piloted us exactly where my wife had said, then idled the engines just as she climbed back into the cockpit. She handed me the monocular and I focused on the spot roughly half a mile away. Through the green-hued image, I saw a long wooden dock with a covered boat port and a white-hulled craft tied off. As Jack had predicted, it was big. A thirty-seven-foot Billfish. A powerful modern fishing boat with a flybridge, but not exactly an ideal getaway craft.

I grabbed my phone and thumbed redial.

"Cutting it close," Maddox said. "I was just about to give the order."

"We're on site and we have visual of the dock and house."

"Any sign of Brier?"

"No sign of anyone. You?"

"No cars in or out. Road's quiet."

"You get ahold of the Guard?"

"Patrol boat's on the way. ETA twenty minutes and they're gonna stand by on the northern opening of the channel in case they try and run for it by sea."

"Good," I said, focusing back on the dock and house.

"We're getting ready to make our move," Maddox said. "Keep your eyes and ears peeled."

"Let me move in first," I said. Before he could voice a protest, I added, "Like Mayor Nix said, Brier's here because of me. He's my responsibility, and if anyone's going to sneak in and take him on, it's gonna be me."

Maddox paused a moment. "How exactly are you planning to sneak up to the place without being spotted?"

"You let me worry about that. You and your guys keep watching the road and forests. He can't get away. I'll be on comms. Channel eight."

"Better make it fast, Dodge."

I handed the phone to Ange and sprang down into the guest cabin. Grabbing a drysuit and Draeger rebreather, I heaved them up onto the main deck and swiftly donned the suit. I didn't have time to do all of the rebreather checks, but I made a habit to inspect and calibrate all of my onboard gear every week for unexpected, rushed circumstances like this. Ange dropped the anchor, careful to keep the splash quiet, and grabbed radios. After zipping up the drysuit, she helped me power on and strap into the rebreather.

"Don't forget your favorite little gadget," Ange said, grabbing one of our Seascooters from below deck. Once my gear was set, I sat on the swim platform and eased into the dark water.

"All good," I said, giving her a thumbs-up while speaking through the full face mask's built-in radio.

Less than five minutes after ending the call with Maddox, I dropped beneath the waves. Descending to the bottom ten feet down, I clicked on my dive light just long enough to power on the scooter and orient myself. Once ready, I switched off the beam and powered the propeller, the powerful little device pulling me through the water across the channel. The scooter, a high-tech model I'd been gifted from a wealthy oil tycoon, had me zipping along at a blazing seven knots, and I managed to reach the other side in just a few minutes.

As the water shallowed to eight feet, I knew that I was nearing the dock, but I couldn't see anything in the darkness.

"Dock clear, Ange?" I said into the radio.

"Affirm."

I pulled out my dive light, made sure that it was on its dimmest setting, and clicked it on. The underwater world came into focus around me. I spun, shining the beam down and forward just enough to get my bearings. I'd overshot the tip of the dock by twenty yards and to the right. Realigning myself, I switched the light back off.

"Relay to Maddox that I've reached the dock."

"Roger that."

The Seascooter having served its purpose well, I left it near the base of a piling and finned toward the hull of the boat bulging beneath the water's surface. I could barely see anything and had to feel along the bottom as I reached the end piling and started removing my gear.

As I turned to grab a swim ladder for support, I noticed something in the water. It was blurry and dark but roughly my size, and it rose up from the seafloor, ending just a few feet from the surface. I kicked toward the object with my arms extended. My hand froze and my eyes bulged as my fingers touched something soft. The shape took form, and I realized that it was a corpse.

"Holy crap," I said.

"What is it?"

I grabbed my light again, aimed it toward the body, and flicked it on. My heart rate ticked up as I gazed upon Vito Bonetti's corpse, his mouth and eyes open and terror-struck. I shined the light down and saw that his lower body was weighted to the bottom by a chain coiled around his legs.

"It's Vito," I said. "Brier sent him to deep six."

Or shallow six, I thought.

He'd drowned with his head just beneath the surface. I swallowed, blinked, and looked away.

"Ange, you there?"

"I've got activity near the house." She paused a moment, then raised her voice. "Two guys heading down the dock, Logan. And fast."

TWENTY-ONE

Nathan Brier stood at the back of the sedan for a moment longer, waiting for the plan to take form. Once it solidified, he rifled through a workbench at the back of the carport. Throwing open two drawers, he nabbed a bottle of Gorilla Glue, then grabbed a nearby broom handle. He pulled a brick from the edge of the footpath, then tossed the items into the trunk of the sedan before turning to Vito's men.

"I'll be right back," he said, slamming the back door shut.

He set the two duffels on the ground and strode for the driver's-side door.

"You're ditching us?" one of the men spat, cracking his knuckles.

Brier stomped over to the back of the car, knelt down and pointed at the tracking device. "You see that? It was planted on the car during your boss's self-proclaimed escape. The man led the feds right to us."

Brier gave the two a brief rundown of his

improvised plan, then said, "You two pack up and head for the boat. We'll motor out of here and meet my guy for a pickup."

The biggest of the two rubbed his chin. "How can we trust you?"

Brier didn't hesitate. He picked up one of the duffel bags and shoved it into the guy's chest. "Take this. There's half a million dollars cash in there. So you know my word is good." Brier glanced at his watch. "Now, go! We're running out of time here."

The man looked at his buddy, then nodded. "You'd better be fast. Or we'll leave without you."

"I will. Now go!"

When the two men disappeared around the side of the house, Brier pulled out his phone and placed a call.

"It's time," was all Brier said when an answer came on the second ring.

After receiving confirmation that his request would be completed, Brier hung up and placed another call. Giving instructions to his second contact, he added that there would be a nice bonus involved if Brier could be extracted right away.

Brier slipped his phone back into his pocket and climbed into the driver's seat. Sliding the key into the ignition, he started the engine and gassed away from the house. He kept his pistol at the ready and his eyes alert, knowing that police could pop out at any second.

They haven't closed in yet, he thought. *They must be waiting for the right time to strike. Standing by on the main road and working to block off our escape routes.*

He cut through the overhanging palm branches and turned onto Niles Road. Switching off his headlights, he oriented the car in the middle of the road, heading south toward US-1. He put the transmission in park and left the engine running.

Hopping out, he grabbed the items from the back. He used the broom handle to secure the steering wheel in place, running the pole through one side of the wheel and out the other before pinning it against the seat and frame. Then he grabbed the brick and plastered one of its surfaces with a thick layer of glue. He'd seen it done without the adhesive but wanted to make sure the weight wouldn't slide off the accelerator.

When everything was set, he slid the gear shifter into drive. Reaching through the rolled-down driver's window, he planted the brick on the gas pedal and swiftly snapped backward away from the sedan as the engine boomed and the car roared away from him, quickly picking up speed. It flew down the long straightaway, roaring like a runaway freight train. Brier hoped that the tracker would momentarily draw attention away from the house. Maybe even strike a parked police cruiser or two. But he didn't have time to sit around and watch the ghost car run its course.

Turning on his heel, he dashed back down the driveway, sprinting as fast as he could through the dark tunnel of foliage and quickly returning to the carport. As he snatched the other duffel bag from the dirt, the sound of smashing metal against metal echoed across the air. Brier smiled as he hustled toward a small shed, threw open the overhead door, and secured the duffel to the back of a parked dirt bike.

Always have a backup plan, he thought as he climbed onto the little off-road vehicle.

As he fished out his keys, the sound of gunfire erupted in the air, coming from the dock. Giving a coarse chuckle as he thought about Vito's men caught in a gunfight, Brier started the 350-cc engine, flicked his wrist, and launched out of the shed.

TWENTY-TWO

I took one final breath from my rebreather, then slipped it off, powered it down, and left it under the swim ladder, right beside Vito's corpse. Ange's words reverberated in my mind.

Two guys heading down the dock fast.

I grabbed hold of the swim ladder, removed my fins, and climbed steadily. With the face mask removed, I no longer had comms with Ange, so I needed a visual on my targets. Rising slowly out of the water, I was greeted by heavy footsteps racing down the planks.

"Get on the boat," a voice grunted.

My body in the shadows, I ascended just enough to peek over the top of the dock. Two tall, wide-shouldered men reached the vessel. One of them climbed aboard while the other tossed a black duffel bag onto the deck, then began untying the lines securing the fishing boat in place.

"We're not waiting for Brier?" the guy on the boat

said.

"Hell no. If that lunatic wants to get himself killed, so be it. Besides, it's only a matter of time before he betrays us. I say we beat him to the punch and make off with our share."

While the guy on the dock untied the forward line, the other strode to the stern and peered at the deck where the bag had landed. Bending down, he unzipped the duffel.

"The hell you doing?" the other man shouted. He jumped over the transom. "We need to fire up the engines and get the hell out of here before police boats arrive."

The kneeling man grabbed something from the deck that I couldn't see and held it up to his buddy.

"Fake money? That son of a—"

The sound of a roaring engine filled the air. It caught my attention in an instant and sounded like it was coming from the main road that cut north to south across the island.

The apparent leader of the two stepped back to the dock and planted his hands on his hips. "We'll get the backstabber when he comes back," he said, grabbing a pistol. "And we'll take all the money he's trying to run off with."

With the sounds of the engine getting louder in the distance, I withdrew my Sig, took aim, and fired a round between the lead guy's shoulder blades. As he lurched to the deck, I shifted to aim at the second thug, who hit the deck just as I had him in my sights.

Racing up the rest of the ladder, I fired a second round as the man dove into the cockpit. The first guy yelled and grunted to his feet, blood flowing from where the bullet had burst clean through and out the front of his body. I cut the distance before he could retaliate and struck him across the face with a soccer kick. His body flailed back and he splashed into the water.

I turned just as the boat's engines thundered to life. Lunging toward the craft, I hurled my body through the air and crashed into the stern as it accelerated out into the channel. I struggled to balance myself, then lumbered toward the cockpit door. The boat dipped back, its propellers churning full speed, then the bow splashed down, allowing me to grip a handrail.

With my Sig raised, I threw open the door and took aim. The pilot's station was empty, and when I took one step inside, the second thug pounced on me from around the corner, swinging a metal fish whacker. I jolted back, but not quite fast enough, and the heavy object struck my gun hand, sending my Sig to the deck. The man turned and geared up for another blow. I sprang toward him, tucking my shoulder and tackling him. He grunted and flew back, our bodies only stopping when we hit the dashboard.

Lifting my assailant off the deck, I shoved him over the panel and into the windscreen. His back punched through the glass, cracking shards loose onto the fiberglass. He struggled to free himself, and I was just about to finish him off when I spotted the dark silhouette of land a hundred yards ahead of us.

With a violent crash imminent, and seconds away, I snagged the throttle and pulled back while rolling the helm to starboard. The boat shook and groaned, and I held on tight as we took the sharp turn, spraying a fountain of water. Narrowly preventing a catastrophic accident, I fixed my attention back on the criminal as the boat slowed. The man had managed to free himself from the broken window and crawled up onto the bow.

With plenty of open water still ahead of us, I let go of the helm and scoured the deck for my fallen weapon. I spotted it near the aft bulkhead and bent down to grab it, turning around in time to watch as the man grabbed a tiny pistol from his ankle. We took aim at each other at the same time but were both beaten to the punch. A high-caliber bullet struck him in the side, sending his body into an uncontrollable spin and throwing him over the bow rail. He splashed into the channel and was floating facedown when I peered over.

I gasped, caught my breath, then slid the drysuit off and pulled out my radio.

"Why do you always wait until the last second, Ange?"

"That's the thanks I get?" she replied as I shifted into the cockpit and motored back to the dock.

"I had him right where I wanted him. Any sign of Brier?"

She didn't answer. When I returned to the dock, killing the engines and jumping onto the planks without bothering to tie off, a chorus of police sirens echoed across the air.

"Ange?" I said, my pistol raised as I rushed toward the shore. "Any sign of—"

"The tracked vehicle just crashed into police cars," Ange said.

As I let her words simmer, a new sound echoed across the air. It was faint, nearly blotted out by the police sirens, but still distinct. It sounded like a small engine. Like a jet ski, an ATV, or a motorcycle. I looked toward the sound, but it was coming from the other side of the house.

"Ange, I think Brier's making a break for it," I said, hustling up the steps to the house's second story porch. When I reached the top, I caught a brief glimpse of a dirt bike flying down a narrow footpath path, then disappearing from view.

"He's heading north," I said.

"I can't... wait," Ange said. "I think I got him. But hell, I got no clear shot."

A moment later, Ange opened fire. I waited for the motorbike to stop, but it kept at it, zipping away from the scene.

"Shit, I missed him," she said. "He's out of my view now, Logan."

As the sound of the engine got quieter, I placed a call to Jane.

TWENTY-THREE

Jane Verona sat in the driver's seat of her parked police Interceptor. With her window rolled down, she gazed down the length of Niles Road.

"Why don't we just move in and get this guy?" Officer Colby Miller said from the passenger seat.

Like all of South Florida, the man was eager to nab the guy who'd threatened his island home and put him behind bars for life. Or even better, finish him off for good with a swift pull of the trigger.

"Backup's moving in from the Gulf to cut off his escape," Jane said.

"Dodge?" Colby said, raising his eyebrows.

"And the Coast Guard, yes."

Colby chuckled. "Mayor Nix's gonna be thrilled when he finds out we're working alongside a civilian again."

"He doesn't know Logan like we do." Jane gestured toward Agent Maddox as the man strode toward her window. "And Homeland's calling the shots on this one, so Nix can blame them if he wants."

"Logan just reached the dock," Maddox said, relaying the message he'd just received from Angelina. "Everyone on your toes."

There were four police cruisers parked, along with three undercover Homeland vehicles. The cars completely blocked off the street. Seconds stretched forever as they waited.

Just as Maddox was getting ready to order everyone to move, a loud rumble shook the calm evening to life. It was the sound of a roaring engine coming from down the long straightaway, and it was getting louder.

"Everyone ready," Maddox said. He grabbed a scope from his hip and focused forward. Jane grabbed a pair of binos as well and spotted a shadowy vehicle flying down Niles, heading straight toward them.

"Lights on!" Maddox ordered.

Every gathered cop did as he instructed, switching on their blinding red and blue lights. They left the sirens off, and Maddox nodded toward an agent, who grabbed a megaphone.

"Stop the car immediately!" the man shouted, his voice booming across the island.

The car didn't slow or deviate from its course. Despite the order, it continued to pick up speed, cranking up over a hundred miles per hour on the side road with no headlights on.

Again the agent gave an order, and again the vehicle kept barreling toward them.

"That's the tracked vehicle," Maddox said, relaying the info from Angelina. "Everyone ready."

When it was within a quarter mile of them, Jane jumped out from her car. "He's not stopping," she stated, grabbing her service pistol.

Colby jumped out as well and stood alongside her as she took aim at the rapidly approaching car.

"Tires," Maddox declared, stowing his optics and withdrawing his handgun in one smooth motion.

He took aim, and on his mark, a line of law enforcement officers opened fire. The cracks of gunpowder filled the air, and sparks shot up from the car's grille and hood as it was peppered with bullets. The front left tire blew out with a well-placed shot, and the car jolted and shook, nearly spinning out of control. When they punctured the other front tire as well, the car roared as it screeched across the pavement, the tire wells spitting out sparks.

When it was within a hundred yards of them, it jerked into a spin, flying in circles. But the car had already gained too much momentum. It flipped, crunched across the road, then tumbled off the shoulder, pummeling into the front end of a parked police car and smashing its hood to pieces before bouncing into the foliage lining the road. Branches snapped as the car crushed a path, then finally settled upside down. The car had stopped, but the engine continued to whine, and the rear wheels continued to spin wildly.

Jane reached the scene first, followed right on her heels by Maddox and Colby. No stranger to navigating a mangrove forest, Jane trudged her way to the vehicle and aimed at the driver-side window. She knew that whoever was inside would most likely already be dead, but she wouldn't think of risking it.

As she crouched beside the driver's door and ordered the occupants to shut off the engine, she realized that there were no occupants.

Grabbing her flashlight, she powered it on and saw that the crunched, battered vehicle was completely empty. Bending lower and shining the beam toward the floor under the dash, she focused on a brick stuck to the gas pedal.

"Holy crap," Colby said as he arrived with Maddox and surveyed the scene. "Brier inside?"

"Nobody's inside," Jane stated.

Both men raised their eyebrows in confusion, and Maddox knelt down beside her.

"They rigged the car to ghost drive," Jane said.

"And locked the steering wheel," Maddox said, noticing the broom handle that had been knocked off the wheel during the high-speed crash.

He looked toward the back of the car, seeing the tracking device still attached near the trunk door.

"Brier knew we were tracking the car," Maddox said. The former soldier leaned into the totaled sedan, grabbed the key in the ignition, and shut off the engine. Then he whipped out his radio and called Angelina. "Brier ghosted the car," he informed her. "Keep your eyes out. He must be making a run for it some other way."

As more officers arrived, Maddox and Jane told three of them to control the scene, then hustled back to the row of parked cars. Once Jane and Colby were back in their cruiser, she fired up the engine and hit the gas, gunning it up Niles. Halfway down the road to the driveway, she got a call from Logan.

"Answer it," Jane said, handing the ringing phone

to her partner.

"Brier's getting away on a dirt bike," Logan said the second Colby answered and put the phone on speaker.

"You got eyes on him?" Jane said, gripping the wheel tight as she flew down the empty street.

"Negative. He's in the thick brush."

Jane eased off the gas as she approached the turn to the house. Having lived most of her life in the islands, and having patrolled the streets for years, she knew the Lower Keys about as well as anyone. Though the Monroe County Sheriff's Office had jurisdiction there, she'd spent time working in joint ops on various incidents and had spent much of her free time exploring their paradise. She pictured the island in her mind clearly. The northern spike of Summerland Key was narrow, just a few hundred yards wide at most places, and there was just the one road in or out. She'd hiked a few trails on the western side of the island, but all the paths eventually wound back to Niles Road.

Logan was infiltrating the house, and with the swarm of police vehicles at their backs heading for the place as well, she knew that if Brier was anywhere near the place, he'd be done for.

He can't head south, can't leave by sea, and he sure as hell can't stay put, she thought. *The only way for him to go is...*

She locked her eyes forward and her expression tightened as they approached the turnoff to the driveway. Instead of slowing and making the turn, Jane mashed the gas harder, flying right by it.

Colby looked over his shoulder, then to Jane.

"That was the place—"

"I know," she fired back, keeping her eyes forward. "We're not going to the house."

Her radio crackled to life and Maddox's voice came through. "Missed the turn."

"You guys check the house."

"What are you doing?"

"Following my gut."

She continued for a quarter mile, thundering over the remote road toward the tip of the island. Niles Road dead-ends at a small canoe and kayak launch, and as the end of the line came into view, Jane let off the gas.

Colby kept looking back over his shoulder. The mass of cop cars had vanished, all of them having turned into the driveway. Jane could tell that her partner was just about to request that they turn back when she spotted movement along the right side of the road just ahead.

"There!" Jane said, pointing through the windshield toward the dark, blurry outline of a dirt bike.

The small off-road vehicle flew across the dead end, shooting up rocks as it turned right and vanished into the encroaching mangroves.

"The trail," Colby said, astonished by the sight.

Jane nodded and clenched her jaw as she slammed the brakes, skidding them to a stop right at the Niles Road trailhead. With boulders and half-buried metal pipes blocking the way, the two had no choice but to jump out and pursue on foot.

They kept their weapons holstered as they raced onto the footpath, the sounds of Brier's bike getting quieter ahead of them. Jane didn't care that their quarry had a vehicle. She knew the trail by heart. It wound up the tip of Summerland for not even a thousand feet before ending at the water's edge.

As they booked it over the path, the dirt bike splashed in the distance, then the engine gurgled and sputtered before it died off entirely. When the growth opened up enough for them to see water, both their eyes homed in on Brier sloshing through the shallows. They hit the shoreline less than a minute after Brier, but the gap had given him enough time to nearly reach the island on other side. With the tide going out quickly, the two officers continued into the water, splashing as fast as they could toward the criminal.

They ran between rows of old pilings, remnants of a bridge that had once stretched to the long, narrow island above Summerland. When the water was waist-deep, Jane looked up and watched as Brier climbed out of the water onto the long uninhabited stretch of groves fifty yards away.

"Freeze!" she yelled, snatching and leveling her Walther.

Colby stopped beside her and reached for his sidearm as well. When Brier ignored her order and continued up the tree-infested bank, she opened fire. Firing a succession of rounds, she managed to hit her far-off, moving, and dark target just before the criminal dropped out of view, her round blasting through Brier's upper back.

She knew she'd struck him, but with her quarry out of sight, Jane holstered her weapon and pressed on through the shallows.

"He won't get far with that wound, Chief," Colby said, following his boss into the deeper water, where they were forced to swim for it through the strong current.

He wouldn't get far regardless, Jane thought as she kicked as hard as she could, following in Brier's dissipated wake. *There's nowhere for him to go on that island. He's trapped, wounded, and finally done for. It's over.*

When her feet struck the bottom, she grabbed her pistol again and raised it to chest height as she trudged up from the water. Just as the two officers climbed up onto the overgrown shore, the distant buzzing of propellers caught their attention. They turned to gaze toward the sounds and spotted the silhouette of a seaplane flying in low from the east, heading right alongside them. Jane gasped as the rapidly approaching aircraft dropped down even lower and tore right past their position, heading for the northern tip of the island.

You've got to be kidding me.

"Come on!" Jane said, lunging into a sprint. Colby sprang forward and caught up to her. "We can still get this guy."

TWENTY-FOUR

Searing pain resonated across Nathan Brier's body as the lead bit into his flesh. The round grazed the muscle just above his right collarbone, spitting a thin spray of blood across the front of his body as he tumbled forward.

Brier cursed from the pain as he landed hard, rolling onto the faint remnants of a path and slamming hip first into a thick branch. He winced, gritting his teeth as he suppressed the urge to scream. Pressing a hand above his right pec, he felt blood dripping out from a mutilated gash in his flesh. The criminal grunted, then spat, his heart thumping audibly in his chest. He caught his breath for half a second, then focused forward.

It'll take more than a damn weak-caliber bullet to take me down.

Shoving the pain from his mind, Brier staggered to his feet, heaved the duffel back over his left shoulder, and hustled through the branches, following the old trail as best he could.

Harvey better show, he thought, pressing on with everything he had. *Or this will all be for nothing.*

Blood soaked the top of his shirt and down his chest as he ran, pumping his left arm only and kicking his legs. Far behind him, he could hear his pursuers sloshing up from the water. Still armed with his pistol, he debated hiding and hitting them with a surprise attack, knowing it would only be delaying the inevitable. Then a sound echoed across the air that filled him with newfound vigor. Poking out into a clearing, he faced southeast and watched as a plane raced across the dark sky, banking and descending straight for him.

Brier smiled and picked up his pace. As he reached the tip of the island, the Grumman Mallard slowed into view and its sleek hull splashed into the waters of the channel. A man waved at him from the cockpit as the twin-engine aircraft pulled alongside the shoreline.

Brier gave the pilot a signal to keep the engines running and splashed into the shallows, heaving as he reached the side door. He pulled it open just as the plane stopped and threw the duffel bag inside. Hearing shuffling and voices from the shore, he withdrew his pistol and fired chaotically toward the bank to cover their escape. Spinning around, Brier gripped both sides of the frame and hoisted himself up into the aircraft. Taking aim once more, he emptied the remainder of his magazine as the pilot accelerated and turned them away from land. Brier's eyes lit up as he managed to strike one of the pursuing officers, knocking the man out of sight. He slammed the door just as the other officer opened fire, pelting the fuselage with rounds.

"Get us out of here, Harv!" Brier yelled.

He lurched into the cockpit as the pilot shoved the throttles, prodding the rudders and gunning them out into the channel. The pilot's long gray hair flowed from the wind howling through a crack in his side window. In his seventies, the weathered-faced man pointed toward the copilot's seat.

"Strap in," he said in his thick southern drawl, then accelerated even more. "We've got a bit of a tight window."

Brier set the duffel on the deck at his feet, then his eyes widened as he saw the stretch of land directly in front of them.

"Why don't you turn into the—"

"You wanna fly this, kid?" Harvey shouted. "We got a cutter incoming. We turn, window of takeoff very well shuts. You're paying me to get your ass out of here, right?" Harvey sneered, then eyed the duffel bag. "Speaking of pay."

"How about you focus on taking off first?"

Harvey snapped his head and glared at Brier.

"Fine," Brier said, wincing as he threw his hand up.

He unzipped the bag and showed Harvey the cash.

"All right, hold on now," he said as they began to bounce over the shifting tide. After two tours in Vietnam, Harvey had spent his next thirty years crop dusting in Iowa before being hired by the private military group known as Darkwater to carry out extractions and insertions. It'd paid better, and the man was brilliant behind the yoke.

As they were pressed against their seat backs, Harvey gritted his teeth and pulled on the control column.

"Come on baby. Come on!"

The craft rose up from the water, slicing into the air just before crashing into the island. Branches whacked the bottom of the fuselage as they roared over the land, then ascended rapidly. Brier gasped and Harvey let out a hearty laugh.

"What I tell you, Nate? No problemo."

He brought them up to just fifty feet, then accelerated to the craft's max speed at that elevation of two hundred miles per hour.

"We'll be clear of American airspace in ten minutes," Harvey said.

"The Air Force blimp?" Brier said, hoping that his other contact had successfully played his role.

Harvey moved his right hand across his neck from left to right in a throat cutting motion. "Albert's offline."

Brier smiled. He'd offered a journeyman who performed routine maintenance on the balloon-borne radar a stack of bills to sabotage it when the time came.

"With Fat Albert indisposed, we should have no trouble making the jump," Harvey continued. "But just in case, I've got an FGM-148 in the back."

"You've got a javelin aboard?" Brier said in disbelief.

The javelin is a fire-and-forget missile with lock-on and self-guidance that was developed by Raytheon and Lockheed Martin primarily for antitank use. Fired from a shoulder-mounted launcher, the advanced missile also has the ability to target and lock on to aircraft.

"I raided Darkwater's secret arsenal a while back. Before the sealed structure was dropped into the Gulf. The massive armory's still yet to be cleared out, so I hear. But I just couldn't help myself from grabbing a few things on my way out the door years ago." Harvey let out another crazy laugh, blaring a gold central incisor. "The beast of a rocket ages like fine wine."

"Nice to see you're still crazy as ever."

Harvey grinned. "Good thing. Only a crazy person could pull off that tight landing and takeoff." Harvey noticed Brier's blood-soaked shirt for the first time. "Jeez, you all right, man?"

"Barely grazed me. Anything on radar?"

Harvey blinked, then peered at the screen in front of him. "Yeah. Two choppers, but they won't catch us. Plus I got a jammer behind me." He reached back, but Brier beat him to it. "You don't wanna tend to that first?"

"I can multitask."

Harvey shrugged as Brier grabbed the jammer from a case, then sat back in the copilot's seat.

Harvey grabbed a first aid kit from a locker and set it at Brier's feet. No stranger to the device, Brier powered on the jammer, pressed a few buttons, then set it aside.

Harvey cackled again as Brier went to work on his wounds. "Just like old times, buddy. Just like old times."

As Harvey flew them over the Gulf, taking a northerly course to avoid Cuban airspace, Brier stitched himself up as best he could. The whole time his mind ran through everything that had happened that evening.

If that fool Vito hadn't gone off on his own, none of this would've happened.

Their plans had failed, and their target was still breathing, an outcome he deemed unacceptable. His anger turned to intense focus as he thought about Dodge. Brier was lucky to have made it out alive, but he felt anything but good. An hour and a half into the flight, Harvey looked up from his instruments.

"Two hundred miles out from the Yucatan. Viva la Mexico! What's next for you when we land? You're free to join me in clubbing, beaching, endless margaritas, and beautiful senoritas."

"Maybe for a few weeks," Brier said, peering out the windscreen. The half-moon cast a sparkling glow over the calm stretch of water.

Harvey spat a wad of tobacco into an empty soda can. "Then what?"

Brier's gaze narrowed. "Then I was thinking of hiring you for another gig." He looked the pilot in the eyes. "Back to Key West to finish the job."

TWENTY-FIVE

I pushed out the back door of the house and rushed down to the dock as police cars closed in, their sirens blaring from the driveway. Ange piloted the Baia across the channel, slowing just as I reached the end of the planks. I leapt over the starboard gunwale, catching myself against the sunbed.

"Sounds like he's still heading north," Ange said, sliding out of the cockpit.

Ange was a hell of a boat captain, but my having spent more time in the islands over the years and doing most of the work on the boat gave me a slight edge. I cut in front of the helm and shoved the throttle, churning up two vortexes and propelling us north into the channel. I had us up on plane in seconds, then roared along Summerland's shoreline. I let loose again, pushing the marvel of Italian engineering to its limits and closing in on the tip of the island just three minutes after Ange had picked me up.

As we rounded the jutting land, a new sound filled the air. Easing back slightly on the throttles, I turned to look southeast. Ange, who'd heard the sound as well and stepped against the rail, pointed into the dark sky. A seaplane was cutting north and flying at less than a few hundred feet.

"Hold on," I said, shifting back forward and picking up our speed once again.

My conversation with Ange days earlier jumped into my mind. Brier no doubt had connections with his former private military group. Though they'd disbanded, he clearly had a pilot willing to work with him.

A wave of anger rushed over me.

He's not getting away, I told myself. *Not again.*

The plane vanished around the island just beyond Summerland for a moment as we closed in. I angled us around and we watched as it slowed a quarter mile ahead of us, and saw splashing between it and the shore. It was Brier, sloshing toward the craft with a duffel bag over his shoulder.

"Ange!" I yelled, but my wife was already on it, grabbing her rifle and aiming it toward the escaping criminal.

She peered through the scope as I tried my best to keep us stable at forty knots.

"No shot," she said, lowering it. "He's behind the plane."

I turned us to port, bouncing right toward the aircraft. Gunfire rattled across the air. As we closed in, I watched as Brier opened fire toward the shore. I felt a sharp pang in my stomach as a dark figure along the bank jolted, then fell out of view, struck by one of

Brier's rounds.

A hundred yards from the tail, I cut back to twenty knots, grabbed my Sig, and sprang up onto the bow. I took aim and opened fire, sparking bullets against the plane's fuselage. Ange managed to fire off two high-powered rounds as well, trying to slow the craft as it roared farther and farther away from us.

The craft's side door shut, and its propellers accelerated. Just as the plane was about to strike an island, it lifted off the ground, zipping into the air and getting smaller as it escaped into the Gulf. I cursed under my breath, then turned to Ange.

"We need to contact the Guard," I said, pulling out my phone.

"Logan!" a voice shouted from the shore.

I froze and focused on the tip of the island. Jane knelt along the water, a man resting in her arms.

"I'll call the Guard," Ange said, snatching my phone.

Remembering that someone had been struck, I cranked the wheel around and motored toward the shore. When we got closer, I realized that it was Jane's partner, Colby Miller, and that he was severely wounded. I spun the Baia so that the swim platform touched the thickets, then gave Ange the controls and vaulted over the side, splashing up beside the two.

"He's hit," Jane said, a combination of terror and rage lacing her words.

Blood blossomed out from Colby's lower abdomen, just beneath his bulletproof vest, and his body shook, his eyes wide as he struggled to breathe. I gripped him under the shoulders, Jane took his legs, and the two of us carried him onto the Baia's sunbed.

Ange had our first aid kit already open on the dinette when we set Colby down.

I'd seen a lot of bullet wounds in my time, and Colby's was bad. The round had torn into his flesh, mushroomed, and pummeled through his lower spine. He needed intensive care and fast if he was going to have a chance.

While Jane and Ange did their best to stop the bleeding, I took a second to run through our options. He'd need a full hospital where they could perform surgeries. That meant either the hospital in Marathon or the Lower Key Medical Center on Stock Island. My knowledge of the islands told me that they'd both be roughly twenty miles away. With distance not a factor, I chose Lower Keys and told the two to hold on.

I accelerated us down Niles Channel, turning south and flying under the bridge. Once in the Atlantic, I turned us southwest and throttled wide open. With open water ahead of me, I kept one hand on the wheel while calling in to the hospital. When I got an operator, I informed them that I had a gunshot victim in critical condition and requested an ambulance to meet us at the boat ramp along the south side of US-1 between Shark Key and Big Coppitt. Every second counted and an ambulance could get Colby to the hospital a lot faster than we could, so I wanted to cut the distance and have them meet us on the way.

Ending the call, I turned back and said, "Ten minutes."

Ange shifted to face me, and the look in her eyes told me everything. The situation was dire. The two fought to control the bleeding and keep Colby stable, but the officer was drifting away, and they were losing him.

I piloted us into Saddlebunch Harbor, banking with a wide turn to maintain our speed. The bridge came into view, cars driving back and forth across it. Near Big Coppitt's shore, I saw the ambulance parked right beside the boat ramp on the long stretch of parking along the road's shoulder.

I eased us right up to the ramp, then killed the engine and helped carry Colby off the boat and onto a gurney. The paramedics wheeled him up the ramp and lifted him into the back of the ambulance. Jane followed, angered by the ordeal. In a blur of activity, she climbed in behind her partner, the doors slammed shut, the vehicle's lights and sirens kicked on, and they disappeared west.

TWENTY-SIX

I cruised us back to Summerland to pick up my rebreather and Seascooter, and to meet with Maddox and a slew of detectives. Once finished, we rocketed back to the marina in Key West, drove across town to the hospital, and strode through the double automatic doors at just after eleven. The waiting area was packed and solemn as Ange and I pushed into the intensive care unit waiting room.

Jane paced toward us first, stepping away from a sea of officers. "They did a CT scan and..." The chief of police paused a moment, trying to keep it together. She was an experienced and well-trained professional, and one of the finest law enforcement officers I'd ever met, but she was still human. And at that moment it wasn't just a colleague whose life was at risk. It was a friend. "He has severe spinal damage," Jane continued, "and has lost a lot of blood. They gave him a transfusion and they just took him in for an emergency surgery, but..."

If she hadn't been in uniform, and if there hadn't been so many other officers around, Ange and I would've pulled our friend in for a hug. Instead we each placed an arm on her shoulder, and I apologized for what had happened.

"Doc says if Colby had gotten through the doors just a few minutes later, he would've been dead before he made it to the operating table. He was that close to the end. So, we have you both to thank for getting him here so fast."

I patted her on the shoulder again, then migrated over to a coffeemaker and filled two cups. The warm, caffeinated beverage felt good entering my weary body. I handed the other steaming cup to Ange just as Agent Maddox and a few members of his Homeland posse entered. He got a quick update from the officers, then made eye contact with me and motioned toward the doors. I followed him back out into the humid evening.

"You did good tonight," he led off. "Nothing stings like injured heroes, but tonight wasn't a failure."

"Brier got away."

"Yes, but three others didn't, including Bonetti, a wanted crime boss."

I sighed. "What's the status on the plane?"

Maddox shook his head. "Don't you ever look at the bright side?" I raised my eyebrows expectantly. I was all for looking at the bright side, but at that moment, after witnessing Colby get shot and watching Brier slip away from me yet again, it was the last thing I wanted to do.

Maddox continued, "Vanished into the Gulf.

Must've had a good jammer, 'cause it became a ghost shortly after takeoff. Heading out of American airspace, flying southwest at over two hundred miles per hour."

"Mexico."

Maddox nodded. "Looks that way."

"So, what's the plan now?"

"We've put an international alert out on Brier. The Mexican government is informed, and their agencies and police will be on the lookout, especially the ones near the coast. And the CIA and NSA will do what they can to figure out where he runs off to. But beyond that... we're Homeland, and he's fled the country. We're not going to fly over there and conduct an investigation on Mexican soil. He'll turn up, Logan."

"That's what I was told six months ago when he fled the scene in Miami," I said. "I guess we'll just have to hope that this time when he turns up, he won't be trying to bomb a sporting event full of civilians."

We both fell silent for a moment, then Ange strode out through the doors at Maddox's back. It only took one look at her cold expression for me to realize that something bad had happened.

TWENTY-SEVEN

I woke up from another nightmare that evening. My face coated in sweat, I breathed heavily and sat up, trying to relax my racing heart.

"You okay?" Ange said, her head nestled into the pillow beside me.

"Fine. Just need some air."

I kissed my wife on the forehead, then slid out from the covers and pulled on a pair of workout shorts. Quietly, I opened the side door and stepped out onto our back porch. Leaning against the railing, with the relatively cool evening breeze flowing against my body, I tried to remember the dream.

I'd never been plagued by routine nightmares before, even during deployments in the Navy. A few of my buddies had, and many had continued to fight back their demons long after their enlistments had ended. I considered myself fortunate in that regard. I'd never had a hard time justifying what I was doing. Wolves existed beyond our nation's gates, hungry and ruthless, and somebody had to stand up to them or Rome would fall.

I'd been proud to be a part of that group, and the demons had been kept at bay. But now, they haunted me. I pictured Brier, and I pictured Colby lying in a pool of blood. His severe injuries had cast a dark spell over the scene when I'd reentered the hospital. Colby was still alive, clinging to life dearly with the help of medical professionals. But even if the strong, proud police officer did pull through, the doctors informed us that he'd be paralyzed from the waist down for the rest of his life.

Many of the officers in the waiting area choked up, and many got angry and desired retribution. I could see it in their eyes. During surgery, he'd gone into cardiac arrest and nearly died on the table. Brier's last act in the Keys, in America, had been to end the career of a nine-year police veteran.

Having swiped my watch from my nightstand on the way out, I checked it for the first time. It was a quarter past three. I should've been tired from the long, eventful previous day. I should've been letting my body rest and recoup, but I felt nothing but energy, fueled by a stronger-than-ever desire to locate and take down Brier.

The bedroom door opened, and Ange stepped out. Without a word, she leaned against the railing beside me, and we stood in silence for a few minutes.

"I know it doesn't feel like it, but you already won, Logan," Ange eventually said.

"Brier's still breathing. And the force lost one of its best officers."

"Yeah, but he failed. He came here to bring you

down, and a bunch of others in the process. We not only snuffed out his plans, but we also took down all of Vito's men that he'd recruited. He failed. Not you."

I hugged my wife, then went back into the bedroom and took a cool shower, laced up my running shoes, and headed back outside. It was an overcast day, with waves of dark clouds closing in from the west. The coverage provided a welcomed respite as I ran down and along the waterfront, then cut inland, passing by the high school again before continuing on toward downtown and resuming my usual route.

I let my mind wander and tried to formulate what I should do next. A big part of me wanted to book a solo flight to the Yucatan and track down Brier my own way. I had contacts in Mexico. They could set me up with whatever weapons I needed, and by greasing the right wheels with cash, I could scour the underworld for news on Brier. It would be like old times.

As a mercenary, I was usually hired to defend mining operations from bloodthirsty rebels, or to help neutralize local uprisings threatening peaceful communities. But occasionally I'd get a classified job offer from a government agency to track down and off a terrorist or wanted criminal.

But things were different now. I had Ange and Scarlett.

What if Brier snuck back into the States in my absence and went after them?

Ange could handle herself as well as anyone I'd ever met, but if something happened to them while I was off playing international hit man, I'd never forgive myself.

The heavens opened up two miles from my house, and I arrived back at our mailbox drenched from head to toe. Lightning cracked, flashing the sky, and thunder boomed and shook the scene. I'd always liked a good rainstorm, and I considered that maybe a higher power was trying to send me a message. That I wasn't all-powerful. That there were things I had to let go of and trust others to handle. That I needed to look after the things and people that I cared about most.

I stretched as I turned into our seashell driveway, my feet squishing in my soaked socks and water dripping down my face. I knew that it would be over soon, that the weather changed fast in the island chain. But with the heavy rains still pummeling into my body, I strode toward our house and stopped when I spotted three vehicles parked alongside my Tacoma. Two police cars and a black Mercedes.

I recognized the Mercedes as the same vehicle that Mayor Nix had climbed into after he'd stormed out from our meeting at Moondog.

As I approached the base of the stairs, the front door opened and Ange stepped out. She wore a worried expression. Not the kind that told me that danger was near, but one that said something was about to happen that neither of us was going to like. Before she got a word out, Mayor Nix stepped out behind her. Her wore a gray button-up and slacks, and his hair was neatly gelled just as it'd been the time I met him.

"Mr. Dodge, please come inside," he said, like a

principal talking down to a student.

The request made my blood simmer a little, and not just because of his tone. Because he was beckoning me into my own damn house. I'd had a long couple of days and a long night, and my patience was thinner than fishing line.

"Mr. Dodge?" the man said again, stepping toward me and holding up his hands.

I scowled at him. "You got something to say to me, Nix? You come down here and say it."

The man shook his head, taken aback by my words. But the look on my face, along with a nicely timed strike of lightning, stiffened him up.

He sighed, took one look around at the pouring rain, then said, "Fine. Have it your way."

He pulled a small umbrella from his pocket, pushed it open, and held it over his head as he strode down to meet me. I kept still, unfazed by the rain battering into me and the grumbling thunder. In my years in Special Forces, I'd grown not only to tolerate discomfort, but to seek it out. The rain and the cold and the wind were my friends.

I gazed eye to eye with the man, knowing that he had a lot he wanted to say. But the last thing I wanted was to sit inside and have him berate me with the cops at his back to provide backup. If he had something to say, he'd have to say it right there.

Just as he opened his mouth, a powerful squall howled through the flanking palm trees and gusted into our bodies. It did a quick number on his umbrella, flapping the metal ribs outward and turning the canopy inside out. He struggled for a few seconds, attempting to fix it. Seeing it was no use, the man tossed it aside, rain now soaking his clothes, ruining his hairstyle, and dripping down his face.

"Fine," he said, removing his glasses. "We'll talk right here in the rain, Mr. Dodge." I kept quiet, giving him the proverbial floor. "This madness has gone on long enough. A shoot-out at a local restaurant and now a severely injured police officer... like I said last time we met, this maniac was here for you. You brought this upon our community."

"No, Nathan Brier did!" Ange snapped from up on the porch.

The door opened and Jane stepped out, followed by two other officers. They all just stood and watched us.

"We need to finish the job," I said, ignoring his statement. He could believe whatever he wanted. I knew the truth. "He's on the run."

"No," Nix said, waving a stern hand. "You need to leave." He stiffened. "It's been agreed upon that your mere presence brings a threat to this island. You will be sent into hiding for the time being. Once Brier is found and dealt with by the proper authorities, you will be able to return. This is for your safety, your family's safety, and the best interests of the islands. It's time for you to leave Key West."

I stared him in the eyes, then glanced up at Jane.

"It's not my call, Logan," she said. "He went to the governor. There's nothing I can do."

I thought about my good friend Scott Cooper. Though his term as senator had recently ended and he was fully engrossed by his new occupation, he still had sway in the political realm. One phone call, and I had no doubt that he could rectify the situation. But as much as I didn't like my first impressions of the city's new mayor, I thought that maybe some time away would be good. For everyone. Maybe I was too emotionally involved in the situation and I needed to step away and examine it more clearly.

Another vehicle pulled into the driveway, its headlights shining into us and its wipers working in overdrive. It stopped and shut off, and Agent Maddox stepped out. He wore a thin black rain slicker and ball cap. No umbrella.

"He trying to twist this like it's your fault?" Maddox grunted, striding toward the two of us. Before Nix could get a word off, he continued, "Because that's crap and everyone knows it. Logan's a hero, and if you try and make people believe otherwise, I'll—"

He had a finger in the mayor's face and was just about to scare the man to death when I stopped him.

"It's all right," I said, surprising everyone. Another lightning strike pierced the sky and cracked, its echo like a ripple across the island. "You can believe whatever you want, Nix." I sighed. "We don't know each other well, but maybe when we do, you'll see the truth. I've risked my life time and time again to protect the people of Key West, and Brier has been the worst threat they've seen in a long time. And now he's gone because of all of our efforts." I motioned toward Ange, Maddox, Jane, and the other officers, then stared back at Nix and added, "Not you." He stepped back, angered and ready to spit out a rebuttal. I beat him to it. "But if my government wants me gone, I'll leave. But just until Brier's found."

Nix straightened and attempted to compose

himself. "There's a flight taking off in an hour to take you and your family to a safe house that only we'll know about."

"It's in the Bahamas," Maddox said under his breath. "There are far worse places to sit tight and wait."

I nodded, and Maddox and I strolled past the mayor, heading for the stairs.

"You'd better hope Brier doesn't find his way back to Key West," Maddox said to Nix. "'Cause if he does, you're going to regret sending away the island's shining knight."

I hugged Ange, who didn't care that I was dripping wet. Nodding to Jane and her officers, we strode inside. Scarlett was standing in the living room and bounded over when I entered. After drying off, changing, and packing our bags, the three of us headed for the door.

"Jack's gonna take care of Atty," Jane said. "He's swinging by in half an hour."

I knelt down and said goodbye to my Lab. The last time I'd been away from him for more than a day was during Ange's and my honeymoon two years earlier.

Loading our stuff into the truck, we drove out of the lot. I glanced at my mirror, taking a final look at my house. Nix had assured me that it would likely only be a couple of days. But the man had no idea what he was talking about. I knew it would be significantly longer as we drove to Key West International, saying goodbye to our island home.

TWENTY-EIGHT

Long Island, Bahamas
Three Weeks Later

I reached over my head on the front porch of our quaint beach cottage, stretching as I gazed out over the hundred-and-fifty-mile stretch of blue that separated the southwestern shoreline from Cuba. The sun was just beginning to peek above the island at my back, and a warm breeze swept across the Bahamian island. I peered right and left, and for as far as I could see was nothing but long stretches of nearly untouched white beaches.

I laced up my running shoes and took off west, striding into a steady jog. After half a mile along the beach, I cut inland when the going got too rocky, winding along a path. Reaching Stevens Bluff, I stopped to gaze around at the island.

Covering two hundred and thirty square miles, the lengthy, skinny island was home to just three

197

thousand people. To put the sparsely populated locale into perspective, Key West has an area of just over seven square miles and a population of twenty-five thousand. Compared to our home, the place felt like the edge of the world, and that was exactly what we were going for. Off the beaten path, far from the eyes and ears of anyone who might be looking for me.

Far from Nathan Brier.

I strode along the top of the short, foliage-infested bluff until I reached the remnants of an old fence. The metal wiring was long gone, but one of the poles remained, holding its ground over the years despite the hurricanes, cyclones, and tropical storms.

My first morning on the Bahamian island, I'd risen before the sun as well and taken the same route. I hadn't thought much of it, but I'd taken out my dive knife and carved a small notch in the weathered post.

Sliding out my knife, I carved another notch, then sheathed the steel. My eyes tracking up the wood, I gazed upon the twenty-two notches stacked above the one I'd just whittled away.

We'd been told before leaving the Conch Republic that we'd likely only be gone a few days, and it'd now been over three weeks and there was no hint of our being able to return anytime soon. Brier was still at large, managing to lurk under the radar in Mexico, or wherever he was in the world by that point. The former SEAL had worked for Darkwater for years, performing off-the-books missions at every corner of the Earth. The man knew how to hide, how to slip between the cracks, leave no trace, and bide his time.

Turning around, I cut back down the path then paced to Queens Highway, a road that runs from one tip of the island to the other. A mile and a half later, I reached my destination in Galloway Landing. I caught my breath while striding down a dirt-and-sand drive that led to a small white house. A sign out front read "Hamilton's Cave." The place was still closed, so I moved around to the back.

"He's already down there," a middle-aged woman who was watering a garden said after barely glancing my way. She smiled, then added, "You eat yet? I've got fresh coconut grits with mango slices."

"You're too kind. I'd love some."

After I chowed down a bowl of the delicious breakfast, she made sure I grabbed a flashlight as I strode down into the largest cave system in the Bahamas.

I'd spent the first few days on Long Island relaxing, working out, snorkeling the coasts, and taking in the scenery with Ange and Scarlett. Then, as it inevitably does in such instances, boredom set in. I wasn't about to complain. Like Maddox had said, there are far worse places to find yourself with an abundance of time than a picturesque Caribbean island. And with the government footing the bill, we had a nice, simple off-the-grid place on the water at no expense.

But at a week into our escape, I began exploring the island more, meeting locals, and trying my best to mesh in with the islander crowd. It wasn't difficult. In my previous travels, I'd found that islanders are among the nicest, most easygoing people you'll ever meet. And Bahamians are certainly no exception.

I'd met Norman Lockhart at Tiny's Hurricane Hole, a local beachfront restaurant, during karaoke night. I'd heard that the man's family had owned land above a cave system for over a hundred and fifty years, so I'd bought him a drink to entice him to open up about it. I'd quickly found out that no drink was necessary. The man was passionate about his private subterranean wonder and had urged me to check it out the following day.

I'd taken him up on the offer and had been venturing underground with him nearly every day for the past two weeks, exploring deep passages and helping him conduct experiments with various plants. It'd proved to be a good way to get my mind off things and also fuel my adventurous spirit, which only seemed to get more robust with every passing year.

I stepped down and clicked on my flashlight, though it wasn't necessary at first. Much of the roof was open, allowing the powerful Tropic of Cancer sunshine to beam through and illuminate the place. There were massive stalactites and stalagmites, vines tangling their way down, and colorful unique shades of rock.

I moved deeper, heading down the main passageway and keeping an eye out for the owner as I headed toward the main cavern. Norman had informed me that he'd found remnants of human bodies dating back to 500 AD. The Lucayans were the natives that had dotted the Bahamian islands prior to the arrival of Europeans, their numbers decimated by conflicts and foreign diseases. The tribes were hit so hard that, by 1520, the Lucayans were completely wiped out. With whole histories of peoples erased, the owner of the cave loved digging up whatever relics he could to help piece together stories of the lost people.

I reached a deeper chamber. It was much darker in there, so I scanned the light around, then twisted back as a horde of bats flapped their wings and took off, some heading higher up and others fleeing to adjoining chambers.

When the creatures calmed down, I pushed across the cavern, careful not to step on the scurrying hermit crabs.

"Norman? You here?" I said, my voice echoing in all directions down the web of passageways.

It still boggled my mind that the man owned the place. Right under his house were miles of caves and passageways, many of which still unexplored.

I called out his name again, and again heard only my echo in reply. Like all caves, Hamilton's wasn't without its dangers. Sharp drop-offs into seemingly bottomless black voids, slippery smooth surfaces, dizzying mazes of turns that could make anyone mad, and let's not forget the rare but possible chance of a weary stalactite giving in to gravity and skewering whatever lay beneath it.

I trekked down another level to a narrower chamber, passing the area where we'd worked the previous day. I was about to call out his name again when I heard a shoe slide against sleek rock, followed by a grunt and a loud heave.

"Norman! Are you all right?" I shouted, picking up my pace as I shined my light forward. I heard no reply as I pushed along a steep crack in the floor. Leaning over, I shined the beam of light, hoping I wouldn't catch a glimpse of the man wedged far below.

Seeing and hearing nothing, I continued to a wide space, then rounded a corner. I jolted back, startled by the sight of sudden movement overhead. Then laughter filled the air. My tensed body relaxed as I focused on the man high above, poking his head out from a cave that wrapped around the other side of the rock.

"I'm sorry," he said, still unable to control his laughter. "I couldn't help myself."

I sighed as he vanished, climbed down, then appeared in front of me.

"You make a habit of attempting to give visitors heart attacks?"

"Most of the time, heck no. But you've been scouring these caves with me for days now. I wanted to spice it up a bit."

"As if exploring unknown underground passageways isn't exciting enough."

The man scratched his gray mustache, then pulled out a hand-drawn map and clicked on his head lamp. "Speaking of unknown passageways, I've got a special vein on the agenda today." He examined the map for a moment, then added, "I was hoping you'd still be around. I'll need someone of your physical prowess. Thought you were only going to be here a few days?"

"Me too. But plans change."

The man shook his head. "Still staying mysterious, huh?" He laughed. "Fine by me."

I strode forward and eyed the map. "So, where we going?"

Norman led me deeper into the forgotten world. Unlike most caves I'd been in, the Hamilton system

202

was a constant seventy degrees year-round, so we didn't need more than T-shirts and shorts. We climbed up steep slopes, crawled into low openings, and squeezed our way through narrow cuts. When we reached a sheer wall of rock, I offered the owner a boost, then managed to climb up it myself. Pushing through an opening so small that we had to shimmy headfirst, we popped out on the other side to a cavity about the size of a normal bedroom.

"Never been here before," Norman said with a big smile on his face.

We pushed up into another chamber before discovering the remains of two half-buried skeletons. He'd brought his small digital camera and took pictures of the scene as well as taking a few samples.

"Incredible," I said, astonished by the sight.

Spelunking with the local pro was efficient at kindling my adventurous spirit, but no matter how much we explored, my mind always drifted back to Brier.

Once we were back on the brighter side of Earth, Norman's wife dished up more grits along with freshly baked bread. No longer probing me with questions, they talked about the history of their place and the island. As they spoke, I noticed a large metal garage near the back of their property for the first time and inquired about it.

"I bought a plane a few years back," Norman said. "A single-engine Helio Courier with floats. Got it from a foreigner who had to leave paradise and sell off all his stuff. Don't get up as much as I'd like to, what with fuel prices, but she's a fun bird and we make trips to nearby islands a couple times a year."

Once we finished eating, I thanked them for their hospitality.

"Same time tomorrow?" I said, with little else to occupy my schedule.

"I've got a big group coming, so we'll have to skip a day. Can't be all play and no work. But we're having dinner at Tiny's tonight if you and your family want to join us."

"We'd love for you to come," his wife said. "There's a popular musician passing through on his sailboat who's playing a set."

"We'll be there," I said, throwing a wave as I strode out the door and down the driveway.

I took one look back at the nondescript house with the small sign.

Oftentimes the coolest destinations and greatest people are the least flashy, I thought.

I was glad that they still received a lot of visitors each year, mainly by word of mouth.

The run back to our beach cottage was harder, the late-morning sun bearing down on me. By the time I made it back to the driveway, I was spent. Scanning toward the small house, I saw that our red Jeep Wrangler was nowhere in sight.

"Where have you girls gone off to now?" I said, gasping for air as I lumbered up the old, faded steps.

When it came to Ange and Scar, you never really knew. Neither suffered from a shortage of spontaneity.

I found a note pinned under a glass on the dining table.

"Gone to the hole," it said in Ange's handwriting, followed by a smiley face and a heart.

TWENTY-NINE

Exhausted, I downed a can of coconut water, doused myself in the coldest water the tropical spigot could spit out, then pulled on my swim trunks and pushed back out the front door. It was only a little over two miles to the popular swimming destination that had quickly become Scarlett's confidently proclaimed favorite place on Earth, but I was done from the run and caving. Shuffling to a shed, I rolled out an old moped, and thankfully, the tiny engine fired up without much hassle.

I enjoyed the quick drive across the island, then propped the scooter against the base of a palm tree. Our rented Wrangler was one of just two cars in the lot. I trekked down a footpath and ogled at a view that's impossible to adequately describe. Dean's Blue Hole looks like a place conjured up by a master graphic designer on a computer. Simply put, the swimming hole is a mesmerizing slice of heavenly paradise on Earth. Sharp limestone cliffs tower around the scene, forming a half-moon around a deep blue circle of water that drops straight down six hundred feet. The other side of the hole is flanked by shallow crystalline waters over a long spread of brilliant white.

Ange and Scarlett were swimming near a small floating dock in the middle of the hole. A man and a woman in wetsuits and fins floated beside them. It only took a quick glance to realize that they were most likely competitive freedivers.

Wanting to take the more exhilarating way down, I skirted around to the opposite side of the cliffs. Stepping back from the edge, I took off into a running start, then hurled myself over forty feet of warm open air. I flew with my arms out, relishing the rush as I picked up speed. Just before striking the surface, I straightened my body and sucked in a breath. My feet pierced the Caribbean, and I torpedoed over ten feet down before slowing to a stop. The euphoria from the free fall, and the feeling of being suddenly enveloped by the clear cooling water, was incredible.

Keeping calm and slowing my heart rate, I steadied myself as the bubbles cleared, the tiny orbs fluttering toward the bright surface overhead. I barely opened my eyes to orient myself, then flattened my body and kicked smoothly toward the floating platform and the long metal chain extending beneath it.

Freediving is all about staying relaxed, streamlining your body to reduce drag, and limiting unnecessary movement as much as possible. You only have the air in your lungs, but you can use it far more efficiently if you stay calm.

As I kicked deeper, it got easier to descend. Around sixty feet down, I reached a point where the pressure mounted too high for my body's buoyancy and it felt like I was being pulled deeper. This can be an uncomfortable feeling if you're not used to it. Most people panic when they first experience it. It's natural, as pushing through this invisible barrier goes against your body's survival instincts. The feeling of being drawn deeper, combined with the air in your lungs compressing and making it feel like your lungs are empty, is a strange one. Staying down requires a great deal of trust and experience.

I descended to what I suspected was around eighty feet, then continued until I reached the vertical chain. The dark abyss loomed beneath me, a seemingly never-ending hole boring into our planet.

Wanting to prolong the dive, I crossed my legs and closed my eyes, pushing myself deeper into the meditation. Hearing a splash overhead, I squinted as one of the freedivers finned down, then gave me a thumbs-up as they kicked past me. A glance at my dive watch told me that I'd been down for just over a minute already. I could hit three without much trouble, and four if I needed to.

I stayed put until the freediver returned, blurring past me, and surfacing just after the three-minute mark. Calmly, I kicked, my lungs throbbing. I blasted the air from my lungs after breaking the surface and took in two quick deep breaths before slowing into a normal rhythm.

"Bravo," Scarlett said, grinning as she treaded water beside me. "You're a show-off, Dad."

I smiled. "Don't act like you can't do that, Scar."

"The jump, yeah. Five minutes underwater? In my dreams."

I swam over and kissed my wife, feeling like it'd been forever since I'd seen her, even though it'd only been a couple of hours.

"Always have to make an entrance, don't you?" she joked.

"And you always have to encourage Scar's lackluster studying habits," I said, shooting them both a fun-loving chastising look.

Scarlett had switched to online classes and was supposed to be working on an essay until I got home.

"Finished early," Scarlett said. "Piece of cake. Besides, it's a perfect day for a swim."

I couldn't help but laugh. My daughter had said the same thing every day for the past three weeks. Even when we'd been holed up and taken cover while a small tropical storm had passed over the island.

"Still bummed out about missing Fantasy Fest?" I said, enjoying my daughter's enthusiasm as she relished the picture-perfect locale.

Every year people flocked to Key West from all over the world to dress up, get wild, and fill the streets with more debauchery than most cities experience in a lifetime. It's known as the craziest extravaganza around, and is a spectacle that has to be seen to be believed. Though Scarlett was too young for me to give her the green light on many of the event's festivities, she'd been looking forward to the street fair and the final parade.

"A little," our daughter said, then did a quick three-sixty turn and took in the paradise surrounding us, and grinned. "But this place isn't so bad."

The two freedivers wearing long fins and sleek wetsuits kicked over to us.

"That was quite the breath hold," a guy with long hair said in a Portuguese accent.

The woman, who had short dyed-pink hair, added, "You're very calm in the water."

"Six months in Coronado will do that," I said.

They both looked at me confused, then Scarlett explained. "My dad was a Navy SEAL. You know, like the badass underwater Spec Ops soldiers?"

"Language," Ange said.

The guy slid down his mask and wiped the damp hair from his face. "That's cool. You ever considered competitive freediving?"

The young man went on to explain that Dean's Hole was the site of an annual contest and that winners received up to a thousand dollars at some events.

"How deep do the winners go?" Scarlett asked.

"Depends. There are different types. Dynamic, free immersion, constant weight, etc. And male and female events. But the record for no limit is like two hundred meters."

My only reaction was to chuckle at the absurd depth. "Over six hundred feet? I think I'm good doing it just for fun. And for dinner, of course."

Scarlett, intrigued by the two, asked them all sorts of questions. Having spent hundreds of hours in the water with Ange and me over the past year, she knew the basics and could dive down to forty feet with fins, impressive for anyone let alone someone her age. But the two professionals ran her through some advanced techniques, and she took to it well.

We spent another two hours at the hole, diving into the mystical depths, exploring around the point, and wading in the beautiful shallows. Scarlett thanked the two interesting Portuguese for all of the help, and Ange invited them to our place for dinner, wanting to hear more of both of their fascinating life stories.

"I told Norman we'd dine with him at Tiny's tonight," I said to Ange. Turning to the two, I added, "We'd love for you to join us as well. The Hurricane Hole serves up some of the best food in the Bahamas. And there's supposedly a talented musician passing through and playing this evening."

They told us they'd meet us there, and we trudged up to the parking lot.

"Well, I've figured out what I want to be when I grow up," Scarlett declared.

"That's good news," I said with a laugh. "Some people never figure that out."

"And some never grow up," Ange added.

Scarlett threw her bag over her shoulder. "A professional freediver. You know they do underwater photography as well? Traveling the world, exploring undersea worlds, meeting all sorts of interesting people along the way. What job could be more fun than that?"

I shrugged. "That sounds pretty amazing. Just always remember the first rule of freediving."

"Never freedive alone," Scarlett said, and I patted her on the back.

THIRTY

We spent the rest of the afternoon at our waterfront abode. Ange sat in a beach chair under the shade of the eave, absorbed by a worn copy of *Robinson Crusoe* that had been tucked away in a small bookshelf in the safe house.

More than a little fitting for the present occasion, I thought as I scanned the remote shore and empty horizon. *All we need is a herd of goats and a talking parrot.*

Scarlett hunched over a glass table, eyeing her laptop and a cracked-open American history textbook. She was reading about NASA and the loss of the *Challenger*, and I'd mentioned that her grandfather, Owen Dodge, had been a part of the Naval Mobile Salvage Unit Two team that had located much of the shuttle's debris.

"That's incredible. Did he find anything himself?"

"Some parts, I believe. I was pretty young, but I remember the joint effort searched over five hundred square miles. But, if I remember correctly, his best find was when he and his buddies dove in the Mediterranean on one of their liberty days years before. Supposedly they found an old sextant."

"Grampa sounds like a great and exciting man."

"He was," I said, thinking back. My dad had dived all over the world for the Navy, so it was hard to keep track of all his trips. "A real legend beneath the waves."

Ange poked her head up from her book. "And I'm the one who distracts her from her studies?" she said with a grin.

I told Scarlett just one more quick sea story, then let her go back to work. Glancing at my phone, I kept hoping to receive a message from Maddox, or Jane, or anyone regarding Brier's status and the status of our brief banishment from our home. But no message came. I sighed and dozed off for much of the day, waking up to Scarlett's occasional excited protestations. After finishing her schoolwork, she researched freedivers for hours.

"Some of them make moola with sponsors," she said. "Or they have YouTube channels."

Ange and I encouraged her passion. No matter how hard something was or how unlikely an endeavor, we wanted her to believe that she could do it. We both made it clear that dreams were just that without a whole lot of action to go along with them. But I'd rather she aim high and miss than aim low and hit.

As the sun dipped into the Caribbean for a rest after its long arc across the sky, we piled into the Wrangler and cruised to Tiny's Hurricane Hole right along Salt Pond Harbor in Thompson Bay. We'd eaten there a handful of times already. With a perfect beach location, hammocks along the surf, palm trees for shade, and a friendly staff, Tiny's was the perfect place to relax, unwind, and soak in the strong island vibes. The place also had rental cottages, a dock, and of course the bar and grill that tantalized taste buds and beckoned hungry travelers from across the island, and from the many sailboats anchored just offshore in the harbor.

We met Norman and his wife at a table nestled into the corner of the covered open porch overlooking the calm evening waters.

We ordered a combination of grilled snapper, jerk chicken, burgers, and some of the best plantains I'd ever had. As the appetizers were set on the table, I noticed a small skiff motor ashore from one of the sailboats. Its hull sliced through the sand, and a man hopped out with a guitar case in one hand. I blinked a few times, then smiled when I realized that I recognized the musician.

He pulled his small craft up alongside a few others, then strode barefoot to the porch steps, his short wavy hair flowing in the calm evening breeze. The owner of the beach club greeted the man before he'd reached the top step, and the patrons clapped as he set up on a small bamboo stage.

"Please forgive my lateness," he said in a faint New England accent as he cracked open the case and pulled out an old Fender. "But I sailed all the way from Maine, so a few minutes tardy ain't bad."

The gathered group chuckled as he checked the mic. "Well, hello Long Island," he said, prompting a cheer from the people gathered on the porch and surrounding beach. "Looks like mostly wayfinding wanderers like myself here tonight. I'll lead off with a tune that I think fits this paradise hurricane hideout to a tee."

The artist, who introduced himself as Scott Kirby, went straight into a calm, island rift that seemed to flow from the strings like magic, echoing the calm heartbeat of the islands. Adding a harmonica to the mix, his smooth tenor put words to the sights and sounds and emotions evoked by exotic beaches far and wide.

"Haven't we heard him play before somewhere?" Ange said, trying to place the singer.

"We heard him at the Smokin' Tuna Saloon earlier this year," I said, referring to the popular new spot in Key West that the musician had helped found. "But if I remember correctly, you were a little far gone that night."

She chuckled, then leaned into my shoulder. "Certainly not the last person to enjoy myself at the Tuna."

Observing the artist, I thought about a rumor I'd heard that he was thinking of dropping a more permanent anchor and settling near his new restaurant back home in Key West. I made a note to ask him once he finished his set, then savored the meal and music, and looked out over the dark water and long stretches of sand. The two freedivers showed up after the third song and the owner pulled out a few folding chairs so they could join us at our table.

The place was packed, and soon the most happening place on the island. It felt good to be there with family and newly made friends. The freedivers went on, telling animated stories from their travels. And Norman told me all about the history of the beach club and the point it rested on, regaling us with stories of pirates hiding out and European explorers.

As I filled up on coconut shrimp and downed my second rum punch, I leaned back into my chair and sighed that satisfied variety that comes in moments of pure contentment. It was a sensation that hadn't taken hold in a while, and it felt good. I couldn't think of a better way to end a day.

Scott took a quick break to catch his breath, but after downing the rest of his drink, he went right into a story about one of the many joints just like that he'd played in all over the world.

As the singer wrapped up his tale, the owner raised his voice at the back of the bar and the group quieted. "There a Logan Dodge here tonight?"

"Logan Dodge," Scott said into his microphone, "Anyone by that name in the house tonight? Bueller?"

I pushed my chair back and stood.

Scott pointed the neck of his guitar at me. "Guess we got a winner."

I smiled then eyed the musician's highball glass that was more melted ice than Bahama Mama. "I'll bring you back a refill."

He threw me a quick laidback salute as I weaved through the tables, heading for the back of the dining area. It wasn't until I was halfway to the owner standing beside the bar that a few gears finally began to spin in my intoxicated brain. I was in the middle of nowhere, on a sparsely populated Bahamian island. And aside from my family and a small handful of government agents, no one knew that I was there.

"You're Logan Dodge?" the owner said.

"I told you he was," the waitress beside him said, then smiled and shuffled her plates of food to their destinations.

I nodded and the man handed me an old corded phone.

"Your friend's footing the long-distance charges, but I'd make it quick."

Utterly confused, I grabbed the handset and held it up to my ear.

"Hello?"

I heard only silence for a second or two, then a voice broke it like a mallet striking a window. "Hello, Dodger."

My eyes narrowed and my body tensed. I gripped the phone tight as I remembered the last time that he'd called me unexpectedly, addressing me by my old nickname that only he had used.

"Enjoying your little vacation, old friend?" Nathan Brier continued. "You didn't honestly think that you could stay hidden from me, did you?"

There were a lot of things that I wanted to say, but I kept my anger in check. No, I didn't think that he wouldn't be able to track me down. A man of Brier's means could find me anywhere if he wanted to. That was why I'd wanted to go after him on my own.

"This has gone on long enough, Brier," I said, my words ice-cold. "Come face me and let's end this. One way or another."

"Oh, I'll end it, brother. You can be sure of that. But now you've pissed me off even more. So we're gonna meet at a place and time of my choosing, or let's just say your little police officer friend won't be the only resident of Key West to find his way into my sights."

"It's over, Brier. Your little reign of terror was done faster than it started. You're on the run and desperate, and probably running low on cash. You—"

"Shut the hell up, Dodge!" he snarled. "Now listen to me very carefully. Either you do as I say, or the downtown streets of Key West will become a bloodbath. Mark my words."

The owner approached me, and I held up a finger, letting him know I'd be another minute. The look on my face told him that something was wrong, and he kept a sharp eye on me.

"You meet me at Rick's Bar on Duval," Brier said. "Eleven o'clock tomorrow evening. No weapons. No damn games. Just you and me."

"You'd never face me on even terms."

"Always so damn cocky, aren't you? Well, let's see if you can live up to your words. Meet me there, Dodge. You're one minute late, I start opening fire on people. Simple as that. As you said, I have nothing left to lose. And that makes me the most dangerous man on the planet."

I thought for a split second, thinking that didn't exactly give me a lot of time.

"Since you know I'm here, you must know that the feds sent me away until you were caught. I try and come back now, and customs will ship me right back."

Brier snickered. "I guess you're going to have to just be a big boy and figure it out. Tomorrow, Dodge. Your end comes tomorrow."

The line went dead.

THIRTY-ONE

Chetumal, Mexico

Nathan Brier pocketed his phone and gave a smug smile as he gazed through the old truck's windshield. He sat in the passenger seat and Harvey drove, cruising them along a dark side street on the outskirts of town.

"How do you know this guy will show?" Harvey said, having listened in to the recent conversation.

"Because he's predictable that way. He'd never pass up an opportunity to try and be the hero."

Harvey took a drag from his cigarette and exhaled out his rolled-down window. "What'd this guy do to get you so riled up anyway?"

"Long story," Brier spat. "You're getting paid double for a simple job. That's all you need to know."

The man stretched his fingers above the wheel and shrugged. "Fair enough." Then he pointed his head forward. "Almost there, amigo."

He slowed and turned into a dimly lit parking lot. Pulling up alongside a big rundown warehouse, he squeaked the old truck to a stop. Just as he did, a wide garage door lifted up, revealing a dark interior.

Harvey took a final drag of his cigarette, then tossed the ember nub out the window. "Like clockwork these guys, I tell ya."

In need of a new bird after Harvey had been forced to make a crash landing in a small jungle lake, as well as ammunition and other items, Brier had no choice but to seek out black market sellers in the region. Harvey had assured him that he'd worked with the mysterious group before. With Logan Dodge still hot on Brier's mind, he wanted to get back into the States as soon as possible so he could prepare for their final standoff.

Harvey switched off the headlights and drove into the warehouse. Before reaching the peak of its track, the door stopped, then fell back down to the ground. It struck with a loud slam, and then the space went pitch black and fell silent as a tomb.

"Just stay still," Harvey whispered. "Like I said, these guys are more skittish than deer. And they like their theatrics."

Nearly silent footsteps filled the air as men closed in from all sides, lurking in the darkness.

"Keys on the ground," a voice spat in Spanish.

Harvey complied. Having already slid the key from the ignition, he reached out and let go, the metal clanking against the floor and echoing across the interior space.

Men climbed into the bed and crawled for a look at the undercarriage, searching every inch of the truck before stopping at the cab. A light flashed on, the beam blinding right into their faces through the windshield.

"Out of the truck, now," a voice barked. As Brier and Harvey slid out from opposite sides, the man added, "Hands in the air, gringos."

The men searched the two visitors as well as the cab.

"I thought you said these guys were your friends?" Brier whispered.

Harvey shrugged. "Loose term."

"Right."

Once satisfied with their search, the leader of the group approached Harvey.

"How the hell are you still alive, you reckless fossil?"

"The fates must have a sense of humor," Harvey said. "You guys got the goods?"

"Money first," he said, shining the light into the man's eyes.

"Sure thing, boss," he said, motioning toward Brier. "Easy on the lights, amigo. My eyes aren't what they used to be, and I'll be useless in the skies if they get much worse."

The guy lowered the light as Brier walked over, slid his bag off his shoulder, then unzipped the main compartment and held it out. The leader, whose appearance was still shrouded in mystery, peeked inside and ran his fingers through the stacks of bills, then nodded.

"Follow me," he said.

Brier and Harvey followed the man across the room and through a side door that led into an adjoining space. Once they were inside, the door slammed shut behind them and a row of overhead lights powered on with the loud click of a breaker.

Brier covered his eyes, then blinked to adjust them. He focused on two rows of industrial shelves covered in stacks of wooden crates. At the back was a colossal garage door, and in the middle of the space sat a parked concrete truck. Right in front of them was a metal table with items sprawled out. A bald Latino in his mid-forties and wearing dark slacks and a button-up shirt stood with his back to them, his hands planted on his hips.

"You've got balls to show your face in here, Nathan Brier," the man said in a stern, articulate voice. "I'll give you that."

Brier froze at the mention of his name. Then the man turned around and the hard former Special Forces operative felt his insides tighten up.

Before Brier could make sense of his confusion, the man continued. "The last time I worked with you, your plan was snuffed out. Your superior officer put a bullet through his skull, and you were disgraced and tossed into prison." The man puffed his chest and blared his teeth. "And as for me and my men, we were forced to flee the area until the smoke cleared. I nearly lost everything because of you. And now... now you come crawling back, looking for help once again. Look around you, Brier," he said, motioning toward the massive warehouse packed with wooden crates. "My operation has grown far beyond what you can imagine." He sauntered toward Brier and lowered his sunglasses. "Give me one good reason why I should not bury your ass in a truck of wet cement, gringo." He stabbed a finger at the parked truck.

Anger and confusion swirled within Brier's mind. He shot a quick glance at Harvey, wondering if the man had betrayed him. But the flyboy looked confused and shook his head, clearly having no idea of the long history between Brier and the illegal arms dealer.

Brier swallowed hard. He'd need to come up with a damn good answer, or he had no doubt that the man would dispose of him. Known simply as El Muerto, the Bolivian born smuggler had a reputation for brutality that stretched across South and Central America.

Brier shook his head. "That was years ago. And Wyatt Holt is the one who messed things up, not me. Why do you think he killed himself?"

The arms dealer chuckled. "You haven't changed. Still pinning things on others." He motioned to his men and they swarmed in, grabbing Brier forcefully.

"You want reasons to keep me alive?" Brier said as they dragged him across the room toward the concrete truck. "I'll give you five hundred thousand of them." He motioned toward the bag that had fallen to the floor. "That's just the beginning. I have more stashed away at—"

"That's it, Brier?" El Muerto said, grinning with enjoyment at the prospect of seeing the American's life come to an end. "Such minuscule sums don't entice me anymore."

A metal staircase was rolled into position, and the massive dome of wet concrete was opened up at the back.

Just as the men lifted Brier up the first steps, he

shouted, "I also know the location of Darkwater's secret arsenal!"

They manhandled Brier to the top and were about to force him over the edge when El Muerto threw a hand into the air. "Stop!" The men froze, and the arms dealer eyed Brier skeptically. "What secret arsenal?" He turned to look at Harvey. "What lies is he spitting out now?"

"A hidden arsenal," Brier said. "Never on the private military's books, and therefore never cleared out by the US government when Darkwater was shut down. We're talking tens of millions of dollars in quality modern firearms. Not to mention advanced gadgetry."

El Muerto studied the man, then shot Harvey another look, the pilot dumbstruck by the shocking turn of events. "You worked for Darkwater for many years. He telling the truth?"

Harvey nodded. "I've seen it myself."

"Why haven't you sold it off, then?" the man said, raising his hands slightly. "Made yourselves a fortune?"

"It's not easy to reach," Harvey said. "I've never been down to it since it was hidden after Darkwater broke apart."

"Down to it?"

"It's resting in over two hundred feet of water."

El Muerto laughed again. "A secret underwater arsenal. That's what you're going with to save your skin, Brier? How can I possibly trust you? Your own country doesn't trust you. You betrayed your own people. How much worse will you betray me?"

"I won't betray you," Brier said. "You have my

word. You will make well over a hundred million dollars from those weapons. Just let me go and give me what I require. Once I'm back in the States and I finish my mission, then the location of the arsenal is yours."

The man thought for a moment. "Your word? No... I can think of a much better way to ensure your cooperation."

He signaled to his men, who forced Brier down to the floor. Muscling him back across the room, they pinned him down against the metal table.

"You have given me the perfect opportunity to test out a new device," El Muerto said as he cracked open a small hardcase. He pulled out a short silver gun-looking contraption with a thick needle poking out from the front. "Keep him still," he said as he handed the device to a man beside him.

Forcing Brier onto his chest, they held his forehead to the metal, then shoved the needle behind his right ear. Brier yelled as the device clicked, then the man pulled it away, leaving a small hole with blood dripping out.

"What the hell did you do to me?" Brier snapped as a square of gauze was pressed to the wound.

El Muerto knelt down to meet Brier's eye level. "We've just implanted a micro-explosive against your skull." He chuckled and added, "That way we can ensure you will do as you say. If you cooperate and tell us the location of the arsenal, we will remove it. But if you do not, we will detonate it... and you will die."

The men holding Brier in place let go, and he slid down the table, a hand pressing the back of his ear.

With another wave of the crime lord's hand, his guards closed in on Harvey, then pinned him down and injected him with a minuscule explosive as well.

"Now," El Muerto said, steepling his fingers, "we can get to the details of your request. Before I give you what you want, I will add one more thing." He stepped toward Brier, whose face was red with anger. "If you mention anything to anyone about where you received these items… I won't kill you. No, your fate will be far worse than death, understood?"

Brier shrugged. "We won't talk. I don't care about your operation. I gave you the money and I've agreed to give you the location of the arsenal. And now I want the damn products."

The man stood toe to toe with Brier, sizing him up. "You're crazy, gringo."

"I'm well beyond crazy."

As Brier had told Dodge on the phone earlier that evening, he had nothing to lose. And men with nothing to lose are the most dangerous kind.

El Muerto turned and held his hand out to the table. "It's all here. The guns. The gas. Action cameras with motion sensors and Bluetooth capabilities. Bulletproof vests. And one pipe bomb." The man motioned to the back of the warehouse. "I have a plane in storage and can have it transported and assembled at a private airstrip three miles from here."

"And the messenger?" Brier said.

Brier had asked for a young, athletic local with no prospects to join them on their trip back to the States.

"Of course," the man said. He whistled, then a lean guy in his early twenties marched into view with a bag slung over one shoulder. "You will go with these men, Rodrigo," he ordered. "I will make arrangements to get you back. When you do, this portion of the money will be yours." He held up a stack of hundred-dollar bills that equaled more than five years' average salary in the region. The young man nodded.

El Muerto turned back to face Brier and Harvey. He gave a cold smirk, then shook his head.

"Big brass balls and strange requests," he said. "On your way. And remember what I said, gringos. You talk and you'll beg for a bullet." As Brier and Harvey gathered the items, the illegal arms dealer added, "Oh, and don't even think about tampering with those explosives we injected. If you do, they will self-destruct. They were designed that way to prevent removal. I am the only one who can safely dislodge them." He placed a firm hand behind Brier's neck and squeezed tight. "Nathan Brier. I'd never imagined I'd work with the scumbag who nearly wrecked me. At least this time I have insurance that you won't screw me over."

He shifted his hand, pressing tight against the tiny explosive device lodged under Brier's skin and staring deeper into his eyes.

They loaded up the truck and the young Mexican climbed into the back. Harvey drove them out of the warehouse, and Brier narrowed his eyes as they pulled out of the compound.

Of all the arm's dealers his pilot friend could've contacted, he happened to call upon one led by a ruthless crime lord who hated Brier's guts.

It doesn't matter, Brier thought, his lips forming a

smile.

He didn't care about the abandoned weapons arsenal. His one-track mind was fixed on revenge and revenge alone. Once his task was complete, he'd give the arms dealer what he wanted, rolling the dice of fortune yet again, and he'd move on knowing that he'd followed through on his vow.

But first… his last chance of a plan that could very well lead to his death, needed to succeed.

But come hell or high water, Dodge will go down with me.

He thought back to his conversation with his old comrade.

I have my quarry coming to me like a moth to the flame. I have the tools and manpower. Now it's time to set up the pieces and strike. Now… it's time for Logan Dodge to face his long-awaited reckoning.

THIRTY-TWO

I held the receiver to my ear, listening to the hum of the dial tone. Once the initial force of the conversation had lessened, I handed it back to the owner and strode down to the sand, needing to get away from the music and people and be alone with my thoughts. I stopped at the water's edge and looked out as a wave lapped up onto the beach and splashed over my bare feet. Brier was calling me out, again. His words ran circles in my mind, the threat to gun down civilians resonating loudest.

I checked the time on my phone. It was half past nine. That meant I had just over twenty-four hours to not only come up with a plan but to conjure up a means to travel over four hundred miles and sneak back into Key West.

Brier had always been an anomaly to me. Even when we'd first served together and I was still following his orders. The man had a habit of making strange moves, of being unpredictable and often going the route that offered the most resistance.

He stayed true to character.

Why in the hell would he want to face off against me in Key West of all places?

He obviously knew where I was.

Why not fly over to the Bahamas and face me here? Or why not get me to travel and meet him abroad somewhere?

Literally any destination would be smarter than his going back to the place where every law enforcement officer for miles had his face fresh in their minds.

I thought for a moment about how Brier would be able to get around without being spotted right away. Then I remembered the significance of the following day in the Florida island chain. Saturday, October 29 was the day of the Captain Morgan Fantasy Fest Parade, the last hurrah of the city's most popular island festival and an event that was predicted to draw over fifty thousand people to the downtown streets. The crowds, costumes, and overall level of intoxication among everyone gathered would make for a great place to blend in.

"You're missing the show," Ange said, bouncing down the steps and pacing toward me. She stopped and took a moment to examine my body language. No one could read me better than her. "Who was that on the phone?" I gave her one cold, serious look that said it all. "You've gotta be kidding me?" she gasped.

"Wish I was."

Her knees bent slightly on instinct, and she scanned the beach in a blink. "He here?"

I shook my head. "No. I don't know where he is. But I know where he'll be tomorrow."

I replayed our conversation, and we both fell silent a moment, her letting the revelation simmer.

"What are you going to do?" she finally said.

"I don't know what the right thing is."

"Yes, you do."

"I could call Maddox and Jane. Get them all on alert. Maybe even cancel the festival."

"That spectacle brings tens of millions of dollars into the islands every year. They're not gonna cancel it. And they'll need you. You know that. They'll need us. I'm sick and tired of this guy. Let's go and get him."

I felt her words. I was beyond sick of Nathan Brier, and I wanted him to finally face the powerful hand of justice as much as anyone.

"And Mayor Nix? The government's order?"

Ange chuckled. "Wouldn't be the first time we've broken a rule. Sometimes it's necessary for the greater good. Put another way, you gotta do what you gotta do."

We strode back up into the restaurant, said quick goodbyes to Norman and his wife as well as the freedivers, then headed for the Wrangler. The local cave owner caught up to us as we climbed in.

"Nobody leaves Tiny's when music that good's playing," he said, sensing that something was wrong. "I know it's not my business, but I've appreciated all your help the past week, and if there's anything I can do to repay the favor and help with whatever's going on, please let me know, friend."

I was just about to thank him for the gesture but wave it off when I thought about our conversation earlier that day. Looking the local in the eyes, I said,

"You mentioned something about a plane?"

He looked back at me, puzzled. "I did. An old amphib Courier like I said."

"She run?"

He nodded. "Took her to Eleuthera a few months back."

"Mind if I borrow it? My wife and I are both experienced pilots—she has over a thousand logged hours. We would pay the going rate as well as gas, of course."

Norman waved me off. "No need. Just be sure to bring her back in one piece. Where you running off to so fast?"

"Key West."

He scratched his chin. "Just watch out for Rina," he said, referring to the hurricane that had emerged from a tropical wave that had rolled across from Africa earlier that month. "She's picking up steam along the Yucatan."

I thanked him for the offer of his baby and said that I'd be in touch and wouldn't likely need to leave until the following day.

"She'll be fueled and ready for you," he said, then I drove us out of the lot, thinking yet again what kind of place the world would be if everyone were as friendly as islanders.

Scarlett leaned forward from the backseat. "Okay, what the heck is going on?"

"We're going home," I said.

"They found Nathan Brier? Can't we finish the guy's set back at the hole first?"

Ange explained the situation while I drove us back to our beach cottage. Heading straight for the back

231

porch, I pulled out my sat phone and punched in Maddox's number. When he answered, he informed me that he was back at Homeland's headquarters in D.C. and that he still had no word on Brier.

"I just got off the phone with him," I said, causing the agent to fumble on the other end of the line. "Yeah, that was my reaction too."

"How the hell… what did he say?"

"That he's going to be in Key West tomorrow evening. And he wants to meet with me and catch up."

"He say anything about a bomb this time?"

"No, but he did mention that he'd open fire on people in the street if I didn't show up on time. And it wouldn't exactly take a crack shot to do serious damage on Duval, especially during the crescendo of Fantasy Fest."

The experienced soldier and government agent paused a moment, mulling it over. "What are you thinking?"

"I called you because you know how men like Brier and me operate," I said. "And because you've seen firsthand how dangerous the guy can be. If we put Key West on alert, fill it with officers and agents from all over the state, or if we try and get this festival shut down, things aren't going to go well. My first instinct tells me to head into town and face him with you and a handful of your best undercover agents nearby. But they're gonna have to be discreet as hell, Maddox. I'd recommend costumes to fit in."

"Costumes?"

I remembered that Maddox had mentioned that he hadn't spent a lot of time in South Florida, and that prior to being based in D.C., he'd spent most of his time on the West Coast and Mexican border states.

"Just Google Fantasy Fest and you'll get what I'm talking about."

"Roger that. How are you planning to get back into the States? It would be tricky for me to help given that it was my team that helped hide you there."

"You let me handle that." I watched Ange crack open her laptop on the dining room table, going into full recon mode. "You and your men just be ready. I'll keep you updated with our plan and progress."

"Copy. Brier's probably gonna have backup again."

"Plan for the worst," I said, and we ended the call.

I headed inside and worked out a strategy with Ange. She had maps open, along with the festival's schedule and weather updates. I called Jack, knowing that he'd be better than any expensive piece of weather equipment at predicting Hurricane Rina's trajectory.

"She won't make it across the Gulf, bro," Jack declared. "With this high-pressure system protecting us, she'll shy away and tuck back. I bet she won't gust much past Cuba."

"The festival's still on, then?"

My old friend laughed. "Those partiers wouldn't be stopped unless a major one hit. It's gonna be a wild night."

You have no idea, I thought.

"You guys finally heading back?" Jack added. "Everyone's anxious to see you guys. Especially Atty."

I informed him that we were heading home,

though not for the reasons he'd hoped. Then I requested his help in getting Ange and me into Key West without being detected, going over what his role would be.

"I'll be there, bro," he said without hesitating. "For whatever you need me for." He paused a moment, then added, "Ironic how after all these years, and all the places you've infiltrated, you're sneaking into your own country."

"This is the way it needs to be. Desperate times—"

"Call for desperate measures. Just give me the call, Logan. I'll be there."

I set my phone on the table and peered out the window at the tranquil Caribbean. The calm before the storm.

I thought over Jack's words, latching onto one sentence specifically. "It's gonna be a wild night."

You got that right.

THIRTY-THREE

The Following Evening

A waxing crescent moon glistened off the waters below as Ange flew us out from over the Strait. She kept the Helio at an altitude of a hundred feet, and five hundred miles into our flight, the dark islands of the Dry Tortugas came into view. Wrapping around Fort Jefferson and putting us on an easterly course, she switched off transponder broadcasting and brought us down to just fifteen feet. The amphibious aircraft was equipped with ground avoidance radar, allowing us to precisely gauge our altitude and keep close to the surface so we could blend in with nearby boats on air traffic control radars.

I glanced over my shoulder at Scarlett who gazed out the window in awe at how low we were flying. We'd debated whether it would have been best for her to stay in the Bahamas, but hadn't liked the idea of leaving her alone at the safe house.

Forty miles beyond the Tortugas, Ange descended slowly, splashing down just west of the Marquesas Keys. Easing us down to five knots, she piloted us into a cut that wove into Mooney Harbor and brought the floats up against the mangrove infested El Radabob Key.

After Ange killed the engine, I hopped out and splashed into the shallows. Grabbing a coil of rope, I pulled the small craft farther out of sight, tucked away from anyone who might cruise by, then tied her to the branches.

"I sure hope Jack's right about the 'cane," Ange said, climbing out from the cockpit. "Otherwise we're gonna owe Norman a new plane."

I gazed southwest and saw a few dark clouds looming on the horizon. "I'd bet the farm on his hunches."

Having spent his whole life in the islands, Jack was fully in tune with the tropical world around him. His weather predictions often surprised me, but he had a spotless track record.

My sat phone buzzed as I climbed back onto the plane and I whipped it out.

"Saw you land," Jack said. "Heading toward the harbor now."

Two minutes later, we heard the low grumble of inboard engines, then Jack's Sea Ray came into view. He pulled up alongside us, carefully navigating in the shallows, then idled the engines.

"Welcome home, Dodge clan," he said, his voice far from his usual laid-back tone.

The three of us carried our gear from the cockpit, locked up the plane, and climbed aboard the *Calypso*.

Atticus sprang down from the bridge, his tail wagging like crazy as he tried to jump onto and lick all of us at the same time. Having not seen him in three weeks, I'd missed the Lab and knew that the time away must've felt like an eternity to him.

I greeted Atticus and scratched his ears, but only for a few seconds. We had work to do.

"Appreciate the lift, Jack," I said.

He brushed off my thanks, then eyed the plane. "You guys have any trouble getting into US airspace?"

Ange shrugged. "I'm sure they've already notified the authorities of the unauthorized landing. Thankfully, this is Florida. Lots of planes and boats coming and going. But we should get a move on quick regardless."

"Say no more," Jack said, bounding back up to the bridge.

He fired up the engines and motored us out from the inlet, around the northern tip of the Marquesas, and east to Key West.

The waters around our island home were bustling even more than usual for a Saturday night. Boats of all shapes and sizes coming and going, tiny floating tiki bars chugging past, party boats, and a few replica pirate ships. As agreed, Jack took us at a leisurely pace to the waterfront and pulled up to one of the few open spaces in the line of docks just south of Mallory Square.

Visitors covered the promenade and filled every seat in the waterfront restaurants. The loud orchestra of music and rowdy partygoers echoed from the downtown streets, centering around Duval.

"You sure you guys don't want me to come with?" he said as I stepped onto the dock and offered a hand to Ange.

"You've done more than enough already," I said.

My wife moved in beside me. "Besides, we need you to look after Scarlett."

"Or I could come, too," our daughter said confidently. "You might need me to watch your backs."

"You guys just head over to the bight and steer clear of downtown," I said, not interested in joking around.

Jack nodded. "Be careful."

I nodded back, shoved off the *Calypso*, and strode up the waterfront alongside Ange. We both wore ball caps and kept our heads down as we meshed into the thick droves of pedestrians, many of whom were decked out in every kind of colorful outfit imaginable. The theme for this year was Aquatic Afrolic, and we passed handfuls of people dressed as mermaids, sailors, and every type of sea creature.

I checked the time and saw that it was 2230, giving me half an hour before the meeting time set by Brier. We'd given ourselves extra minutes to prepare for the encounter and don the necessary apparel. Not our usual choice of black tactical clothes, but something more fitting for the occasion.

We headed into a variety shop that we knew from experience had a large section devoted to costumes. Many of the getups were taken already, but we weren't picky. We just needed items to conceal our faces and still leave us with proper range of motion, ruling out the full set of medieval armor on display.

I grabbed a Zorro mask along with the matching hat and cape. It wasn't in theme, which was why it was still available, I assumed. Donning it right away, I turned and spied Ange grabbing and throwing on a sparkling silver-and-purple masquerade mask.

I paid with the mask on, the kid behind the counter not questioning what would usually be a strange act. This was Fantasy Fest in Key West. It wouldn't come close to being the strangest thing he'd see that night.

Once ready, we left through different exits, splitting up as we cut five blocks across town toward the meeting place. While I took the left side of Duval, heading northwest, Ange would cut around and approach from the opposite direction and the right side.

For someone who's never experienced the final night of the festival, it's difficult to do it justice. Simply put, it's complete and utter chaos. I imagine it's what Port Royal, the famous buccaneer hangout in the golden age of piracy, looked like when swashbucklers arrived laden with gold and anxious to spend it in one night. A cloud of cigarette smoke hovering over the scene, women dressed in scanty outfits, guys dressed in nothing but thongs.

I passed by a man dressed in an old dive helmet with a fish tank strapped to his chest, then cut onto Duval, the parade passing right by. I glanced at a float filled with hula dancers wearing coconut bras and grass skirts. People covered the balconies and streets, laughing and cheering and all acting like they'd checked their inhibitions at Homestead on the drive down.

Had I been there under different circumstances, I'd

be enjoying myself, smiling along and watching the spectacle in awe. Instead, I was focused and alert to everything going on around me, ready for Brier to pop out at any second or to try and take me down from a rooftop. I tried to blend in with my walk, moving as casually as I could, but on the inside, I'd never been more focused.

One block from Rick's Bar, my phone buzzed in my pocket.

"Cute costume," Brier said when I answered.

"Let's get this over with," I said, cutting straight to the point.

"Easy, Dodge. I'll be killing you soon enough."

"Come out and face me."

Brier laughed. "You need to look around, take a lesson from the people surrounding you and lighten up. The night's just getting started." Before I could interject, Brier added, "Now, stop. About-face, then enter that haunted house two doors down."

I turned and narrowly avoided a Pomeranian being driven around in a remote-controlled car and a conquistador on stilts.

I eyed the door into the haunted house, then Brier said, "I'll meet you on the second floor, brother."

The line went dead. I looked back up, and as I strode for the door, a man slipped out wearing a hood and carrying a backpack. He took one look my way, then froze and bolted into a sprint, weaving through the people and heading away from me on the sidewalk. I took three steps after him, then Ange booked it across the road, sprinting right in front of a float adorned with fake marine life.

"I'll get this punk," she said, barely looking my

way as she raced toward the mystery man. "You get Brier!"

Her voice was nearly drowned out by the chaos surrounding us.

Who the hell was that? What's he up to, and why did he leave right after Brier called?

My foe was playing tricks on me, that much was certain. Part of me wanted to race after him with Ange, to take him before he had the chance to hurt her or utilize whatever was in his bag. But Ange's words rang true, and as I looked back to the door of the haunted house, I knew that I needed to focus on Brier.

I sprang toward the door, gripped the handle, and pulled it open.

THIRTY-FOUR

Nathan Brier double-checked that all of the knots were tight, then stepped back from the terrified woman. Wearing a Key West Police uniform, Brier had sweet-talked the tipsy college-aged girl down on the first floor, then told her that the upper level was a great place for a make-out session. Once upstairs, in the area of the business that was closed off for repairs, Brier had slammed the door, then knocked her across the head and tied her up.

"Please… please let me go…" the woman cried.

Her dark hair was a mess, and tears streaked the thick pink eyeliner down her face. She wore only a matching pink bikini, and she was coated with smears of various-colored paints.

"Shut up," Brier snapped, wrapping a hand around her throat and squeezing so tight that her eyes bulged. "Or I'll wring the life out of you. Got it?"

She was barely able to give a slight nod, and when he let go, she coughed and wheezed for air.

Brier eyed the girl. "No, you can't be counted on to keep quiet."

He snatched a roll of duct tape and ripped off a length. Stepping behind the shaking woman, he pressed it around her mouth. Not sure if it would be enough, he wrapped two more passes of tape, pulling so tight against her neck and strands of hair that she squealed.

She was tied to a wooden beam near the edge of the cramped, dark room. Directly in front of her was a maze of mirrors, each reflecting off each other. Footsteps approached, and Brier turned to see Harvey.

"Everything's set," the man said. He glanced at his watch. "Nearing time. What if he doesn't show?"

"He'll show," Brier snapped, then turned to peer out a dirty window that looked out over a chaotic stretch of Duval.

As if his confidence had manifested his expectation, he spotted a man dressed in a Zorro costume, weaving through the throng of people. The guy was tall, athletic, and wide-shouldered. But more than that, he had an air about him, a way of movement and analyzing the crowd that Brier could spot a hundred yards away. It was training ingrained into their every action. It was Logan Dodge.

He waited until his rival had passed the door to the haunted house, then called and informed Dodge of the change of plans. As Logan turned and moved back his way, Brier gestured toward a young man in the corner.

"You're up, kid," he said to the guy in Spanish.

The young man nodded, tightened the straps of his

backpack, then put on his hood and hustled around the maze and across the room to the stairs. Brier listened as the kid moved down the old staircase and watched as he popped out onto the sidewalk below. Logan froze in the crowd, observing the young man with the backpack for a moment before taking off. Brier's eyes shifted to focus on the road as a woman ran across the street and said something to Logan before chasing down the kid.

Brier chuckled, then shook his head. He turned to Harvey. "All right. This is it."

He looked over the woman once more, relishing her fear. "Don't worry," he said in a soft tone that cut like an icy dagger. "It will all be over soon. You will help me in my quest for justice, and your death will serve a purpose." The sadistic criminal brushed aside her hair. "So beautiful. Such a shame."

Staring her in her teary eyes, he turned away and cracked his neck, preparing himself for the bout that he'd been looking forward to and planning for nearly a month.

Harvey grabbed two gas masks from the floor, donned one, and handed the other to Brier.

"Cue the gas, Harv," Brier said, tightening the mask over his face.

Brier gave a sinister smile as the man followed his command, lumbering across the room.

THIRTY-FIVE

"It's five dollars for the fright of your life, Zorro," a short, chubby, pimple-faced kid in a zombie costume said as I pushed into the establishment.

The sound of mechanical ghosts and skeletons, recorded screams and fleeing bats, and real shouts of terror filled the dark interior of the haunted house. Smoke billowed out from the corners, coating the floor in a dense fog.

The cashier twirled his glowstick, then pointed at the sign over his head. "Ten if you want the bonus room of ultimate scare. You alone?"

I looked around, amazed that Brier had chosen a place that wasn't just open for business but filled with people. But I remembered that he'd mentioned I'd find him on the second floor.

"You see the guy with the backpack just run through here?" I said, taking him aback. "Any idea who he was?"

The kid shook his head. "Lots of people in and out

today. Hundreds. Thousands! It's been a wild night."

I pulled a twenty from my wallet and planted it on the counter. "Where are the stairs?"

Again the kid looked puzzled. "Second floor's under construction. It's all blocked off."

"Where?" I said, sliding the bill to him.

He pointed to the back far corner. "That way, man. But like I said, it's closed. The start of the trail of terror is this wa—"

He kept babbling on, but his words died off as I stomped into the darkness. A witch popped out at me, then a skeleton sprang out from a casket and screamed in my face. I didn't blink as I pushed through the haunted house, avoiding the occasional visitor before reaching a staircase.

It was blocked off by a rope and a sign that said "Area Closed." I stepped over the sign and made quick work of the steps. Coming to a closed door at the top, I gripped the knob and pushed it open. More smoke poured out, covering me in a thick white cloud. I waited for a moment as it dissipated slightly, then pushed onward, letting the door shut behind me.

I felt suddenly lightheaded and off-balance as I stepped into a nearly pitch-black room. Ahead of me, I saw the dark outline of what looked like a partition that didn't quit reach up to the ceiling. The dizziness turned to vertigo as I scanned around the room, and I realized that something was very wrong. It wasn't just fog spewing out from machines at the edges of the room. It was some form of mind-altering gas, and it was wreaking havoc on my mental faculties.

I threw off my mask and cape, folded the fabric, and pressed it to my face to try and filter the gas.

Striding away from the fog toward what I quickly realized was a mirror-covered divider, I yelled for the coward to show himself.

"Come out, Brier!" I said. "You got what you wanted. I'm here. Now come out and face me."

My mind in a haze, I peered around in the darkness, expecting him to hop out and strike me at any second.

I heard a mechanical click, followed by a bright bulb showering me with light. Blinking, I spotted a portable work lamp on a stand. A lean man with leathery skin and long gray hair stood beside it. He had a black gas mask strapped over his face and stared straight at me.

"Who the hell are—"

"Nice of you to stop by, Dodge," Brier said.

I turned as my old brother in arms strolled toward me from the opposite side of the room. He wore a police uniform with a bulletproof vest, and had a gas mask strapped over his face. Closing in on me, he gave the other guy a nod and the stranger shut off the fog machines. When the smoke cleared and the gas began to dissipate, Brier removed his mask and shot me a cruel gaze.

Feeling disoriented and having a hard time staying on my feet, I said, "You told me we were going to fight fairly. What the hell is this shit?"

"Just a little nitro," Brier said with a smile, referring to nitrous oxide. "And you said that you were coming alone." He wagged a finger at me. "You should have known better than to bring your pretty little wife into this. I just wish I could be there to watch as she's blown to pieces."

The image of my wife chasing after the guy with the backpack jumped into my mind. I'd been worried and protective and conflicted before, but now it was being pushed to the extreme.

"It should be any second now," Brier said, stealing a peek at his watch. "Kaboom goes Mrs. Dodge."

Unable to stand there and listen to the twisted maniac spew out garbage any longer, I lunged toward him. My head spun, and I was severely off-balance, but I didn't care. It would take a hell of a lot more than a little nitrous to prevent me from engaging Nathan Brier.

I tried to fake left, then swoop back for a right hook, but I lost my footing. Brier avoided my attack and struck me across the cheek, the blow sending me to a knee.

I shook my head and blinked like mad, trying to free myself from the effects of the potent substance. Lunging toward the man a second time, I threw a jab, then shoved my knee toward his gut. He blocked the first attack, then avoided my knee and swept his leg, knocking me to the floor with a loud smack.

Brier knelt down in front of me. "You have no idea how pathetic you look right now," he snickered. "You just had to make this whole thing hard for yourself, didn't you?"

Gritting my teeth, I flipped over and launched toward him like a provoked bull. He slugged me in the side, grabbed me by the shirt, and manhandled me back to the floor.

The confusion reached a climax, and I saw nothing but a blurred image of Brier surrounded by circling stars as my head hit the hardwood.

"I remember that day," Brier snarled, grabbing two fistfuls of my shirt collar and leaning over me. Veins popped from his forehead and arms. "I remember it like it was yesterday. I needed you. You were my brother and you left me hanging out to dry. Well, now it's time to return the favor. It's time for me to fulfill the vow I made eleven years ago in that military courtroom."

His hands slid up and wrapped around my neck. I gagged as he pressed hard, crunching my windpipe. With his left hand pinning me down, he reached back and grabbed a twelve-inch Ka-Bar. As he struck it down, I saw only a quick blur of motion and jerked my head to the right. The blade barely sliced my left cheek and struck into the wood.

Feeling the haziness begin to fade a little, I elbowed him in his left eye, then thrust upward with everything I had, tossing him off me. He spun and landed on his feet. I propped myself up, and before I could remove the knife, Brier charged. I charged right back, yelling as I threw my shoulder into his chest. The collision knocked the air out of both our lungs, and we grappled, throwing knees and punches and beating the hell out of each other. At one point I managed to snag a Velcro strap and rip the Kevlar vest off him, exposing his upper body.

Avoiding a right uppercut, I retaliated with a strong side kick that launched him to the floor. With the gas numbing the pain from the blows I'd been dealt, I pushed through the confusion and threw myself at him. But before I could finish the job, the man in the corner of the room slid a pistol across the smooth floor. Brier caught the weapon, his body shaking and his lungs gasping for air, and aimed it right at me just as I was about to take him down for good.

Brier didn't hesitate.

The moment he had the pistol leveled, he pulled the trigger, and I expected the lead round to burst into my body and tear up my insides. The exploding gunpowder rattled my eardrums in the tight space, and I heard a rapid, loud whistling sound as the bullet flew past me, puncturing the door at my back. Brier had somehow missed, and now that he was within arm's reach, I wasn't about to let him flex his finger a second time.

I snatched his wrist and jerked him around, nearly cracking the bones as I forced the weapon from his grasp. It bounced to my feet and I shoved Brier off me with a powerful grunt. Eyeing the fallen weapon, I lunged toward it just as the light clicked again and the space went dark once more.

I nearly tripped, my body battered and my mind still recovering from the gas. But I remembered where the weapon had been and managed to find it in the blackness. I grasped the pistol and whirled around to a knee. The light clicked back on, casting a glow over the scene.

Brier had vanished, along with his accomplice.

"You think you've beaten me, Dodge?" Brier shouted from the middle of the room. He cackled, fighting back the pain I'd dealt him. "You're too weak to finish me off. Too soft to deal the fatal blow. That's why you'll never defeat me."

Catching my breath and focusing forward, I held the pistol out in front of me with both hands and stepped slowly toward the opening in the massive mirror. As I entered, I realized that it was a maze, with all the walls reflecting off each other and making it dizzyingly impossible to figure out the right way to go.

As the effects of the gas began to wear off, pain radiated from across my body, but my vision was still hazy. In the dim light, I could barely see where I was going. But I had Brier's pistol, and its sights followed the path of my eyes, my finger on the trigger, ready to take down the sadistic criminal once and for all.

I made my way confidently through the world of confusion and disarray, the injuries doing their best to hold me back. With every sharp corner, I expected to see my old comrade and put an end to the charade, but the rows of mirrors and dead ends and passageways seemed to never end.

Then, I heard the shuffling of footsteps in front of me, just beyond my line of sight around a jutting mirror's edge. I crouched low, wanting to pop out and take down my assailant from an unexpected plane.

"Come out, come out, Dodger," Brier said, fumbling with what sounded like a firearm.

I took in a deep, calming breath, doing everything I could to clear my mind. My vision remained blurred, and fog coated the bottom of the space. I couldn't see well in the dim light, but that wouldn't matter. It was all about to end.

Gripping Brier's pistol, I narrowed my gaze and poked around the corner. Brier was there, standing at the end of a short passageway in the mirrors. He held a submachine gun in his hands, aimed straight at me.

The moment I had him in my sights, I pulled the

trigger, firing a round just before he could. The crack shook the space and a flash burst from the muzzle. Having aimed right at Brier's chest, I gasped as the round hit its mark but didn't strike flesh. Instead the round burst through Brier's reflection in a mirror, shattering the wall of glass. Instead of Brier moaning and falling uncontrollably to the floor, I heard a muffled, high-pitched whimper.

As the wall of glass fell away, I spotted a woman right on the other side of the mirror. Her head was down, and blood flowed out from a bullet wound to her exposed chest.

THIRTY-SIX

Angelina watched from across the street as her husband stopped, then turned around, a phone pressed to his ear. She observed him carefully through the throng of rowdy pedestrians, packing Duval tight and partying as if the world were about to come to an unpreventable end.

Ange crept to the edge of the sidewalk, watching the scene intently. Logan advanced in the opposite direction of the original meeting place, and she traced his trajectory as he paced toward the entrance to a haunted house. The second she locked eyes on the door, it swung open and a lean man wearing a sweatshirt and a backpack stepped out. The hooded man turned and looked straight toward Logan, then cut right and bounded as fast as he could manage through the chaos. Ange didn't hesitate. Just as the man bolted, she jumped into the street, sprinting in front of a colorful float, then cutting off her husband.

"I'll get this punk," she said, barely glancing his

way before returning her focus to the fleeing mystery man. "You get Brier!"

She pursued him along the sidewalk, zigging and zagging and fighting for openings through the festival. The man turned down Caroline, and Ange dashed right on his heels. She had no way of knowing who he was or what he was up to. But given the guy's reaction, she wanted to figure out for herself what he was doing before she read about it in the news that evening.

The guy was fast, flying down the less crowded side street. But Ange could keep up with the best of them, and she knew her town better than most. Cutting across the backside of a real estate office, she managed to close the distance to just thirty yards by the time they hit Truman Annex.

She followed the guy as he ran across Front Street to the downtown parking garage. Instead of bolting for the stairs, the guy leapt onto a low-lying tree branch, then hurled his body and grabbed hold of the railing on the second level. In a flash, the wiry young man flung himself up and over, vanishing from her view.

Who the hell is this guy? she thought as she planned a quick parkour route, using a sunshade instead and managing to heave herself up and over.

The garage was packed solid but mostly devoid of people. She hustled between two cars, then spotted the guy as he rounded the corner, sprinting for the upper level. She raced after him, following right at his back as they rounded their way up to the top. When she reached the roof, and the night sky welcomed them, Ange thought she had him. She removed her

Glock and hustled across the top of the lot, raising her weapon toward the fleeing man as he continued toward the northwest corner of the structure.

"Freeze!" Ange yelled at the top of her lungs.

The man didn't break stride. Racing behind an SUV, he sprang onto the guardrail and jumped, his body soaring off the parking garage and landing hard against the metal roof of the Margaritaville Resort.

Ange holstered her weapon, nearly in disbelief at what she'd just seen. She ran for the edge and, without questioning whether she could make it or not, picked up as much speed as she could and launched herself over the gap. Her upper body slammed into the corner, and she nearly jerked back and fell to a path thirty feet below.

Gripping tight, she managed to pull herself up the smooth roof and jump to her feet. Pushing to the crest of the building, she peeked over the point just as her quarry slid down the opposite side. He fell ten feet, landing on top of a delivery truck parked along the walkway. Rolling with the fall, the man dropped onto the roof of the cab before sliding off and landing in the plaza.

Ange grabbed her radio and exclaimed, "He's heading north along the water toward Mallory."

Maddox gave a reply of "Copy that" as she clipped the radio back to her waist and vaulted over the peak. She quickly picked up speed, sliding down the metal roof with the bright lights, music, and noise around her. Digging in slightly with the soles of her shoes, she managed to slow herself just before falling and rolling onto the roof of the truck. Snatching the edge, she shifted herself off, then eased down and let go, landing on the brick sidewalk.

She followed the man around the heart of the resort, racing along the promenade. Fatigue set in for both of them as she stayed on his tail across the wooden footbridge to Mallory Square. Four hours earlier, during sunset, the place would've been jam-packed elbow to elbow with people coming together to say an enthusiastic last goodbye to the sun. With the party having moved inland, they only had to avoid a few clusters of visitors.

The man cut through a row of palm trees, heading for the parking lot. But he stopped in his tracks when a black BMW roared into the lot, flying straight toward the man. With Ange closing in at his back and Maddox cutting off his inland escape route, the man looked around frantically for a moment before sprinting back toward the water and turning north again.

Ange closed to within ten yards of him, close enough to withdraw her weapon and open fire. But the narrow promenade in front of the Ocean Key Resort was lined with dining tables and vacationers, making a shot far too risky.

But we have him, she thought, her heart racing and her body coated in sweat.

With Maddox hightailing it to the other side of the resort, the runner would only have one way to go.

Sure enough, just as the man rounded the corner, he froze yet again. Ange spotted Maddox and his partner closing in from the other end of the promenade. The spooked quarry dropped his bag near a crowded corner bar, then darted onto the two-hundred-foot long Sunset Pier.

Ange pushed through the people, grabbed one of the bag's straps, and swiftly unzipped its main compartment. Her eyes locked onto three sections of capped water pipes tightly bound together. An attached LED screen was counting down, and had just hit the five second mark.

With no time to disable the pipe bomb, Ange turned and shoved toward the point.

"Everybody down!" she yelled before striding forward and hurling the bag as far as she could out over the water.

The moment it left her hand, Ange hit the deck, wanting to create as small of a target as possible. Hearing the seriousness in her tone, most of the gathered people dropped down as well and gasped in confusion. Just as the bag dropped out of her sight, a powerful explosion shook the ground. A blast wave tore across the scene, knocking people down as flames burst from the backpack. Tiny, jagged pieces of metal shot out, pelting the side of the boardwalk and the resort's upper rooms and shattering windows a hundred yards away.

Ange looked up, catching her breath following the blast wave which had knocked the wind out of her. Fortunately, the bomb had fallen over the wharf just before exploding, the wall of pilings protecting the people. But even the indirect wave had felt like being punched in the chest, and it took her a moment to get her bearings in the chaotic aftermath of the blast.

People cried out and lay on the ground, scrambling to flee. Thankfully, she didn't see anyone bleeding. Looking through the chaos, Ange spotted the bomber's silhouette as he neared the end of the dock.

The man was preparing to dive into the water and make some kind of escape when the *Calypso* pulled alongside the planks with Scarlett at the helm.

Jack was standing on the bow with his compact Desert Eagle raised. When the bomber reached for a weapon, the islander opened fire, the round pummeling into the man's chest and sending him toppling over the edge and into the water.

THIRTY-SEVEN

I stared at the woman's motionless body for a brief moment, my heart thumping, my mind trying to make sense of what had just happened.

What... what have I done?

I took a step toward the woman, then remembered that Brier was still on his feet. I'd hit my mark, but my target had been nothing more than my enemy's reflection. And a carefully chosen one at that. Before I could wrap my head around the situation, and before the wave of emotion fully set in, Brier taunted me again.

"Look what you did, Dodge!" the man said, his tone laced with intensity. "You've just killed an innocent woman."

I moved toward the sound, his words fueling my desire to end his life even more. I weaved through the final stages of the maze. Just as I was about to exit, I caught another reflection of Brier raising his submachine gun. This time, I dove right, landing on my chest just as he opened fire.

A stream of rounds rattled the air, bursting through the maze and shattering the mirrors all around me. Shards flew out in all directions and rained down like a heavy storm. I rolled twice, reaching the edge of the maze and popping to a knee. Catching a faint glimpse of Brier as he moved along the end of the maze, holding the trigger and lighting up the place with lead, I took aim and fired, burrowing a round into his left thigh. Brier yelled and flew back, shooting a trail of rounds into the ceiling before the sound of gunfire was replaced by a familiar mechanical click.

His mag was empty.

Brier moaned and scurried as I rose and closed in, my emotions running high as the sight of the woman's motionless body came into view in my peripherals once again. I fired another round at Brier as I sprang toward him, aiming for his shoulder. The bullet hit its mark, and he released control of his weapon just as I reached him. The moment he laid eyes on me, I smacked him across the jaw with the pistol, knocking loose a row of teeth as he grunted and fell to the ground. Blood dripping from his mouth, my old brother in arms broke out into a maniacal laugh.

"You've played right into my hands, Dodge," the man said. He spat a spray of blood as I dropped down and grabbed a fistful of his shirt. "She's dead," he added, gesturing toward the woman. "You killed her and now… now you will be forced to feel as I felt. Now you will be the one disgraced by your own people."

I punched him in the cheek, my anger swelling

over.

He cackled some more. "That was my plan. Not just to kill you. It was to do what you did to me."

He hissed the last words, crimson oozing from his teeth. I yelled and punched him again. Hearing shuffling to my right, I turned just in time to see Brier's accomplice making a break for the door. I aimed and fired, my rage making me focused and precise. The bullet tore through his hip, and he yelled and stumbled to the floor just out of sight.

When I turned back to Brier, the man gripped my wrists with all the strength he had left. He managed to keep the pistol aimed away from him. But I knew Brier, and I didn't need to glance at his left ankle to see what was latched to it. He always kept a spare knife.

Leaving my left hand to continue the struggle for the gun, I reached for his ankle with my right and withdrew a blade. Jerking the gun aside and bouncing it across the floor, I manhandled him to his feet and stabbed the knife through his chest. His body went rigid, and he took quick, shallow breaths. His head hung and he only stayed on his feet with my help, the blade still lodged in his upper body.

"You've lost... Dodge...," he barely got out. Looking up with dying eyes and red covering much of his face, he gurgled, "Still... can't... finish me..."

I let go, stepped back, and slammed my right heel into the knife's hilt. The blade drove deeper, and the force knocked Brier backward. His body crumpled and he only managed a grunt as he crashed through the window, flipping as he tumbled out of view into the night air.

The sounds of the parade rushed into the room, nearly drowning out Brier's body thumping and cracking against the pavement below. I stepped to the window and looked down for only a second, just long enough to see him lying dead, facefirst in the middle of Duval. Crowds swarmed around him and looked up toward the window.

I turned and sprang toward the woman. Kneeling beside her, my heart racing and my body weary from the encounter, I rested her head on my leg and pressed a finger to her neck. She was beautiful and young, and she smelled of perfume.

My eyes traced down from her face to the horrendous wound to her chest, the mutilated flesh from the violent bullet impact and the blood oozing out down her tanned stomach and bikini.

My bullet.

From the shot that I'd fired.

A wave of emotions unlike anything I'd ever felt before overtook me. My hand shaking, I felt for a pulse once more, hoping for any sign of life. But in my heart I knew…

I felt nothing. No pulsating vein. Nothing but flesh. She was gone, lifeless in my arms.

I broke down, completely losing it. In the chaos and confusion, I'd killed an innocent woman, and the gravity of the situation completely overwhelmed me. After I dug out my phone and called for an ambulance, my phone fell from my hand and I collapsed over the woman, struggling to breathe and unable to see through the darkness and my blurry eyes.

"Logan!" a voice said, though I was too far gone

to distinguish it.

A light switched on, and in a whir of activity that I couldn't make out, footsteps approached, and a figure dropped down beside me. I blinked and turned, and hands draped over me. It was the warmth, the inexplicable sensation that told me who it was.

"Ange," I said, wrapping my arms around her. I fought to rid myself of the blurriness and looked into her beautiful blue eyes.

THIRTY-EIGHT

Everything happened so fast, it was tough for me to make sense of things. Sirens filled the air. Police and paramedics flooded into the second floor of the haunted house. People scattered, and streets and sidewalks were emptied as the crime scene was closed off.

I stood in the corner, watching intently as the woman I'd shot was photographed by investigators. Following my statements, she was zipped into a body bag and carted on a gurney out of the room. My last glimpse of her was her piercing green eyes. They seemed to look at me, and they sent a chill down my spine so powerful I nearly vomited.

Ange stayed by my side through it all, seeing how fazed I was by what had happened. She'd seen me take on hardened criminals again and again over the years. Standing toe to toe with the world's vilest and most despicable. She'd seen me kill and defend myself on the verge of death before. But this… this was different. This was me taking an innocent life by accident, and it was tearing me apart on the inside.

I was open with the detectives from the start, telling them, Agent Maddox, and the other Homeland agents everything that had happened.

"I shot her," I told them. "I entered the maze, saw Brier's reflection, and pulled the trigger. It was my bullet that killed her."

Maddox placed a hand on my shoulder for a moment, seeing how hard I was taking it.

"It's not your fault," he assured me. "Brier clearly set you up. He's dead now thanks to you." He looked toward Ange. "And thanks to you, Mrs. Dodge, that bomb didn't go off in a crowd and take down droves of people."

Ange had told me what had happened, giving me a rushed rendition of her chase and the climactic explosion. Thankfully, no one had been seriously injured. Many had suffered minor wounds and trauma, but they'd live thanks to Ange putting her life on the line to save complete strangers.

I thought over Maddox's words. He was right. It was an accident. One that I wished again and again that I could relive and keep myself from pulling the trigger. But that didn't matter. It didn't change what I'd done. I'd killed her, and I'd forever have to live with that fact. I'd see her face in my mind forever.

"Who was she?" Ange said.

In the chaos and barrage of questions, I hadn't thought to ask it myself. Part of me wanted to know, but another part of me knew that it would make it even harder to bear.

Maddox shot me a solemn look. "You sure you

two want to know?"

"We'll know sooner or later," I said.

He nodded. "Her name's Heidi Collins. She's from Tampa. Twenty years old and was down here with friends for the festival."

Twenty years old? I thought, feeling like I'd been struck by another blow to the gut. *Just a few years older than Scarlett. With her whole life ahead of her.*

My legs went wobbly, and I stepped back, leaning against the wall. Ange didn't bother asking if I was all right. She just closed in and wrapped her arms around me again.

Brier had done his job well. As he'd told me just before I'd stabbed him and kicked him out the window, he'd returned to ruin me. To make me feel as he had felt. As relieved as I was to be rid of the man, he'd succeeded in inflicting trauma that would haunt me for the rest of my life.

Two agents approached and ushered Maddox away. I watched as the three spoke for a minute, then rushed across to the opposite side of the room and stared into a dark corner of the ceiling. Another man came over with a ladder and messed with something that I couldn't make out attached to the wall.

I tried to catch my breath as I scanned over the scene. A sea of broken mirrors lay all around the room. The glass that remained in place was cracked, the pieces clinging on for dear life.

I gazed to my left at the pool of blood that had come from Brier's accomplice, a man who'd been helped by paramedics, then taken into custody right away. I still didn't know who he was, or who the bomber was. By the time anyone could get to the young man who'd run off with the backpack, he was dead, his corpse floating in a sea of red at the base of Sunset Pier.

My attention shifted back to Maddox as he strode toward Ange and me.

"We've got a bit of a problem," the man said in his low, serious voice. I looked beyond him at the agents, who were carefully removing what looked like a small action camera from the ceiling. "Apparently Brier rigged the camera with a motion sensor. It was recording when we found it."

Seconds after the words left his lips, Maddox's phone rang, and he answered.

"Yes, sir," he said, then held up a finger to us and stepped away. "What?" He spoke a short while longer, then stepped back to us, eyeing his smartphone. "You've gotta be fucking kidding me."

"What is it?" I said, wondering what could possibly be going on.

Brier was dead, that much was certain, so whatever it was it couldn't be that bad. Maddox twisted the phone to show us an image of a video. I couldn't see much, but it was clearly footage from the camera in the corner, a bird's-eye view of the maze.

"This shit's circulating all over the internet," Maddox said. "Brier rigged the video to be livestreamed and it's going viral."

Ange and I leaned forward as Maddox played the clip. It was short. Just thirteen seconds. The beginning showed me navigating the final stages of the maze. I had a hard time watching it, reliving the moment all over again and wishing I could stop what was about to happen. The footage seemed to slow down as I watched myself pop out around the corner, take aim and shoot the mirror.

From the camera's angle right above the mirror, you couldn't see Brier's reflection. Hell, you couldn't even tell that it was a mirror. All you could see was a thin line separating me from a helpless woman tied up and gagged. The bullet drove right into the woman and she collapsed. Then the clip ended. A caption above the video said, "Navy Veteran Shoots Hostage."

I swallowed hard. The caption was a lie, but based on the clip alone, it looked like just that. Like I'd popped out and shot the helpless girl intentionally.

THIRTY-NINE

It was nearly three in the morning by the time Maddox dropped Ange and me off at our house. Jack's blue Jeep was in the driveway beside my Tacoma, my friend having driven Scarlett home and stayed with her while we dealt with the aftermath. It was late, and it'd been a long, emotional night, but I wasn't tired. My mind was running as fast as it could, going over everything that had happened and wondering what was going to come of it.

Before leaving the scene, we'd called in to the Guard, and they were working with a local boat towing company to bring Norman's plane over to Tarpon Cove Marina and tie it off near Ange's Cessna for the time being.

As we were leaving the scene, one of the other Homeland agents had pulled Maddox aside again.

"What are we going to do about him?" the man said, not quite out of my earshot. He gestured my way as I stood beside Ange near the door to the stairs.

"What are you talking about?" Maddox grunted.

The man held up his phone. "The video—"

"The video changes nothing."

"Sir, with all due respect, that's not what it looks like."

Maddox eyed the man. "Is there anything else?"

The guy sighed. "You're gonna have some explaining to do if you let him walk tonight, that's all I'm saying. I believe Dodge as well. But this… this is going to cast the eyes of the nation—hell, the eyes of the world—onto what happened here tonight."

Maddox stopped and put his car in park. It'd been a silent drive across town. All of us had a lot on our minds. I hadn't checked the news myself yet, but I knew that the few articles that had already been posted in just the few hours since the incident painted me as a villain. I was a murdering, trigger-happy veteran.

Ange and I had fought hard over the years to stay under the radar, never wanting to reveal our actions to the press and going to great pains to ensure that others received the credit for whatever we accomplished. Since the article in local papers after the discovery of the lost Aztec treasure three years earlier, neither of us had been featured in any news outlets. And we liked it that way. But that had all changed in an instant, and there was nothing I could do to stop the spread.

"I'm gonna be in town for a few more days," Maddox said. "Dealing with the fallout. Buttoning up this operation for my report." He paused, then turned and looked me in the eyes. "I'm sure I speak for Chief Verona as well when I say that I'll do everything I can to make this better for you and your family. But there's a storm coming. A bad one. No doubt about that. This shit hit the fan and you guys are going to face some heavy fire. Scrutiny from all over the world."

"I understand," I said.

The truth was, I didn't understand. How could I? How could anyone understand? With humanity diving headfirst into the age of social media, no one could predict how big a story could grow or how fast it could morph into something else altogether. I wasn't worried for myself. I could handle whatever criticism or lies or insults or anything else were thrown my way. I was worried about the repercussions for my family, friends, and the whole island community. The people that I cared about who'd suffer because of this mess.

"If there's anything you need, I'll do what I can to help," Maddox finished.

I thanked him, and Ange and I stepped out, trudged up the stairs, and entered the house. Jack was lying on the couch with a Mexican-style blanket over his body and Atticus curled up at his feet. The two awoke and rose, despite our opening the door quietly.

I greeted Atty briefly, then we strode over to Jack as he slid his legs off the couch and rubbed his eyes. His smartphone and a laptop sat on the table in front of him.

After a brief silence, he said, "I'm sorry, guys." He shook his head. "This garbage is out of hand."

I shut the laptop. "Thanks for believing me."

"Are you kidding? I've known you since you were eleven. I know you'd never hurt a soul unless they deserved it." He looked down. "But this is heavy, bro. This is hitting nationa—"

"Jack," I said, cutting him off. "It's been a long day. I think it's best if we all get some rest."

He nodded and rose.

"Heard you took down the bomber," I said.

Jack shrugged. "Scarlett and I stuck around, and she wanted to listen in on the radio channel just in case. It was all her doing. I just went along. We motored over when Ange gave the guy's position."

"You did good, Jack," Ange said. "You and Scarlett both did."

He ran his hands through his messy hair and headed for the door. Gripping the knob, he turned back. "I'm not the only one who believes in you, Logan. Your island family is here for you. Some conchs will buy into these lies and it might be hell around here for a little while, but many people know you and know the kind of man you are. We'll stick up for you. We don't know any other way."

My usually easygoing friend solemnly stepped out, shutting the door behind him.

Scarlett emerged from her bedroom, gravitating like a zombie straight for us. We went in for a long family hug, then she asked me what had happened. She believed in me and my innocence, but I told her the story anyway, letting her know about the scuffle and the cameras, drugs, and trickery. She was nearly a woman after all. And she was our daughter. She'd be facing the aftermath of it all as well, and she deserved to know the truth.

After taking a moment to let the story sink in, she said, "Perception is often mistaken for reality."

I nodded. "How old are you?"

She smiled softly.

She was right. Stories can be easily twisted. People see a headline or a well-timed image and make assumptions based on it.

I didn't sleep. Not even a wink. Even after grabbing a bottle of tequila and downing four shots, I couldn't shut off my mind.

It never ceases to amaze me how powerful the mind can be. Once a potent enough thought takes hold, it festers and grows and can become all-consuming. If you don't put it in check, dark thoughts and powerful emotions can take over your life. And as determined as I was to bounce back, I knew it was going to take time.

I stayed up until the sunrise, then sat in the hammock while watching the early light trickle over the channel. Ange and Scarlett brought me breakfast at the backyard dining table. Seeing me looking at my phone, Ange took it away and tossed it across the lawn.

"I think you've had enough of that," she said.

I hadn't wanted to read what was being plastered all over the internet about me, but I couldn't help it. I needed to see what I was up against.

"Did you sleep at all?" she added as she set a plate of mango waffles doused in syrup and a fresh mug of coffee in front of me.

"No. What's the occasion?" I said as she dropped a plate of bacon down as well.

I was the morning person in the family and usually handled breakfast. Scarlett set a pitcher of orange juice and three glasses and we all sat down.

Ange gave her best attempt at a smile. "I just figured we were all due for something good."

Scarlett remained silent as we went at the food. Not having eaten anything since our light early dinner the previous day, I realized just how hungry I was when the aromas hit my nostrils.

While we ate, a vehicle pulled into the driveway, a powerful, grumbling engine I'd recognize a mile away. I glanced up at Scarlett, smiling for the first time in what felt like ages. I watched as the lightbulb clicked on, then her eyes lit up and she jumped to her feet.

"My baby!" she exclaimed.

She ran barefoot around the house as the engine shut off. Ange and I rose as well, following at a more leisurely pace to the front of the house. Scarlett's blue Bronco was parked beside my truck, its exterior repaired, washed and waxed. It looked like it was parked in a showroom with the morning light reflecting off it.

Cameron climbed out from the driver's seat. He held the keys up to an ecstatic Scarlett, but she just jumped into the kid's arms.

"It looks perfect," she said, then they kissed.

It froze me in my tracks. Ange placed a hand on me and laughed. "She's sixteen."

I remembered what I was like as a sixteen-year-old, then tried to forget it. If it'd been any other time, I might have reacted differently. But with all that was happening, Scarlett and a boy was lower on the list of my worries. Besides, I'd let the kid know who was boss the first time we'd met. He knew where I stood and what I was capable of, and above all, I trusted

Scarlett. He seemed like a good kid.

Cameron looked up the moment their lips met, his eyes staring at mine as they pushed off each other.

"Hey, Logan," he said. "Hi, Ange." He looked at the vehicle, then added, "My uncle sends his regards. Says he emailed the invoice and you already took care of it, so here you go." He held out the keys and Scarlett snatched them.

"Looks great, Cameron," Ange said. "And congrats on the victory."

We'd listened to the rematch between the Key West Conchs and Marathon Dolphins via satellite radio in our Bahamian bungalow. Though not as close as the first bout had been, and thankfully not nearly as memorable, the hometown boys had come away with the W.

Before Cameron could reply, Scarlett cut in. "Care to take a joyride?" She admired the Bronco once more, and added, "I feel like it's been forever since I've seen anyone."

We'd spent three weeks away from Key West less than a year after Scarlett had moved there. She'd had just enough time to make friends, given her outgoing personality, and then she'd left.

Cameron looked down, rubbing the back of his neck. He turned serious, then glanced toward the front of the driveway.

"You guys left your house yet today?" he said gravely.

"No," I said. "We were just eating breakfast."

"Have you eaten yet, Cameron?" Ange asked. "We've got extra."

The kid swallowed, then looked toward the

driveway again. "You're gonna want to see this."

He gestured toward the road and we followed him down the crushed seashells. Halfway to Palmetto Street, I spotted something spray-painted on our driveway. We stopped right before we hit the pavement. There at our feet, in bold red letters, was one word.

KILLER.

FORTY

After snapping a picture of the message, I uncoiled a garden hose and sprayed it down. Most of the paint dripped through the shells, flowing away into the ditch. Then I used a shovel to cover up the residue. When there was no sign left of the word, we headed back to the house.

"Who do you think wrote it?" Cameron said.

I shrugged.

"We can go hang with friends some other time, Dad," Scarlett said.

"No, you two go. Don't worry about that." I wound the hose back up and stowed the shovel. "People who leave messages like that do it because they're too scared to say it face-to-face." I kissed my daughter on the forehead. "Shoot us a few messages to keep us updated."

She said she would, and the two teenagers climbed into the Bronco and rumbled down the driveway.

As Ange and I headed back to the yard and cleared

the remnants of breakfast, she said, "Sure nice to see people giving you the benefit of the doubt. Doesn't the legal process count around here? Not like you've been convicted of anything."

"Like our mature daughter said, people are gonna believe what they want to."

"You're not worried?"

"About you and Scar, yeah. But I'm more worried how this is going to affect our personal lives. If someone wants to get in my face and start something about this, I'd be more than happy to take them on. But let's just hope it doesn't happen."

After doing the dishes, Ange suggested that we head over to the marina.

"The *Calypso* got pretty messed up from the blast last night," she said. "And you know Jack, his boat could be destroyed in a 'cane and he'd still try to repair it himself."

"Sounds like a good idea," I said.

When we arrived at the marina, Jack was in the water in full scuba gear, working on the starboard hull of his Sea Ray. When the fragmentation-laden pipe bomb had gone off, some of the shrapnel had struck and damaged Jack's boat during his daring approach.

"I'm sure the government will comp this," I said to my friend as we eyed him from the dock.

Jack turned, grinned, and removed his regulator. "You know how it is trying to get money from the government," he chuckled. "I'd much rather put in the sweat and foot the bill myself."

I donned a set of scuba gear as well and splashed in beside him. Ange manned the deck, handing us whatever tools or materials we needed. There were four good-sized gashes along the fiberglass, and two more grazes near the bow. Fortunately only one was below the waterline, and it wasn't deep enough for the *Calypso* to take on water.

We sanded and applied epoxy, then coated on small pieces of fiberglass cloth before eventually applying a finisher to make it nice and glossy smooth. And in between, while waiting for it to dry, we grabbed scrubbers and went to work on the grime below the waterline. It was due for a cleaning, and we both agreed that since we were already down there, we might as well clean it. It's not easy work. With a suction cup in one hand to keep steady and scrubbers in our other, we worked back and forth, wiping the grime away. But few things get me out of my head more effectively than some good old-fashioned manual labor, so I relished the task.

While growing up, whenever I'd complain that something was hard, my dad, the wisest man I've ever known, would say things like: "You think this is hard? Try spending a day digging a ditch or roofing a house. Then you'll know hard."

He was right. And though what we were doing wasn't as grueling as some labor jobs, it was more than enough to work up a good sweat and fatigue muscles not normally used.

Just as we were wrapping up the patch jobs, Ange returned with fresh lobster rolls from DJ's. She brought them up to the flybridge. As Jack and I climbed out and removed our BCDs, we had another visitor.

"Don't you two ever sit still?" Harper Ridley asked, eyeing us through big sunglasses.

She wore yoga pants and a ball cap, always doing her best to shield her pale skin from the sun, and she had a bag slung over one shoulder.

"We're just about to," I said. "Care to join us for lunch?"

"I bought more than enough," Ange said, her head popping up from the bridge.

Harper waved us off. "Thanks, but I can't stay long. Been a busy day and there's a lot more to do still."

"I can imagine," I said, unzipping my wetsuit. I patted myself down with a towel, then threw on a faded Rubio Charters T-shirt.

"You guys all right?" Harper said, mostly to Ange and me.

I draped my towel over a rail and sighed. "As good as expected. Trying not to think about it too much."

"I'm sorry."

"What's up, Harper?" Ange said.

She paused, then adjusted her glasses. "We had an interesting visitor this morning at the office. A well-known freelance journalist stormed in all smug, like he was a big shot walking into the rookie league locker room. He stepped right into the middle of the office and proclaimed that he'd give five thousand cash to anyone who could give info on Logan Dodge."

I pinched my bottom lip and looked out over the harbor.

"What happened next?" Ange said, intrigued.

"We all told him to take a hike. Told him that's not how we handle things. And you know what this guy said? He called us a tiny, insignificant operation, then stomped out cockily."

"Thanks, Harper," I said. "I appreciate the *Keynoter* having my back."

She bit her lip. "It won't matter. I'm sure we're not the only office he walked into and made that offer. He'll find people to talk. Just a matter of time. With this story getting so big already, it won't be long before you'll be followed every time you leave the house."

I thought about that for a moment. I'd expected it to get bad, but not that bad, and not so fast.

"Before there's even a charge against him?" Ange said.

Harper shrugged. "Unfortunately, yes. Seen it happen again and again. The footage is... it's not good."

Harper had to take off, and Jack and I climbed to the bridge and ate lunch. It seemed like one piece of bad news after another, but I tried my best to remain positive and enjoy the company and the delicious food.

After lunch, I called Maddox for a quick update. He informed me that the older accomplice from the haunted house was being kept at the Monroe County Detention Center. He'd been questioned but had yet to supply anything that could offer more proof that Brier had schemed to frame me, or how they'd managed to acquire the gas, the bomb, and the plane to fly back to Key West.

When I asked where things stood with me, he told me that there was nothing conclusive yet but to be ready for anything. The same thing Jane said when I called her. Livening the mood a little, she also informed me that Colby was making great strides with his physical therapy and that they were fighting to keep him on. Though his patrolling days were over, the man was still eager to serve and could be put to work at the station.

When we returned home later that evening, Scarlett was doing schoolwork at the dining table, having dropped Cameron off at football practice.

After a few minutes telling each other about our day, I grabbed a notebook, pen, envelope, and roll of stamps, and headed for the door. "I'll be back in a few hours."

Ange, already knowing what I was up to, just gave a slight understanding nod. Scarlett was about to ask where I was going when Ange stopped her.

"Why don't I teach you how to make conch chowder?" she said to our daughter as I pushed out the door.

I climbed into my truck and drove southwest as far as you can in the continental United States. Entering Fort Zachary Taylor State Park, I pulled into a space in the first lot I came to and strode down a shaded path. The park had one of my favorite beaches and picnic areas in the Keys, second on my personal list only to Bahia Honda. But I wasn't heading for the beach.

Instead I cut toward the fort, throwing waves to a few rangers as I passed by. I'd spent a little time volunteering at the compound over the years, so I knew most of the staff. Striding into the grassy heart of the fort, I continued to the other side, wound up a staircase, and took in one of my favorite views in the world.

Built in the mid-1800s, Fort Taylor remained in active military use until 1947. The three remaining fifty-foot-tall walls rise up from a partial moat just up from the beach. It's a great place to go to get a nice 360-degree view of the island, distant waters, and outskirts of the Key West Wildlife Refuge.

I headed to my favorite spot atop the northwest bastion, climbed onto the parapet, and sat against the back of a wooden-framed placard that displayed a map of the harbor. The sun was growing weary, nearing the end of its arc across the crisp blue sky. I peered north over my right shoulder toward the downtown waterfront area and all the people gathering along the promenades. I'd never found a better place to relish and commemorate a sunset than Mallory Square, but occasionally I preferred to observe the colorful evening wonder in silence.

I took in a deep breath of the fresh ocean air, savoring the cool rush into my body, then looked out over the water. Tilting my head down, I pulled out the notebook and pen and leafed to the first empty lined page. Closing my eyes, I took a moment to gather my thoughts, the sun's rays warming my face. Once I was as ready as I'd ever be, I put ink to paper and let it flow, trying my best to be as transparent as I could and to truthfully express what was in my heart. It wasn't easy, and a rush of emotions came over me as line after heartfelt line covered the page.

By the time I blinked out of the trance, I had two and a half pages written, and my hand hurt. I sighed and looked up just as the final embers of sunshine went out with a whisper. A chorus of far-off cheers filled the air. Conch shells blew and music played, and people clapped. I admired the sky, still glowing in soft shades of red and gold, and watched the boats come and go.

As the day ended, giving way to night, I remembered a poem that I'd first read while watching a sunset in Kuwait. While helping to evacuate survivors in a Kurdish village prior to Operation Desert Strike, I'd witnessed things that no one should have to see. It'd been my good friend Scott Cooper who'd given me the poem as I'd sat on a rocky hill, gazing out over the desert, my twenty-year-old self trying to make sense of the cruelty I'd witnessed.

"Maybe this will help," he'd said, handing me the small leather-bound collection of handwritten poems. "It sure helped me."

I'd opened it to a bookmarked page and began to read.

> What do you think has become of the young and old men?
> And what do you think has become of the women and children?
>
> They are alive and well somewhere;
> The smallest sprout shows there is really no death,
> And if ever there was it led forward life, and does not wait at the end to arrest it,
> And ceased the moment life appeared.

Whitman's immortal words emerged from deep within my soul, but for reasons I can't explain, the final lines eluded me. I looked around, searching for the words that lay just beyond my reach, as if hoping to spot them on the horizon.

With darkness falling over the Conch Republic, I made my way back to my truck. I ripped out the sheets and folded them into an envelope. Pulling up a message on my phone from Maddox, I copied an address he'd sent onto the front, then pressed on a stamp and drove over to the nearest postal collection box. Idling, I rolled the window down and took one final look at the letter addressed to Doug and Caroline Collins, then dropped it in.

A lawyer would have no doubt told me that sending the letter to the woman's parents was a bad idea. But I knew it had to be done. They needed to know what had happened, and how much it was eating me up inside.

I put the truck in drive and pulled back onto Truman Avenue. As I did, the words I'd forgotten from the poem elbowed their way into my mind unexpectantly.

> All goes onward and outward . . . . and nothing collapses,
> And to die is different from what any one supposed, and luckier.

FORTY-ONE

On the drive home, I got a call from Ange saying that I should head over to Salty Pete's for dinner.

"Scar and I are already here," she said. "I know you might not feel up to it tonight, but I really think you should. There's a fun surprise here for you."

After the busy day, and especially after spilling my heart onto a page for half an hour, what sounded best was a nice quiet evening at home. Nothing in the world sounded better. But Ange insisted, and I've learned that the less I question my wife, the more harmonious life generally is. So I agreed to stop by but said that I'd need to call it a night earlier than we usually did when at Pete's.

I drove into the lot and parked along the hedge. While striding for the door, I spotted Atticus relaxing in his usual spot. My Lab trotted over like we hadn't seen each other in ages. It's amazing how good he is at picking up my mood. It was a bond that went back thousands of years. Man and dog, looking out for each other.

After I greeted him, he followed me until I reached the steps, then nestled back into his place, watching me intently.

"I'll bring you out some fish, boy," I said, then pulled open the door.

As usual, I was greeted by the ringing of a bell. The hostess had her back to me, and I froze midstride when she turned my way.

"Mia?" I said, my lips forming the biggest grin they'd made all day.

I gravitated toward my friend and wrapped my arms around her. The twenty-six-year-old squeezed me tight, laughing as I held her.

"You look great," I said, loosening my grip.

The last time I'd seen her in the islands, she'd been thirty pounds underweight, pale, and with dark circles around her eyes. The local's drug-dealing boyfriend had gotten her addicted to opioids. And after I'd dealt with the boyfriend and then the smuggling operation, Mia had agreed to be admitted into a rehab facility up in Homestead. The program was designed to last upwards of three months if necessary, but Mia explained that she'd taken well to the program and that the doctors had agreed on her release after just over a month. Pete, his team at the restaurant, and the rest of her island family would look after her and make sure that she continued down the positive path.

"Thanks to you," she said.

I couldn't describe how good it was to see her healthy. And there was something much deeper, an underlying shift in her persona. Her glow had returned, along with her vibrant enthusiasm and zest for life. Mia had been the lifeblood of Pete's place for years, the smiling face that made everyone's day when they strode in out of the hot tropical air. Mia, combined with the smells from Oz's cooking in the back, gave the place a homey and welcoming vibe that epitomized what the islands were known for.

Ange and Pete strolled over from beside the kitchen. As they did, I threw a wave to Oz, who peeked through the order window. The big Scandinavian was built more like a brown bear than a human and had fully recovered from his scuffle with Vito and his thugs.

"It was a group effort," I told Mia, glancing at them. I hugged her again, then added, "It's so great to see you."

After we spent a few minutes catching up, Ange invited her to have dinner or to go out on the boat with us whenever she wanted.

"It's indescribable having our brightest star back in Key West where she belongs," Pete said.

"And it's great to be back," Mia replied.

As I strode alongside Ange and Pete across the dining room toward the staircase, I couldn't help but notice a few sour glances my way. The quick dirty looks reminded me of the message that had been spray-painted in our driveway that morning. I didn't take it to heart or let it affect me. As everyone had said, we were in for a big mess after all of the articles and clips that had already gone viral.

When we reached the second floor, I was glad to see that Pete had already fixed up the place following the shoot-out. The broken glass cases had been replaced, the bullet holes patched up, and he'd installed a new sliding glass door.

"Sorry I wasn't here to help with the place," I said to Pete.

"Nonsense. If it weren't for you and all you've done around here, we'd have been out of business years ago."

We ate dinner at our usual corner table up on the balcony. Isaac, Scarlett, and Cameron huddled together, Jack's nephew helping the high school senior with college admissions stuff. The talented athlete was being recruited by a few in-state colleges, including the University of Miami. And even popular out-of-state colleges were showing interest. It didn't surprise me, and I hoped he'd pick somewhere relatively close by so we could catch some of his games.

We ate trays of steamed royal red shrimp coated in Key West Spice seasoning and dipped in melted butter and house-made cocktail sauce. I changed up the tastes by lathering oysters on the half with horseradish, mignonette sauce, and a squeeze of lemon, relishing the combination of flavors.

The main dishes included grilled grouper and snapper fillets, blackened jumbo scallops, and crab-stuffed ravioli, downing it all with Key limeade and my favorite mojitos on the island.

It was a great, relaxing evening with friends, and I was thankful for all of them. Jack and Lauren showed up after wrapping up their sunset charter, and even Frank Murchison, a professor friend at the local community college, stopped by.

"Wait until I tell you what happened in the Virgin

289

Islands," the tanned middle-aged man said.

The adventurous archeologist went on to explain how he'd been held hostage by a Russian criminal so that the man could blackmail his daughter, who'd been looking for Captain Kidd's lost treasure. It was a long story, filled with the professor's usual blend of danger and excitement, and ending with a revelation that a mutual friend of ours, Jason Wake, had been the one to save him.

"What are the odds?" I said, smiling as I thought about the young man, who was quickly making a name for himself in the covert operations department.

We all continued to regale each other with stories long after the last of the food had been eaten. Losing track of time, we didn't load into the Tacoma and cruise home until after ten. It had been a fun dinner, and an amazing revelation to see how far Mia had come.

A stretch of advancing clouds reached us on the drive home, the skies going from clear to dumping rain in a matter of seconds. I slowed and flicked the wipers on full speed. Halfway across the island, my phone buzzed in my pocket. It was Jane.

"Logan, where are you?" she said, her tone serious.

"Just wrapped up dinner at Pete's and on our way home. What's going on?"

She paused a moment, then said, "We'll meet you there."

I reached our driveway five minutes later, turning off Palmetto and crunching onto the seashells. The headlights beamed through the downpour and rustling palm trees. Like déjà vu, the drive was filled with a line of cars: two police cruisers, the mayor's Mercedes, and Maddox's blacked-out BMW. I slowed to a stop beside Maddox's car, eyeing the four vehicles skeptically as I shut off the engine.

"What's going on?" Scarlett said from the backseat. She'd been so tired that she'd dozed off to the sounds of raindrops, but she went wide awake when she saw the idling cars in our drive.

Local officers, including Jane, stepped out and moved in toward the truck. Maddox and a fellow Homeland agent also flooded out, along with Mayor Nix.

"Dad?" Scarlett said, leaning forward. "What—"

"I don't know," I said. I turned back to look at my daughter and an anxious Atticus wagging his tail, then looked to Ange. "Do me a favor and wait here."

A flash of lightning coated the scene in white light, and an earsplitting crack filled the air. The inclement weather felt strongly like a sign. A parallel that alluded to that morning weeks earlier when I'd returned from a run, slogging up the drive and soaked from head to toe, only to be welcomed home by unwanted news.

I leaned forward, gazing at the dark skies through the rain-splattered windshield, then gripped the handle and pushed. It was just a quick summer rinse. There one minute and soon to move on. But its crescendo was timed perfectly with my exit from the truck, dousing me in thick, heavy drops as an eruption of thunder shook the heavens.

I planted onto the driveway and shut the door behind me, standing tall and unfazed by the storm. My attention went first to the chief of police. "What's going on, Jane?"

"A load of shit, that's what," Maddox said. "But it'll all be ironed out, Logan. You can be sure of that. This garbage won't stick."

I looked at Jane and the other officers as they closed in on me, water soaking their uniforms.

"What's he talking about?"

Mayor Nix cleared his throat. "He's talking about something that's nearly twenty-four hours overdue."

I looked up at the man who was still standing behind his car, rain splattering and dripping down his yellow poncho.

Before I could reply, Jane said, "Logan, it pains me to say it, but you're under arrest pending further investigation into the death of Heidi Collins."

Thunder rumbled again, rolling across the island as if to add emphasis to her unsettling declaration.

She nodded to the officers on either side of me, then they cut in close. One, a big guy who I recognized but had never met, ordered me to turn around as he pulled out a pair of handcuffs. I complied, pressing my chest against the side of my truck as he bound me, the cold steel biting at my wrists as he tightened them.

While I was being restrained, the other officer gave me a quick Miranda recitation, then they turned me around and prodded me toward the open back door of the nearest police cruiser.

"Remember, he is to be held without bail, Chief Verona," the mayor said, eyeing me suspiciously.

Maddox placed a hand on my shoulder. The passenger door of my Tacoma pushed open, and Ange strode around the hood, looking like she was ready to scold each of them and then take them all on. But I shot her a look and shook my head. Her face contorted with equal parts anger and sadness, my wife froze for a moment, then pressed a hand to her mouth as the storm drenched her.

I turned to look toward Scarlett who eyed me from the backseat, bawling her eyes out beside a now-agitated Atticus.

"It's going to be all right," I assured her as they ushered me into the back.

I stared into my wife's blue eyes as they slammed the door shut. Jane and another officer got into the front of the cruiser. She put it in gear, then backed up and accelerated down the driveway. Peering back over my shoulder, I took one final look at my wife, then my whole world vanished in the dark tempest.

THE END

Note to Reader

Many of you no doubt recognized a familiar name in this story. Scott Kirby is a musician who really did help found the Smokin' Tuna Saloon back in 2011. For those not familiar with his music, Scott truly captures the essence of the islands in a way that few artists can.

During the brunt of the pandemic social distancing, Scott performed livestream shows from Key West, and I listened to one of those shows nearly every day it was so good at transporting me to faraway beaches and aqua blue surf. I'm forever grateful for his words, voice, and passion. You can check out his website, scottkirby.com, for more info and upcoming tour dates.

And if you're curious about what live show I'm referring to, I'll be posting it to my Facebook page: facebook.com/matthewrief.

Thank you, my loyal readers. I hope you enjoyed this adventure.

LOGAN DODGE ADVENTURES

Gold in the Keys
Hunted in the Keys
Revenge in the Keys
Betrayed in the Keys
Redemption in the Keys
Corruption in the Keys
Predator in the Keys
Legend in the Keys
Abducted in the Keys
Showdown in the Keys
Avenged in the Keys
Broken in the Keys
Payback in the Keys

JASON WAKE NOVELS

Caribbean Wake
Surging Wake
Relentless Wake

Join the Adventure!
Sign up for my newsletter to receive updates on
upcoming books on my website:

matthewrief.com

About the Author

Matthew has a deep-rooted love for adventure and the ocean. He loves traveling, diving, rock climbing and writing adventure novels. Though he grew up in the Pacific Northwest, he currently lives in Virginia Beach with his wife, Jenny.

Made in United States
Orlando, FL
10 August 2023

35955397R00178